Bullets, Blood & Stones

The journey of a child soldier

donna white

ISBN: 0-9952805-0-9
ISBN-13: 978-0-9952805-0-2

For Charlie

This story is based on actual events using information obtained through interviews with former child soldiers from Joseph Kony's Lord's Resistance Army in Uganda. In certain cases incidents, characters, locations and timelines have been changed for dramatic purposes. Certain characters may be composites, or entirely fictitious.

Excerpt located on page 59 and 60 taken from: *Pawns of politics: children, conflict and peace in northern Uganda*. Rory E. Anderson, Fortunate Sewankambo, Kathy Vandergrift (2004). Mississauga: World Vision, 52. Used with permission.

Cover design by H. Leighton Dickson

PRAISE FOR BULLETS, BLOOD & STONES

"Donna White has written a book about one of the world's biggest injustices, the issue of child soldiers. An issue that's often hard to understand and tell, she ... give(s) voice to the children who have and continue to be haunted by this experience and at the same time connecting young people in North America to the humanity of their peers on the other side of the world."

- **Michel Chikwanine**, former child soldier and author of Child Soldier: When Boys and Girls are used in War

"Bullets, Blood and Stones, imaginatively brings the Child Soldier issue to life—bridging the gap between here and there, between us and them in a compelling fashion that will appeal to young readers and adults alike."

- **Patrick Reed,** Director/Producer Fight Like Soldiers Die Like Children

"Donna White has written a book on child soldier as if she was in Uganda for all the years the war had been there. Her book is so inspiring and touching psychologically, spiritually, socially and physically. This is the book about what innocent children in Northern Uganda and Eastern went through."

- **Oroma Christine,** Head Counselor at Gulu Recovery Center for Former Child Soldiers

"Donna White has written a book about one of the most powerful and troubling subjects there is in the modern world: child soldiers. She has also added a supernatural element which makes the book even more accessible to teenagers of all socio-economic backgrounds. This is an important book. Read it. Now."

- **David Henry Sterry**, best-selling author of Chicken

Prologue

A family tie is like a tree; it can bend but it cannot break. ~ African proverb

When the soft rumble of the drums and the chanting of the village elders began, Dembe knew it was time.

A thin gnarled hand pushed the zebra hide aside, allowing the morning light to invade the dark enclosure. Kaikara, the village *jago,* peered into the hut and spoke. “Come, Dembe. Your mother is ready to go.”

Dembe crawled out of the opening and followed the old chief to where four elders sat on the ground beside a body covered with leaves and long grasses. The drums and the chanting ceased.

Dembe looked down at the face of the woman who had honored the great earth mother with his birth twelve rainy seasons ago. He knelt beside the body and gently ran his fingers over his mother's face. He drew in a long unsteady breath and bit his lower lip, trying to keep the sorrow hidden behind his eyes. His anguish betrayed him. Tears rolled down his face and dropped onto the cold cheeks of his *maa*.

He searched his mother's face and saw the shadowed images of his own siblings—three brothers and two sisters who were now quiet and resting in the red soil, the same red soil that begged for rain from the cloudless skies and left in blood-colored twisters that flew across the savanna.

Dembe wiped his fallen tears from his mother's face. He was alone now. He could not afford the indulgence of self-pity. He would not be weak like his father, who had turned his back on the village and walked into the setting sun six days past.

The old man knelt beside him and removed a small sack from Dembe's mother's neck. He placed the pouch around Dembe's own and smiled softly.

"It is now your duty to carry the stones, Dembe," the *jago* said. "They were protected by your *maa*, and her *maa* before her. For generations your ancestors have been the guardians. And now it is up to you."

The man's breath escaped as a sigh. "You have lost greatly during the famine and illness that has set itself upon our people. But let it be known to you that this honor of carrying the stones is yoked with the task of keeping them safe. They must never, never be taken, or lost, or destroyed. They must remain forever a part of our village, for hidden in them are the powers of the ancients. It is told they will bring our people peace. A peace that will come through a child, a child who will uphold goodness despite the evil that surrounds him."

Kaikara stood and raised his gaze, searching the sky and the hills and the trees. "There will be more terrible times ahead of us. With the withering of our meager gatherings from the earth, there will be many men who will struggle to fill the bellies of their women and children, and war will engulf us from all sides. You must always be on your guard, Dembe."

Dembe closed his eyes and lowered his face to Kaikara's feet.

"Come," the old man said, extending his hand to the boy. "We must bring your mother to her *kabedo me kuc*."

Four men lifted the corners of the hide that lay under Dembe's mother, taking a lead in the procession of the men, women, and children to his mother's final place of rest, past the outlying trees. After they laid their burden onto the ground, each man gathered a handful of dirt and sprinkled it on the body. As the soil fell on Dembe's mother, a soft wailing from the women rose into the still air, punctuated by the harsh, steady beat of the drums.

Dembe looked at his mother one last time.

"Come, Dembe," Kaikara said, placing his hand on the boy's shoulder.

The two brought up the rear while they walked back to the village. The wailing and drumbeats carried them forward.

When the silence came, it echoed louder than the chorus of mourners. The drums stopped mid-beat, and the women's anguished cries stuck in their throats. Dembe raised his head, catching Kaikara's eye. But the silence, stark and powerful, was split as recognition dawned. The women's keening turned to screams of fear and panic. Torches sparked across the sky, arcing above the villagers' heads and landing to erupt on the dry grass roofs of their huts. The war hoots of the *lamone* flew across the empty plain. They filled Dembe with terror.

Kaikara turned to Dembe and grabbed his arm. "The enemy has come! You must run, Dembe! Go!" He spun Dembe around to face the hills. "You must not let them take the stones!" The women and children rushed toward them. Kaikara pushed Dembe away from the path. His voice grew louder. "Run! Go to the hills! Hide in the caves!"

Dembe stood rooted to the spot. He glanced from Kaikara, to the hills, and back to the old man's face, covered with fear.

"Go!" Kaikara shouted.

Dembe knew what he had to do. He clutched the sack of stones tightly to his chest and turned away from Kaikara, away from his people, away from the village, and ran. His feet pounded the hard clay ground as he headed toward the hills. His lungs burned and his heart beat with the rapid rhythm of a war drum. He had never felt so afraid and fearless all at once. His determination was as solid as the stones he carried around his neck.

Dembe rushed to the path that led to the hill. As he slowed to climb the slope, he turned and glanced behind him to see if he had been noticed. He had. A young man caught his gaze and set off along the path to the hill. His *tong* was poised and ready.

Dembe slipped on the loose rocks. He tumbled down the hill and crashed into a large boulder. He struggled to his feet and glanced back. The *lamone* was nearly upon him. The man had stopped. His feet were firmly planted. He drew back his arm and launched his *tong* with a long fluid arc. Dembe watched the lethal weapon hurtle toward him.

The spear pierced his side, ripping into his flesh and sending a thousand burning barbs through his body. Dembe stiffened. His face contorted, teeth clenched, as a primal sound escaped his lips. His hand moved to his side, sticky and hot with blood.

He wrapped his hand around the long stick and ripped the spear from his flesh. A surge of blood gushed from the wound. He lay for a moment, gasping for breath. Dembe clutched the spear and forced himself to stand, ignoring the pain that magnified itself as it coursed through his body. His knees shook. Blackness covered his eyes. He adjusted his grip on the spear and threw it at the man pursuing him. It fell uselessly to the ground. He ran.

Dembe threw himself headfirst into the brush and found the hidden entrance to the cave. He fell on all fours and crawled into the darkness. He struggled farther and farther into the cave's interior. The cool, dank air wrapped around him, and he was aware of nothing except total blackness.

His breath came to him in short quick pants. He stopped in mid-crawl and listened. The sound of legs and knees scuffing on the stone floor came closer and closer.

This is the end, he thought.

He grasped the cave wall and lifted himself. He would meet his attacker like a man, standing, glaring into his eyes. Not like a cowardly young boy.

And then he felt it.

There at his fingertips was a small opening, hidden in the side of a rock that jutted out from the wall. It was small—too small for a man. But large enough, perhaps, for a boy.

He had no choice. He squeezed his slight frame through the opening and coaxed his body forward until the narrow tunnel gave way to a wider cave. He crawled to the side and propped himself up against the cool, moist wall.

The *lamone* would not find him here. He would leave and Dembe would stay here with the stones.

He clutched the sack to his chest. He heard faint footfalls—pacing—near the small cave entrance. They faded as his attacker left the cave. Dembe breathed a deep sigh of relief. He could rest now, and tomorrow, when the warriors were gone from his village, he would show his people the stones were safe.

And all would be well.

Chapter 1

Knowledge without wisdom is like water in the sand. ~ Guinean proverb

Scott crouched and felt forward with his hands. "Great," he muttered under his breath. "I just love tight places."

He hoisted his pack onto his back, turned on the headlamp that was on his helmet, and peered into the dark tunnel. The light pink-colored stone walls reflected small flecks of crystals, shining, creating a soft glow.

Scott called out. "You there yet?"

Nothing. He yelled again. No response.

He drew in a deep breath and closed his eyes. He imagined black mambas curled in hidden crevices and bat colonies hanging from the ceilings of caves. He shivered. "Ah, great. Well, at least if the ceiling caves in, they won't have to go through the trouble of burying us."

He crawled into the tunnel.

As he inched forward, Scott breathed in the stifling, dead air. He craned his neck, trying to see what was in front of him. A faint flicker of light passed over a wall and then disappeared. "What's it like up there, Dad?" he yelled.

A muffled voice carried down the passageway. "It's getting narrower up here, Scott. Watch your head."

Scott sucked in his breath and exhaled through his nostrils in a noisy huff. He did not want to be shown up by his dad. He knew he would never hear the end of it: "Yeah, brought my son to Uganda to explore a newly discovered cave, and what does he do? Spends the day at the entrance worrying about spiders and bats and snakes."

"Wuss," Scott said, directing the comment at himself. "Fifteen years old and you're still a wuss."

Several feet in, the passageway narrowed to a small culvert-style opening. Scott took his backpack off and shoved it ahead. He gripped the dirt floor with the toes of his boots and pushed forward, wiggling his shoulders and stomach, grabbing hold of any crevice or rock to pull himself closer and closer to the cave. He paused for a moment to catch his breath.

"I really, really hate tight places," he muttered again. He urged his body forward.

"It's right here!" Scott's dad yelled.

After a few more feet, the passageway opened up into a huge agora. His dad opened his backpack and took out a flashlight. He flicked the switch and aimed its beam at the ceiling, waving it back and forth.

Scott stood and turned around and around. His mouth dropped open, and he exhaled in awe. He grabbed his own flashlight and turned it on. The whole cave filled with light.

The ceiling of the cave was covered with massive stalactites—long pointed fingers, reaching down toward the ground. A cascade of whites, pinks, and reds erupted in varying intensities, filling the cave with a soft glow. The cones glistened, their smooth surfaces wet and slick. It was as if they had been waiting thousands of years for someone to finally see their magnificence.

Scott and his dad stood silently, their heads tilted upward, the beams of their flashlights exposing what darkness had covered for many years.

So this is what it feels like, Scott thought. *That feeling of discovery, of seeing something no one has ever seen, or at least not for a long, long time.* He gave a brief nod, as if to reassure himself. No, he would never grow tired of exploring and discovering new things. He was sure of it.

"Didn't I say you wouldn't be disappointed?" his dad said, resting his hand on Scott's shoulder.

"Yeah," Scott said, keeping his eyes on the shining cones. "Yeah."

"This may be one of the smaller caves in Uganda, but it sure is the prettiest. Kind of nice to be one of the first to see it, hey?"

Scott's dad shone his flashlight onto the walls and sent its beam from one side of the cave to the other. He paused at the far-right corner. "Ah! There it is! Dr. Moran told me he'd found an opening into a smaller cave just over here."

Scott peered at the small hole. "Ah, you go ahead, Dad. I don't mind waiting here and checking this out some more."

"I'll be back in just a bit. Stay here. Don't wander off." Scott's father tucked his head into the small opening and crawled in.

Scott shone his flashlight onto the walls, searching for a drawing or painting created thousands of years ago by primitive man. His beam crept along the rock, bringing more tiny flecks of clear stone to life. He rubbed his finger over a small lump, brought it to his nose, and sniffed. It was a familiar smell. He licked the tip of his finger and smiled. It was a salt cave.

He inched his way along the edge of the wall and marveled at how the rocks formed large vertical steps that "walked" around the agora. Mesmerized, he followed the stairs and searched each crevice. He looked high into the ceiling and examined each and every crack along the floor. He knew he had to do this kind of thing very slowly and meticulously; his father had stressed it over and over again when they went on their first outing years ago. Quickly overlooking a fold in the wall or a shadow from the light could mean missing something very important.

Scott followed a small crack on the wall with the beam of his flashlight until the crack split in several different directions. Slowly, he retraced the paths, following each fissure until it ended at the floor. He inched farther along the wall until his beam revealed a large crack at the highest point of the ceiling. He turned his flashlight to high beam and aimed it into the darkness, exposing a flat area of darkened red stone. "Nope. No opening there," he said.

He shifted his position and aimed the light farther along the wall. His hand stopped in midair. "What the?"

He leaned closer and waved his flashlight across the wall, first to the right and then to the left. He tightened his grip on the handle and held his breath. "What do we have here?"

It was easy to miss, and Scott understood why he didn't find it the first time he circled the cave. While he walked in a clockwise direction, the shadows from the stair hid the entrance quite well. But when he turned and circled the cave in the other direction, the light from his flashlight didn't bounce back to reveal a cave wall. Instead, the light was swallowed up by the darkness of a small enclosure.

Scott reached in and felt along the edge of the opening. It was just wide enough for him to squeeze through.

"Figures," he mumbled. He rested his head against the wall and sighed. It had always thrilled him to see new things, discover secrets hidden for thousands of years, whether it was on a search with his dad or in a corner of a museum in one of the many countries he visited. But this was different. He was afraid. Plain and simple. And he hated himself for it.

"You'd be one pathetic excuse for an archeologist if you didn't go in, Scotty."

Scott shook off the tingling sensations of fear and inched his way into the tiny opening, feeling ahead with one arm while shining his light into the tunnel with the other. Half crawling and half crouching, he shivered as he felt his way along the damp walls.

Several feet in, the tunnel opened into a smaller cave. Scott aimed the beam of his flashlight at the ceiling. The space was tall enough for him to stand in. He rose and scanned the roof and the walls, determining the size of the enclosure. It was tiny, barely wide enough for two men to stand side by side with their arms spread.

He waved his flashlight across the floor. His hand froze in mid-swing.

White.

He sent the beam back.

Bone white.

Scott shone his light onto the ground and brought the beam up the cave wall. His hand stopped. Two hollow sockets stared at him from an empty void.

He took a small step back. Leaning against the wall, half sitting, half lying, with its arms crossed over its chest, was a skeleton.

A huge smile crept over Scott's face. Within seconds he was kneeling at the skeleton's side.

He set his flashlight on the ground and reached out but then quickly pulled back. He had heard of great artifacts turning to dust the moment they were touched by an all-too-eager archeologist, and he didn't want to destroy anything. This skeleton could tell him stories if he stopped and examined it closely.

First, he looked at the legs, starting at the feet, inching his gaze along the bones, watching for any clues as to the identity of the ancient remains. He had learned a lot from his father, and he was now confident as he took on the role of examiner instead of student.

He continued onto the sacrum in the pelvic area. “Bones aren’t fused. Can’t be older than eighteen or . . .” He paused and took an approximate measurement of the body. “Must be four, maybe four and a half feet at the most. Maybe eleven, twelve years old. Hard to say. And the hips? No.” He shook his head. “Too young to tell if it’s a boy or a girl. But no, it’s probably a boy, judging from the bone thickness.”

The ribs were next. He began at the bottom, near the pelvis. “False rib, unattached, twelve, eleven, ten . . . true rib, attached, seven, six, five . . .” He stopped counting and peered closer. The fifth rib on the left side was much shorter than its counterpart on the right. It was broken. Shattered. The missing piece lay on the ground, giving evidence it was a complete break. “Ouch,” Scott whispered. “That must have hurt a bit.”

Next he examined the skeleton’s arms. They were crossed over his chest as if they were protecting something. *His heart, probably*, Scott surmised. *Many people instinctively clutch at their heart as they die.*

He leaned over the clasped hands. A small frayed piece of leather peeked out from the fingers. *What's he got here*? Scott wondered.

At that moment he forgot everything his father had stressed since day one: don't disturb anything, don't touch anything, and above all, don't remove anything. All of his inhibitions were gone. He had to see what was clasped so tightly in those hands.

He aimed the flashlight beam onto the skeleton's hands and got to work. Carefully, slowly, he pried the bony fingers open one by one. It felt as if time stretched on for hours, but at last Scott was able to see a small leather pouch tied with a leather cord nestled in the skeleton's hands.

He lifted the sack and sat briefly cradling it in the palm of his hand. Gently, very gently, he pulled the cord loose and opened it.

Five round green stones glistened within the dark folds of the leather pouch.

He passed his fingers over them one by one. They felt cool and smooth, their color reminding him of the fresh new needles of an evergreen tree.

He held one of the stones and brought it closer to his flashlight. A faint silver thread ran across it as he turned it over and over.

He looked at the skeleton and tried to picture the boy whose life had ended in this cave. Who was he? Why did he grasp the bag of stones so tightly when he took his last breath? And why did he die here?

Maybe the stones were the boy's talismans, his good luck charms. Maybe they were used for some ancient ritual. Maybe the boy thought they held some magical power. Scott could only speculate, but he knew ancient people had some pretty strange beliefs.

He closed his hand around the stone and placed it back into the pouch.

Suddenly, Scott was outside the cave. An intense heat surrounded him, and his lungs filled with smoke. Flaming torches flew over his head. People screamed and ran in different directions. Guns fired. A young girl turned and rushed toward him, her eyes wide, her arms outstretched.

And then it was gone: the girl, the guns, the fire. Everything. Scott sat absolutely still, gasping for air. "What the hell was that?" He gazed across the dirt floor and stared at the skeleton and then at the sack of stones.

His hand shook as he reached into the pouch and picked one up. It was cool to the touch. Nothing was different. Nothing was unusual.

He coughed. The smoke burned his nostrils, stabbed his lungs.

The smoke was real. Wasn't it?

The gunfire, the screams, echoed in his ears over and over again.

It was all real. Or was it?

Scott dropped the stone back into the pouch, just as he had done before, and waited.

Nothing happened.

No smoke, no fire. Nothing.

He stared into the dark recesses of the skeleton's eye sockets. "Is there magic in your stones? Is that why you're holding on to them so tightly?"

Scott shook his head. "Now you really are crazy, Scotty. Seeing visions, talking to a skeleton . . ."

"Scott!"

He tore his backpack open, wrapped the sack of stones in a spare T-shirt, and tucked it into the bottom.

He didn't think about what he was doing or why he did it. It was a quick decision, made so fast and with such certainty that he had no chance to think twice or change his mind.

Scott poked his head out of the cave entrance and called out. "Over here, Dad! I found another cave!" He hoped he could hide the tremor in his voice.

His father squeezed his slim body into the opening and inched into the cave. He stopped in mid-crawl as he began to focus on the skeleton. "Oh my . . ." he whispered.

He bent over the skeleton and glanced at it from head, to foot, and then back again. "It's perfect. Absolutely perfect," he said, taking out his glasses. "Must be a child, say ten or twelve years old. Too young to tell if it's a boy or a girl. Looks like an injury of some sort, a trauma to the fifth rib."

His eyes grew wider as his face broke into a huge grin. "How did you find this opening, Scott? Dr. Moran must have missed it, and he's usually very thorough."

Scott shrugged. "I just circled the cave a few times, but when I went in the other direction I spotted the hole."

"Wow." His dad thumped him on the back. "Your first find. This is quite a big thing."

Scott looked at his father, forcing a smile to his face. He glanced from his dad, to the backpack, and then to his dad again.

It was a big find, bigger than his dad could imagine. But he couldn't tell him about the stones. Maybe it was because he knew his dad would pass the vision off as something caused by the excessive heat or the stale air in the cave. Or maybe it was because he wanted to keep the discovery all to himself and try to make some sense of it. Either way, he wasn't going to follow any archeologist's code of ethics and place the stones in a glass box in a museum for everyone to see.

No, there was something to these stones, and he wanted to find out what it was.

Chapter 2

He who is destined for power does not have to fight for it. ~ Ugandan proverb

Scott stepped into the shower and cringed.

"Argh!" He shrieked, plunging his head under the frigid stream. "Why is everything hot in Africa except the water?"

He scrubbed shampoo into his scalp. A stream of red clay and water trickled down his legs and flowed down the drain. After he lathered a bar of soap over his body, he stepped back under the shower and rinsed. His teeth chattered and his body shook as he turned the water off.

Scott pulled a towel from the rack and rubbed himself dry. His body enjoyed the pleasant, just-right temperature for a moment, until the heat of the room hit him with a friendly reminder of the unbearably hot African climate and the complete lack of air conditioning in the hotel.

"You all right in there?" Scott's dad yelled. "You sounded like you were auditioning for the soprano section in a church choir."

"Very funny, Dad. Ha ha." Scott's eyes almost rolled to the back of his head. "Next time I need a shower, I'm going to stand outside with my shampoo and soap and wait for it to rain. At least it'll be a bit warmer."

"Ah, that might not be such a bad idea," his dad said as he looked at his watch. "We'll be heading to the Akello Hotel in Soroti in a few minutes, so make sure you have your bag packed before we go. There won't be much time before we head to the airport. It's a long drive to Entebbe."

"Yep, I'm working on it," Scott said as he walked into the room.

"Oh, and by the way, I just got off the phone with Dr. Moran. I told him everything about the cave and the skeleton. Said he can't wait to meet you."

Scott grinned. "Already hobnobbing with the upper brass, Scott. You're good."

He gathered several pairs of mud-encrusted mountain pants and T-shirts, rolled everything into a big ball, and stuffed it into his suitcase. Then he threw on a newly pressed cotton shirt and a pair of pants and looked in the mirror. He nodded at his reflection. With all of the red dust washed away, he could finally see his blond hair and the tan that had resulted from spending two weeks in the hot African sun. “Exit one caveman and enter one Scott Romo, explorer and discoverer extraordinaire,” he said with a grin.

“You ready?” Scott’s dad asked, poking his head into the bathroom. “Because I just saw our jeep pull up.”

“Yeah, I’m ready.”

Scott glanced at his backpack. *Better leave them here,* he thought as he locked the door and put the key in his pocket. *They’ll be safe*.

He jumped into the back of the jeep.

The driver held out two prehistoric cassette tapes. “What will do for you, Mr. Scott? Mr. Joel or Mr. Elton this time?”

Scott laughed. For the whole duration of his stay in Uganda, the driver had asked the same question every morning before they headed out, giving the same two choices of music from his somewhat limited eighties music selection.

“Oh, let’s live on the wild side this time, Mr. Okwe, and listen to Mr. Joel again.”

“Mr. Joel it is, Mr. Scott,” the driver said as he popped the cassette into the tape player.

Scott leaned his head back and closed his eyes.

The image of the young girl running toward him flashed in his mind. Her eyes were wide, her arms reaching out to him. The blasts of the guns pounded his eardrums, deafening him. Piercing screams shook his very core, and his heart beat rapidly against his chest. Scott's eyelids flew open and he drew in a quick breath. He let it out and slowly drew in another and another. His hand tightened over his heart. He waited for the pounding to slow. He looked at his dad and Mr. Okwe, now deep in conversation. They hadn't noticed.

He smelled a whiff of smoke and turned his head toward the open window. A group of young boys gathered around a small cooking fire in a nearby field. A boy waved, his hand rapidly fanning the air as he grinned. Soon all of the boys in the group were waving. They jumped up and down, shouting and laughing. Scott smiled and waved as the jeep sped past, leaving a trail of dust behind them.

As the vehicle ambled along the potholed road, the lights of the town came into view and a sign indicated they were now entering the town of Soroti. Small houses built with clay and bricks began to appear, as well as several shops; their raised awnings revealed candlelit interiors. Men dressed in crisp cotton shirts and pressed pants pointed at the items they needed to purchase while their wives stood quietly beside them.

As they entered the main street of the town, the jeep slowed until it barely crawled, dodging bicycles, motorcycles, pedestrians, and motorcycle taxis, commonly known as *bodabodas*, as they weaved through the tight spaces between cars and heavily laden trucks.

"Now that guy's got it all figured out." Scott's dad laughed.

A young man wearing rollerblades zipped in and out between the cars, holding on to the backs of vehicles of unsuspecting drivers as they pulled him along.

"That would be illegal back home," Scott's dad told the driver.

"But crazy good," Scott said. "How come we never took a *bodaboda* anywhere?"

"Because they aren't safe, that's why. The way their drivers fly around everyone without looking. And see," Scott's dad said, pointing at a *bodaboda* driver passing them, "they don't even wear helmets. I'm surprised there aren't any accidents."

"But there are the accident, Dr. Romo and Mr. Scott. Yes, many bad bad accident. And it is not good for the tourist to sit on the back and hang on. The driver can go one way and you will go the other! It is better that you stay safe with Mr. Okwe." The driver laughed and stopped to allow a man dressed in a business suit to pass by. The man had a live chicken tucked under one arm while he held his briefcase in the other. "Eeh! That man is a happy man! Look at the fine fine chicken he bring home to supper tonight!"

Scott grabbed his camera and took a picture. "Nobody will believe me if I don't have proof," he said.

The jeep crept forward and stopped again. This time a family of goats hurried across. Scott took another photo.

He began to take pictures of almost everything around him: the traffic signs, the billboards, and the people. He even managed to get a good shot of a mother and father and their three kids crammed together on one motorcycle heading toward the marketplace. Scott aimed his camera at the sidewalk where a group of girls were sitting on the ground near a shop. He took a photo of them as they lay on their blankets, wrapping themselves to guard against the chill of the approaching African night. A short distance from them was a larger group of boys gathered together, placing their blankets on the ground. A boy covered two children with a blanket, then sat at the end and looked up at Scott, who pointed at the camera and then at the boy. He smiled and nodded. Scott took his photo.

As the jeep ambled along, the scene repeated

itself over and over again. More and more children lay on the sidewalks, covered in their old blankets. And more and more of them walked down the streets, carrying their blankets on their heads. Older boys and girls carried younger boys and girls on their backs. Some children walked alone, others in groups.

"I didn't realize there were so many orphans in Uganda, Mr. Okwe. Is this because of AIDS?" asked Scott.

"Eeh? No, no. These are not the orphan. These are the night commuter. They leave their village every evening to come and sleep in the town. Some sleep beside the storefront, some on the sidewalk, and some, if they are lucky, find a business that open their door for them to spend the night."

"Why would they do that?" Scott asked.

"To stay safe just," the driver said matter-of-factly. "To stay away from Kony." He spat out the window in disgust.

"So Kony's out here, is he? I thought he was farther north right now," Scott's dad said. "In Sudan."

"Eeh, that Kony, we do not know where he go, but yes, he is near to the village now. That is why the children are footin' here."

"Kony? Who's Kony?" Scott asked.

"Kony? He can only be the devil who come to

kill his own brother and sister. That is all he can be. He is like the snake. Very evil. Very cunning."

The driver inched forward and parked next to the hotel. "Here you are, Dr. Romo and Mr. Scott. I will be waiting here for you when you are ready to leave."

A well-manicured hedge surrounded the hotel while two columns flanked the glass doors. Bright lights, evenly spaced along the pink walls, displayed the name of the five-star hotel: AKELLO. To the left of the building, an easel announced the grand event of the evening: SOROTI CULTURAL SOCIETY PRESENTS A MOST GLORIOUS DISPLAY OF UGANDAN TREASURES AND ART. ALL WELCOME. Scott and his father climbed out of the jeep and entered the hotel. As the doorman accepted a tip from his father, Scott couldn't help but turn around. The glass doors, richly trimmed with brass plating, depicted the scene of the children lying on the street, huddled under their threadbare blankets.

Dr. Moran spotted Scott and his father at the entrance and smiled, bowing his head in acknowledgment. He strode toward the pair and grabbed Scott's hand in his own massive and calloused palm, shaking it until Scott imagined his shoulder dislocating from its socket. "My God, Scott! So young, and you've already discovered your first piece of ancient history! I remember my first find—a mere fossil from a diplodocus. It really wasn't anything wonderful, come to think of it now. I mean, how many fossils of a diplodocus do you see in museums nowadays? I'm sure everyone must have at least two or three in storage. But to me, it was the thing I always wanted to find. Something I was the first to see."

Scott smiled. He knew exactly what Dr. Moran was talking about.

"I heard you're looking into going to the University of Toronto when you graduate from Grade 12."

"Yes, I hope to get accepted there, sir."

"A great university. Many fine graduates come out of there, including yours truly, of course." Dr. Moran's voice trailed off. "Yes, only fifteen years old," he said, shaking his head. "I wonder what you're going to discover next." Then, placing his hand on Scott's shoulder, he ushered him and his dad into the exhibit.

Scott's mouth fell open when he saw the statues, clay pieces, masks, and other artifacts that covered the walls and display stands in the room. He could not imagine anyone, not even his best friend Rob, understanding how cool it was to be here at this exhibit. He was looking at hundreds of priceless artifacts, each gently taken from the ground that had hidden it from human eyes for thousands of years. A new thought came to Scott: *Will they put the skeleton I found on display in some big museum? Now wouldn't that be cool! Homo sapien, 1000 AD—or something like that—Lower Soroti, Uganda. Discovered by Scott Romo.*

He left his father and Dr. Moran so he could check everything out.

It was the masks that first caught his attention. African masks had to be the weirdest of all the masks Scott had seen in his short span of museum visits. The grotesquely distorted wooden faces, combined with an odd assortment of grasses, beads, and colors reminded Scott of some sort of insane Picasso painting. The one he was looking at now was no different. The bulging huge red eyes, set on either side of an elongated nose, stared back at him. The sharp triangular teeth and straw hair added to its strangeness. This guy was having more than a bad hair day.

The shields caught his attention next. Some were made from tree trunks and brightly colored, others made of pounded metal. Some circular, others elongated to protect the whole body. And of course there were the spears, piercing shafts of metal tied to long poles, barbaric and lethal.

Scott declined a glass of pineapple juice a porter offered to him and made his way to a gathering of people around a display set in the center of the room. A tall ceramic figure of a beautiful African woman stood before him. Small thin wisps of braided hair were piled on top of her head, her chin jutted forward, and her face was set with a piercing look of determination. Her right foot, poised in the air, stepped over a massive black mamba snake, dead at her feet.

A display card next to the statue read WHEN WE WILL FIND PEACE in bold black letters.

Scott studied the sculpture. The beauty of the woman's face, the strength of her being, commanded his attention and that of all those who stood with him. Not a murmur was heard. No gasps of awe. No shouts of exclamation. Just total silence.

A lone woman wearing a brightly colored African dress stood off from the group, her gaze directed at the people and the statue that stood in their midst. An elderly woman turned away from the statue and walked toward the woman, her head lowered and eyes to the ground. She bowed at the woman's feet and dropped to her knees. She took hold of the woman's hands and drew them to her face. She pressed them against her wet cheeks, rose, and left.

One by one each onlooker turned their gaze to the woman and came to her side. One by one each clasped her hands, their eyes downcast and solemn. One by one they left, saying nothing, leaving in silence.

Scott stayed, not daring to move, wondering what sadness the statue had delivered to its audience. As he looked more intently, he realized the woman in the art piece looked much like the woman in the bright dress. The faces were the same: their brows were drawn tight, their eyes were fixed forward, and their mouths mirrored each other in a silent strength.

He startled, feeling the hand of the woman rest gently upon his shoulder.

"You do not know what this is about, do you?" the woman asked.

Scott heard the faint lilt of her Lugandan accent and the now-familiar way in which the Ugandan people spoke. Scott shook his head, lowering his eyes, looking away from her hypnotic gaze.

"The woman represent all of the mother who have lost their children to this horrid war. The snake is Kony, the leader of the Lord Resistance Army, the army that has stolen so many children and forced them to become soldier and killer." She paused and drew in a deep breath. "And I do believe someday there will be peace. That is why I created this. To show the world there is hope. Someday the children will return to their mother, and someday they will catch this devil, and he will be made to suffer for all of the pain he has thrust upon his own people. And someday I will see my own son again, and I will hold him and comfort him . . ."

Scott looked up, surprised to see a slight smile creep across her face. He stood, startled.

But it wasn't the smile, so out of place in such a solemn environment, that made him gasp. It was the necklace that hung from the beautiful woman's neck. A small and delicately fashioned chain of gold, from which hung five smooth, polished green stones. Exactly like the stones he had taken from the hands of the skeleton in the cave and that were hidden in his backpack.

"Blandine," Dr. Moran said, coming up beside her and greeting the woman with a kiss on each cheek. "I see you have met my colleague Dr. Romo's son. Scott, I would like to introduce you to Aluko, Blandine," he said, using the traditional way of introducing a person by placing their surname first. "She is an artist here in Uganda, and a dear friend of mine."

Dr. Moran turned his gaze to the statue that had captured so many people's attention. Like all of the others, he stood in total silence, respectful of both the art and its creator.

"Oh, Blandine," he finally said as he enclosed both of her tiny hands in his, "when will this come to an end?"

He guided her outside and onto the sidewalk.

This woman, who stood so stoically, appeared now to fold in the doctor's embrace as he wrapped his massive arms around her tiny body. Briefly, she held on to Dr. Moran, then stepped back and bowed her head. She patted the doctor's hand, walked to the sidewalk's edge, and stood next to a fruit peddler's cart.

"Well, Scott," his dad said, coming up behind him and interrupting his thoughts, "we have to get going. We'll just have enough time to get back to the hotel and catch a couple hours of sleep before we have to drive to Entebbe."

Scott nodded and walked out the doors while his dad followed him onto the sidewalk. Dr. Moran shook his dad's hand. "We'll see each other again soon, I hope."

"Of course. Perhaps in another year or two. I'll email you the report as soon as it's completed."

"Wonderful. And perhaps next time you'll come during the rainy season. Then you can see the Pearl of Africa at her finest," said Dr. Moran.

"Pearl of Africa? Now that was Churchill who called Uganda that, wasn't it?"

"Yes, I believe it was when he visited our country in 1908, or was it before that? Now let me see . . ."

"I'm sure it was before 1908. Didn't he write his book, *My African Journey*, then?" Scott's dad pulled at his chin, deep in thought.

"Ah, if you'll just excuse me for a moment, I'll let you guys talk." Scott walked to the edge of the sidewalk and stood beside Blandine. He peered into the cart. "Don't think we'll be heading to Entebbe anytime soon," he said quietly.

"Have you had an orange during your stay here, Scott?" Blandine asked.

"Yes. Yes, I have."

Blandine placed a coin in the fruit peddler's hand and picked out two oranges. "They are so sweet when you can pick them right from the tree and eat them, but I am sure these will do."

She passed the ripe fruit to Scott, then began to peel her orange.

Scott glanced from his orange to the stones on her neck. The green color, the size, the slight silvery sheen—yes, there was no mistaking it. They were identical to the stones he had found in the cave.

"You find interest in my stone? Am I correct, Scott?"

He took a slight step backward. "Yes," he said. He dropped his gaze and stared at the cracked pavement at his feet.

"You seem to me to be very unaware of what is Uganda, but yet you have an interest in all that you see. I am right, yes?"

Scott nodded.

“There is a story about the stone. Would you like to hear it?” She stared into Scott’s eyes, searching his face until the corners of her mouth turned up, revealing the same slight smile she gave him in the museum.

“Yes,” he said.

“Come, sit,” she said, sitting on the edge of the cart and tapping the worn wooden board beside her.

Scott sat.

Chapter 3

He who loves the vase loves also what is inside. ~ African proverb

Blandine popped the last slice of orange into her mouth and licked her lips. She clasped her hands together and placed them on her lap, then drew in a deep breath and sighed. "Like most Ugandan children, I grew up listening to many story. Every evening, when the day was done of it care and obligation, our family sat around a fire and our grandmother and grandfather told us the story their grandmother and grandfather told them. I think your culture call these story legend or myth. But to us these story were as alive and real as the person who told them.

"When I turned thirteen year, my mother told me a story I had never heard before. She repeated it to me every night until I was able to repeat it to her, word for word, gesture for gesture. It has been many year since I told the story, but I know it very well."

She patted Scott's knee and began. "Long ago there was a beautiful young woman who had taken many heart from the men in the village. It was said her beauty could not be compared with anything. Her eyes were like those of a young kob, deep brown, golden, forever searching and gazing, delighting in the beauty of the world. And her skin! Her skin glowed like the browned grass as it captured the ray of the rising sun.

"Many man wanted her for their wife, and many tried to prove they were worthy of her. But she would only turn her eyes to one man, and it was this one man she agreed to have for her husband.

"When people from the neighboring village heard she had promised herself in marriage, they assumed the man she chose was the strongest and most handsome of the tribe. But when they came that day to celebrate the marriage, they were quite disappointed. The man was neither of these, and none could understand how such a beautiful woman could marry such a plain and ordinary man.

"The first day of marriage should be filled with the joy of togetherness, but from the moment the young woman and the young man wed there was nothing but worry and fear in their life. Each of the men who were denied the young woman love sought to end the life of the man who possessed such a firm hold of it.

"One day a venomous snake that never strayed into the village was found hiding in the blanket of the young man bed, it tail tied to the center post of the hut. Another time, while the young man was walking through the jungle, several large fruit, still green and not ready to fall from their high loft, came crashing down onto the ground, just a hand space away from the man head.

"And there were many other frightful thing that happened each day that bore down on their life until the man became so fearful that he shut himself in his hut. He would only leave the security of his home when his beloved wife called to him and asked to keep her company while they ate near the fire and watched the sun set in the distant hill.

"And so it came to pass that the young woman became pregnant and gave birth to twin, a boy and a girl, and they were doubly blessed.

"When it came time for the village witch doctor to lay the name upon the children, the couple was very afraid, for they believed many of the evil trick were his doing. After all, he had been the greatest pursuer of her love and the most shunned.

"When the time came for the ceremony, the

woman laid the boy and girl at the *lajok* feet and stood back to hear the name he had chosen for her children. But when the *lajok* looked onto her children face, he leaped back and let out a piercing scream. 'There is great evil here!' he shouted. 'A powerful *jok* has entered your child body and has claimed it for it own. The spirit will use your child to do much evil in our village!'

"The order the *lajok* gave to the new mother ripped her heart: she was to take both children to the *Lagoro Rock*, a place where all of the tribe sacred festival were held, and, under the light of the new moon, she was to lay them flat on it cold surface and wait for the evil spirit to cry out from the child. Whichever child cried would be the child she must kill.

"He handed her a knife and told her she must leave with the children at once.

"When the woman turned to her husband to seek comfort from his face, she saw only bitterness. The husband glared at the *lajok*; the corner of the man mouth were upturned in the smallest hint of a smile.

"The young woman placed the knife in her pouch and gathered her children in her arm. She left her village and walked until the sun had set and the full moon rose into the blackened sky.

"She did not place her children onto the bare

rock to hear which child would cry. Instead, she found a nearby cave, lit a fire, and nursed her children until they fell asleep. As she warmed her body with the heat from the fire, she thought of what she must do. A plan had formed in her head as she walked away from her village, but she did not know if she could summon the courage to follow through with the terrible task.

"Closing her eyes, she drew in a deep breath and plunged her face into the fire. She held it in the flame until she smelled the sickening stench of burnt hair and flesh.

"When she saw her hideous reflection in a pool of water, her grief was immeasurable. Her wailing filled the cave, and the tear that rolled down her disfigured face burned as they touched the reddened flesh.

"As each drop coursed down her cheek it fell onto the fire until the fire became a small whiff of smoke and then was no more. When the fire was stilled, the rock that lay beneath the gray coal had cracked and broken and now lay as a pile of smooth, polished stone.

"Weary from her pain and suffering, the woman held her children to her breast and fell asleep on the cold ground. The dream that came to her that night, however, did not allow her any rest. The *lajok* was well aware of her disdain for his command and sent an evil spirit to do what she had failed to do. All through the night the spirit wrestled with the woman, attempting to pull a child from her grasp, inflicting horrible pain on her, sending demon into her mind, torturing both her body and her spirit. But it could not match the strength of the mother. She fought a good and courageous fight and won.

“When the early-morning light spread it first ray onto the darkened earth, Lagoro, the spirit of all that is good and right in our world, visited the sleeping mother and looked upon her with great happiness.

“Gathering the stone from the fire, Lagoro placed them into three sack and tied a sack around the neck of the boy child, the girl child, and finally the mother. She lifted the woman hand and held it to her own, smiled, and left.

“When the woman woke she felt the weight of the sack on her chest and held it in her hand. When she saw that the same sack hung from the neck of both of her children, she knew Lagoro had visited her that night and blessed their life.

“She wrapped her children to her body and returned to her village. When the people saw her, they screamed. Many turned and covered their eyes, and many fled at the sight of her disfigured face. All except her husband. He greeted her with a loving embrace, then bowed at her feet—something a man had never done before a woman—for he knew she had sacrificed her beauty for him.

“When the *lajok* heard of the woman return, he ran to the family hut and found the woman holding her children under an acacia tree. Ripping the boy child from her arm, he pulled a knife from his side and held it to the child heart.

“She cried and fell to her knee, lifting her palm up to the *lajok*, begging for his mercy.

“The *lajok* stopped and stared at the woman, his eyes wide and his mouth open. He dropped his knife, placed the child on the ground, and ran as he had never run before.

“The woman stared at the *lajok*, her husband, and her children, then at her upturned palm.

“There, in the middle of her right hand, lay a blackened ring the size of a walnut, singed into her palm. It was the mark of protection from Lagoro, and no one, not even the highest *lajok*, could harm her.”

Blandine let out a sigh and smiled. “I love that story. I think it is my favorite out of all the story I hear as a child. It tell of a mother unselfish love for her husband and her children. I can understand that, just like all the mother who have also lost their children to Kony. I only wish each mother had her own protective mark.”

Tears ran over her cheeks. A quiet moment passed until she wiped them away with the back of her hand.

"So is the story true?" Scott asked.

"True? What is the truth? There are many story that have been passed on from one generation to the next, the elder passing it on to the younger. But as each generation accept the story, it lose it strength and the story turn from truth to legend, from legend to myth—a myth to entertain the children around the fire at night. Nothing more."

"But the stones on your necklace? Do you think they're Lagoro's?"

Blandine looked intently into Scott's eyes. "That is what my ancestor have said each time they pass the stone on to the next child. And as a child we do accept it as the truth. As an adult, I am not too sure."

"But the stones the children carried. What does the story tell about the children and their stones?"

"Now that I do not know. There is another story I have heard about a great famine and a woman who sent her children away, one east and one west to search for green land, each bearing a powerful gift from the god. But there is nothing to say it was the same children or if the gift they held was the stone."

Blandine paused. "My mother called the stone

tyero or *tumu* stone." She stopped and ran her fingers over her necklace. "Now what would that word be in your language? Sometime there are word in our language that cannot be found in yours. Perhaps the word is . . . sacrifice? But no, that does not come close to it enough. It is more than that. Sacrifice—not given willingly—but yes, given still. And then it become willing. Is there a word for that in your language?"

Scott's brow creased in deep thought. Finally, he shook his head. "I'm not too sure about that. I don't think I've heard of an English word that means anything like that."

"That is too bad," Blandine said.

Scott's dad and Dr. Moran walked toward the cart.

"Well, Scott. We better get a move on. I'd love to stay and talk longer, but we've got to get going," his dad said. He turned to Blandine and introduced himself. "You kept my son's attention for a long time. You must have had something quite interesting to tell, but then again, anything about Africa is interesting."

She laughed.

"I hope we can meet again," Scott's dad said.

Blandine took his hands in hers and held them. "Yes, that would be lovely. But please bring your son with you. I am sure he would enjoy coming back again."

"Of course. Once you've been to Africa, you can't wait to see her again."

Scott shook Blandine's hand. "Thank you for the story, Mrs. Aluko. I enjoyed it very much."

Dr. Moran grasped Scott's hand and gave it a firm squeeze. "And thank you, Scott, for sharing your discovery with us. You have no idea what this means." He paused and shook his head. "No, I'm sure you do know what this means. Let's keep in touch, shall we?"

Scott nodded and smiled, then climbed into the jeep. He turned in his seat and watched Blandine reach into her purse and place a handful of coins into the fruit peddler's hands. As the jeep pulled past the museum, swarms of children gathered around the storyteller. She laughed as she passed her newly purchased oranges into the children's outstretched hands, grinning at their smiling faces and cheerful shouts of laughter.

Somewhere a beating drum caught Scott's attention. The *rum-de-rum-rum, rum-de-rum-rum* sound filled the air. Soon the boys and girls lifted their arms and began to pound the earth with their energetic jumps and twists.

Scott drew every image and every sound into his mind, trying to hold on to every part of Uganda he could before he had to head home.

When the town was out of sight, he turned around and stared into the dark African night. Somewhere out there was a troop of children, including Blandine's son, forced to fight and kill for a madman. And there, left behind in the town, huddled on the sidewalks and the storefronts, lying on the cold ground, were hundreds and hundreds of children who left the comfort of their homes and family to find protection from a man named Kony. A man who was compared to a snake. A black mamba snake, the deadliest and most feared snake in Uganda.

Scott closed his eyes and drew in a long deep breath. He couldn't help but wonder: With so much horror and pain in Uganda, what reason could there be to dance?

Chapter 4

Instruction in youth is like engraving in stone. ~ Moroccan proverb

The first thing Scott thought of when they pulled up to their house in Toronto was his toilet. There were three bathrooms in the house, one for each of them, and he couldn't wait to enjoy the luxury of being able to rest his butt on a plastic seat on a porcelain throne. There was no way he could enjoy such a relaxed "position" in Uganda. He just couldn't get the knack of aiming his butt over a bicycle-seat-shaped hole in the ground. If he'd had a few more weeks there, he may have gotten used to the ice-cold showers, the tough chicken, and the red dirt that always blew in his face, but he knew he would never grow fond of traditional Ugandan toilets.

He heaved his suitcase onto the sidewalk and breathed a sigh of relief.

"Nothing like home sweet home, hey, Scott?" his father said.

"Yeah," Scott said as he pulled his suitcase down the walkway. "Nothing like home sweet home."

He walked down the basement stairs to his bedroom, closed his door, and dropped his backpack on his bed. He rubbed his eyes and let out a huge yawn. The thirteen-hour flight to London and then the nine-hour connecting flight to Toronto, plus all the stopovers, had made for a really long, long weekend. And with school starting the next day, Scott had to change his body clock from African time to Canadian time ASAP. He'd be slightly embarrassed if he fell asleep in his first-period Grade 10 social studies class.

But sleep would have to wait.

During the flight home Scott couldn't keep his mind off the stones. And it wasn't easy resisting the temptation to take them out of his backpack when it lay only a foot away, tucked under the seat ahead of him.

Many thoughts bounced around in his head. The story Blandine had told him: Was it true? "What is the truth?" she asked him. Strange. Really strange. And yet . . . it could have some truth in it. Couldn't it? No. Highly unlikely.

And the stones given to the children. Could the

skeleton be that of the boy or girl who got the stones from the god Lagoro? But ancient African tales were just that: tales told to children to teach them lessons about life. This story showed young girls that beauty wasn't important. That true love didn't rely on beauty. Nothing more to the story.

And that thing that happened in the cave, when he suddenly found himself in the middle of some kind of war or battle or . . . What of that?

Scott rationalized it all. He told himself he'd been light-headed. *And who wouldn't be?* he thought. It was a hundred degrees out there, and the air in the cave was dead. Stifling dead.

He told himself he'd probably blacked out and some scene from a war movie he had once watched replayed itself in his mind. Nothing more.

But as each argument played out in his head, a nagging doubt confronted his voice of reason. It had to be real. It felt so real.

There was only one way to find out. He would try the stones again. And then he would tell Rob. Only a good friend would take him seriously on this.

Scott opened his backpack, pulled out his T-shirt, and carefully unwrapped the leather pouch. His hands shook as he pulled the cord away.

He opened the pouch and stared at the five stones. Green, round, and polished. A faint shimmer of silver passed over them as the room's light reflected off their shiny surfaces.

It was now or never.

Scott grasped a stone in his hand, held it for a moment, and then dropped it back into the pouch, just as he did that afternoon in the cave.

He closed his eyes, his body tensed, and he waited.

Nothing happened.

He opened his eyes and picked up a different stone, held it, and dropped it back into the pouch.

Nothing.

He tried each stone.

Nothing. Nothing. *Nothing.*

Scott sat back.

"I could have sworn . . . But maybe . . ." He pulled out his laptop and googled "green rocks and minerals." The page showed a variety of stones and gems including emerald, fluorite, malachite, and amazonite, but nothing even came close to having the same hue of green—or the shimmering silver color—of the stone when he had turned it over and over with his fingers. *Too weird,* he thought.

His mind drifted to the story—or myth—Blandine told him. *There's got to be more to the story,* he thought as he typed in "Ugandan legends myths stories."

Scott sifted through the items and searched for

the story the artist had told him while he sat beside her on the edge of the orange cart. There were plenty of tales about kings, evil spirits, and animals that talked, but nothing about a woman who plunged her face into a fire and received a sack of stones as her reward.

How about . . .? He typed in "Blandine Aluko." *Maybe there's something about the stones in her necklace. Can't hurt to try.*

The number of items about the woman was staggering. As Scott sifted through the newspaper and magazine articles, she took on an interesting and compelling personality. Not only was she a popular artist in Uganda, but she was also very active in her role as a spokesperson for the many children who had been abducted by the Lord's Resistance Army, or LRA, led by Joseph Kony.

One article described the time Blandine's son had been captured while he was spending the night at a friend's place out in the countryside. "I had heard of Kony, and I had heard of his horrid way of creating his own army of brainwashed children. But I did not know he had traveled so far into the interior of Uganda. I would never have let my son go there if I had known of the danger. I would never have put him at risk . . ."

Scott clicked onto another article and read: "We must not stand idly by while this awful man continue to lead his army into all our village and school to abduct our children. No mother or father should have their children torn from their arm, and no child should be forced to become a soldier. If our government cannot do anything about it, then we as parent must do what we can to stop Kony."

Scott went to a different site—one that spoke about Blandine's involvement with a recovery center in Gulu, in northern Uganda, for former child soldiers. "I have come against a brick wall," Blandine told a reporter from the *Daily Monitor*. "I do not have a tank or machine gun, and I do not have an army. But I have compassion, and I will do what I can for the children who manage to escape from the LRA. This recovery center we have created will welcome all children and provide them with medical attention, counseling . . ."

Scott scrolled to the next page and found a picture of Blandine wearing the necklace with the smooth green stones. Of course, nothing was written about it, only some information about the important fundraising event that was held at the prestigious Grand Imperial Hotel, with all proceeds going toward the recovery center.

Scott opened another tab, typed in "Joseph Kony," and read about the man whose name caused their Ugandan driver to spit in disgust: "Head of the Lord's Resistance Army . . . a guerrilla group . . .

violent campaign . . . abducted sixty thousand children . . . displaced over two million people . . . number eight on the world's ten most wanted . . . unimaginable crimes against his own people, especially children . . . some as young as seven or eight years of age . . ."

"Scott?" A faint knock came from his door. "Are you still up? Can I come in?" His mom poked her head around the door.

"Sure, Mom."

"It was lonely here for the last two weeks. I missed you guys, you know?" She leaned over and gave him a squeeze and sat down beside him. "I still can't get over you finding that skeleton, though. Your dad's real proud of you—even if he's burning with jealousy that he didn't find it first." She laughed, patting him on the back. "Quite the thrill, eh?"

Scott nodded.

"What are you looking at?" She stared at the laptop screen. "Why are you looking at this site about Joseph Kony?"

He yawned and told his mom about the night commuters searching for places to sleep on the sidewalks and storefronts during the night. He then described the statue and his encounter with the artist.

"Yeah, I know about Kony. That's what

happens when you work in the humanitarian field. You tend to know about all of the injustices going on in the world. Even the ones that don't make the headlines. But I didn't know he was anywhere near where you and Dad were staying. When I asked at our office what was going on with Kony, they told me he was in Sudan. Maybe I should have been a bit worried about you," she said, tousling Scott's hair, "but you were with Dad so I knew everything would be fine. As it is, we've been working with one of the northern Uganda offices for years now, helping to fund the recovery center in Gulu. I'm working with their relations team right now, seeing how we can get more support from our government."

The wave of fatigue that had been slowly creeping over Scott disappeared. Of course his mom would know about Kony and the recovery center. She was heavily involved with African relations where she worked.

He searched back on his laptop and found the picture of Blandine. He pointed to the photo on the screen. "Do you know this woman? Her name's Blandine Aluko. She's the one who made the statue."

"Blandine Aluko? Yes, I've heard of her. She's been instrumental in setting up that recovery center in Gulu for the kids who manage to escape. Her son was abducted years ago by the LRA. She's thrown herself into this center completely. Working there, holding fundraisers, speaking out to the press. A remarkable woman."

"Yeah. She seemed to be very well respected by everyone at the museum."

"I've got a book in my briefcase the Ugandan office has written about Kony and child soldiers and the recovery center if you want to see it. I brought it home from the office to do some extra reading," she said as she walked to the door.

"Sure, Mom," Scott replied. He was curious about this so-called war he had known nothing about until just a couple of days ago.

Scott's mom returned moments later, clasping a thin paperback to her chest. "The book gave me nightmares." She thumbed the pages with one hand. "Maybe it's from being a mom and imagining losing your child like that." She drew in a deep breath as she stared at the cover. A crude crayon drawing of a war scene, obviously drawn by a young child, was positioned under the book's title: *Pawns of politics: children, conflict and peace in northern Uganda*. The scene showed a group of children, their hands tied behind their backs, being forced to leave their burning village. "I don't know what I'd do if that ever happened to you. I'd go insane with grief—I know I would." She passed the book to him reluctantly. "But," she said, pausing, "you know I've never been one to keep you sheltered from the goings-on in the world. Go ahead and read it, but there are a lot of frightening things in there."

* * * *

Scott woke and stared at the clock on his nightstand: 1:27 a.m. He had slept only three hours. He hated time changes. It would be 8:27 a.m. in Uganda. The roosters would have crowed there hours ago.

It always took him days to adjust, but the winter holidays were over and now he had to get back to the reality of school and homework. Scott rolled over, turned on his light, and grabbed the book his mom had given him earlier that evening. Maybe a bit of reading would help him fall asleep. *Besides*, he thought, *how bad could it be?* He'd watched plenty of war movies and read a few books about WWI and WWII and some of the recent wars. Sometimes his mom could be so melodramatic.

He turned the pages and began to read a passage his mom had highlighted:

I was in Primary 2 when I was abducted. I was coming home for lunch and as I rounded a bend, eight rebels suddenly appeared and aimed a gun at me. They dared me to run else they would shoot me. They took my books and tore them all, and tied me up. One person was given to guard me and asked me if Ugandan People's Defense Force soldiers likes patrolling that route. I denied but they maintained their ambush.

At five o'clock in the evening, I heard gunshots and after a short while, four rebels were shot dead by the UPDF. When the others came back, they then decided to kill me because I had deceived them and made them lose four soldiers.

They tied me up again but one of them decided that I should not be killed. I had lost all hope of living again, and my heart pounded loudly, and still, I believed they would kill me during the night.

Scott shut the book, placed it on the nightstand, and started to think: *Primary 2. That meant Grade 2. The kid was seven, maybe eight years old when he was taken.* He shook his head in disgust and thought back to the way the driver spat on the ground when he said Kony's name. *If I were ever to see this Kony guy, I'd do more than just spit,* he thought.

Scott lay down and tried to make himself sleep. Sleep—sweet, peaceful sleep. Soon his eyelids began to close. And in that dreamlike moment, halfway between sleep and wakefulness, he found himself heading off to school, down the cement sidewalk, walking with his friend Rob. As they walked, the sidewalk gave way to a hard-packed red clay ground. He heard the sounds of children playing and shouting everywhere around him.

"Scott! Over here! Pass the ball!" One of Scott's classmates jumped, trying to gain more height as he stood near the basketball net.

Scott reached for the ball that lay on the ground and threw it with all his might. It whizzed through the air, twisting and turning. He stood mesmerized as the black lines of the ball became thicker, more pronounced, and began to twist and fall from the ball. To his horror, long thick black snakes pulled themselves from the ball and fell to the ground. Hissing and slithering toward his classmates, the snakes quickly wrapped themselves around their wrists and ankles, pulling them to the pavement. Scott let out a stifled cry as the school bell rang and the rest of the children walked into the school, ignoring the bodies of his friends as they lay on the ground.

"Scott!" Rob cried as a snake wrapped itself around his neck and began to squeeze.

"Scott! Scott!" The voice became louder and clearer. "Scott! It's time to get up. You'll be late for school!"

He rubbed his eyes with the back of his hand. His heart throbbed and he was drenched in a cold, prickly sweat. His mom was right. There were a lot of frightening things in that book.

Chapter 5

If you close your eyes to facts, you will learn through accidents. ~ African proverb

"You're late, Mr. Romo."

Scott looked behind him, expecting to see his father. "What?"

Social studies class—he'd stepped into Mr. Smeld's classroom, where everyone was addressed as an adult: Mr. Romo, Mr. Brown, Miss Black, Miss White.

Mr. Smeld repeated himself. "You're late, Mr. Romo. Go get a late slip."

Scott did an about-face and headed to the office. "Now this is stupid," he said under his breath. "I'm already late."

Five minutes into the class, Scott handed the pink slip to Mr. Smeld and searched the room for an empty seat. There was only one, the second seat from the front, where he'd be staring into the huge hulking figure of Bruce *Jerk*-ins.

"Lovely, just friggin' lovely." Scott slid into his seat.

On the board in bold letters Scott read "Grade 10 social studies discussion groups." *Oh great*, he thought, *Mr. Smeld's four corners discussion groups*. His grade eleven friends had warned him about these supposedly interactive, peer-directed chat groups.

Scott opened his binder and pulled out a piece of paper.

"Thanks," Bruce said, turning around and grabbing the paper from his hand, "I forgot mine."

Scott glared at Bruce's back.

"Now if you could get into the groups I assigned you, read aloud the article I'll be giving each group, and then begin your discussion. You'll have to assign someone in your group to record your opinions. Okay, everyone. Let's get started."

Mr. Smeld walked over to Scott's desk. "Mr. Romo, you'll be joining this group here," he said, pointing to Bruce and two girls sitting in the next row.

Scott's head slumped onto his chest and he sighed while doing a mental review. First there was Bruce: all bulk and no brains. Then Vicky Tiff, who was cute but a bit of a drama queen. Finally, Hailey Rubenstein, a nice-looking redhead, smart and on the student council but with no time for boys. At least, that's what Scott had determined since she ignored every boy in the school, including him.

This is going to suck, he thought, taking a handout from Mr. Smeld.

"Okay. Who wants to read first?" Hailey said, looking at each member of the group.

Scott could see those "fine" leadership qualities already being put to use.

He and Vicky looked at their papers. Bruce had already put his "creative" talents to work and had transformed his handout into a paper airplane.

"Well," Hailey said, unfazed, "then I'll start. Jump in when you want."

After a couple of paragraphs, Scott began to read. He found the Wikipedia article interesting because it was something he was a bit familiar with. His mom often brought up world issues to discuss at the dinner table since they affected her work so much.

"'The war in Darfur began in February 2003 when the Sudan Liberation Army and the Justice and Equality Movement group took up arms, accusing the Sudanese government of oppressing the non-Arab Sudanese in favor of Sudanese Arabs . . .'"

Bruce drew a couple of swastikas on the paper airplane's wings.

"On the other side of the conflict are the Sudanese military and police and the Jangaweed, a Sudanese militia group recruited mostly from the Arabized indigenous Africans . . .'"

The plane flew over Scott's head and did a perfect nosedive into the garbage can.

Vicky began to read: "'There are various estimates on the number of human casualties, which range up to several thousand dead, from either direct combat or starvation and disease inflicted by the conflict. There have also been mass displacements and . . .'"

"Blah, blah, blah," Bruce said as he crossed his arms over his chest, leaned back in his chair, and looked up at the ceiling.

"'Coercive migrations, forcing millions into refugee camps or over the border and creating a large humanitarian crisis.'"

Vicky stopped. She was obviously upset about what she had just read. She looked down at the paper and sighed.

Hailey read the question. "It says here we have to discuss this statement: 'Should our government provide military and financial assistance to the people of Sudan?' Well, Bruce, what do you think?" Hailey said, with the emphasis on "you." She looked peeved. Hailey liked to take things seriously, and she obviously didn't take too kindly to Bruce's artwork on the plane. Her last name was Rubenstein. Go figure.

Bruce took his plane from the garbage and opened it. "I don't get it," he said.

"What's not to get?" Hailey asked. "It's simple. The Arab people in Sudan are killing the non-Arab people, and thousands of people are dying. It's simple. And stupid. Almost as stupid as your pathetic Nazi airplane."

Scott stared at Hailey and then at Bruce. He had never seen anyone, at least not anyone in their right mind, stand up to Bruce.

"You know, Hailey, it's a good thing you're wearing a training bra or I'd hit you."

Hailey glared at Bruce, then picked up a pen and started to write. It seemed she was working hard not to let Bruce get to her.

Vicky jumped in. "Well, I think it *is* stupid. I've seen this on the news. I saw this long road filled with people, and mothers carrying their children. They showed this one boy who was nothing but skin and bones. Now tell me why shouldn't we help them?" A slight tremor caught in her voice.

"'Cause it's like this," Bruce cut in. "It's the survival of the fittest. The strong survive, the weak die."

Scott's eyes flew open as he stared at Bruce.

"Besides, the world's overpopulated as it is. Get rid of 'em all. If they wanna kill each other off, let 'em."

This time Hailey couldn't keep her cool. "They don't want to fight, Bruce." Her words came through gritted teeth. "These are men and women who just want to raise their children and keep them safe."

"Oh, I don't know 'bout that. Have you seen some of the weapons those women hide under those long dresses they have to wear? Those bushka things? I wouldn't trust any woman—"

"It's called a burqa, and we're talking Sudan, not Afghanistan," Hailey said. She glared at Bruce.

Scott shook his head. Years of hating Bruce through elementary school and high school had culminated in a final realization: Bruce had graduated from being a stupid bully to being a real stupid asshole.

Finally Scott spoke. "I bet you wouldn't think like that if the problem was right here, and you and your family were being shot because you were from the wrong group."

"That's where you're wrong, Scotty," Bruce said, smiling as he leaned over the desk. "I'd be the one doing all the shooting. It's all survival of the fittest."

Hailey, Vicky, and Scott stared at Bruce and shook their heads.

Bruce had just won the least-popular person in the group award.

"Okay everyone, return to your seats and let's hear your opinions on this."

Chairs scuffed across the floor as the class looked up at the board, where Mr. Smeld had written "democracy" in huge red letters.

"Now remember," Mr. Smeld continued, "we live in a democratic society, and that means we're all entitled to our opinions, and we can voice them because we all have freedom of speech. So that being said, let's have a show of hands. Raise your hand if you think our government should provide assistance to the people of Sudan."

All hands went up except for two or three. Bruce leaned back in his chair and crossed his arms over his chest.

"And raise your hand if you think our government should not . . ."

Bruce raised his hand, high into the air.

"Okay, then, Mr. Jenkins," Mr. Smeld said as he walked to Bruce's desk. "Looks like you're in the minority here. I'm interested. What makes you think we shouldn't send aid to Sudan?"

"'Cause it's every man for himself, Mr. Smeld.

Survival of the fittest. It's like I said to the group. If people wanna go 'round killing each other, let 'em. The world's overpopulated as it is. Nothin' like a little war now and then to get rid of a few thousand or more."

Instantly the class was in chaos. Students yelled at Bruce while Mr. Smeld tried desperately to quiet everyone down.

Bruce had just won the least-popular person in the class award.

Chapter 6

Never marry a woman who has bigger feet than you. ~ Mozambican proverb

Scott closed his eyes and rested his head on his locker door. It had been a long day.

"Hey, there you are. I was looking for you at lunch. Where were you?"

Scott turned his head and opened one eye. Through thick black-rimmed glasses a pair of brown eyes stared back at him. A grin that could have been pasted on any goofy comic book character revealed a set of silver braces and orange elastics.

"I fell asleep on the gym bleachers. I'm still on Ugandan time."

"So how was it? Did you get me anything?"

Scott laughed. Leave it to Rob to get right to the point.

"It was great, and yeah, I got you something." He reached into his jacket pocket. "Here."

Rob read the label out loud. "'Chew 4 U. A Tongue Sensation.' No way! You brought me bubblegum from Africa?"

Scott gave his head a slight shake and smiled. He liked this quality about Rob. He was one of those guys who would think he'd won the lottery if he found a quarter left in a soda vending machine.

"I know you can't have any right now because it'll stick to your braces, but I figured you can have it later, when you get them off."

"Heck, no. I'm not waiting! This is great!" Rob ripped open the package and popped a black square into his mouth. "I don't think I've ever seen bubblegum this color," he said, blowing a huge black bubble. "Thanks! You want a piece?"

"No, that's okay. I've got another package," Scott said, patting his pocket. He paused and lowered his voice to a whisper. "We've known each other for a long time, right?"

"Yeah."

"And I can trust you with anything, right?"

"Course. What gives?"

"I've got something else I want to show you, but . . ."

"But what?"

"But you have to promise not to tell anyone, and I mean *anyone*. Promise?"

"Yeah. Promise. I'll sign an oath in blood if you want me to."

Scott turned his back to the hall and faced his locker. He reached into his pocket and pulled out the leather sack containing the five stones.

His voice was barely above a whisper. "I found it in the hands of a skeleton in a cave my dad and I were exploring."

He opened the pouch and pulled out a stone. Rob moved in closer.

"In the hands of a skeleton, eh? That's kinda cool."

"But there's more."

Scott told Rob everything from beginning to end: from prying the sack from the skeleton's hands and hiding it in his backpack, to seeing the same type of stones on Blandine's necklace, to telling him the bizarre legend she'd told him as they sat outside the hotel. He purposely omitted the part about the vision in the cave. That would have to wait. For a moment.

Rob stared at the stones, then at Scott, and back to the stones again. His chewing grew more and more intense. "No! That's crazy! I mean, you're kidding me. You find the stones and then the same types of stones—almost exact replicas—appear on some lady's necklace? That's just too weird."

Scott smiled. It felt good to finally share his story with Rob and see the look on his face.

"Did you see any other stones like them anywhere else?"

Scott thought about this briefly. "No, I saw some turquoise stones and some malachite. They're both greenish-colored stones, but nothing this shade of green."

"But isn't your dad gonna kill you when he finds out you've taken 'em and not told him about 'em?"

"Yeah. But there's more to the stones." Scott paused. "Try this for me, okay? Open up your hand." He placed the stone in the palm of Rob's hand. "Now hold it and put it back into the pouch."

Rob did exactly as Scott asked.

"Anything happen?"

"What do you mean, 'anything happen?'"

"I mean, did you see or hear anything strange?"

"No. Should I have?"

Scott stared at the stones and closed the bag. His shoulders dropped. "No, I guess not."

"You're really weird, Scott. I think you need some more sleep."

"Yeah. You're probably right. Are you going home now?"

"No. I got basketball practice."

Scott pocketed the stones in his jacket and walked down the hall, dragging his feet.

"I'll meet you at our spot at eight thirty tomorrow, okay?" Rob yelled.

"Uh-huh," Scott mumbled, feebly waving his arm, barely able to keep his head up.

He turned the corner and walked right into Hailey Rubenstein.

"Hey! Watch where you're going!" she yelled. Two heavy bags fell from her grasp and landed on the floor.

Scott looked at the bags, waiting for the wrath of Hailey to be unleashed. Instead, she picked them up and gave Scott a quick smile.

Was he imagining this?

"That was some class, huh?" she said. "I just loved it when everyone started tearing Bruce apart. Stupid jerk. He deserved it after saying all that about 'survival of the fittest' and 'overpopulation.'"

Scott gave his head a shake.

"I think I'm going to enjoy that class. I wanted to take it, but I wasn't quite sure what it'd be like having Mr. Smeld as a teacher," Hailey continued.

Scott slowly looked up. "Yeah, Smeld is kind of strict," he finally replied.

"I'll say. You were halfway in the door when the bell rang."

“Yeah.” Scott tried to fathom the idea he was actually having a conversation with Hailey Rubenstein, academic wonder and red-headed goddess of Poplar Grove High School.

“Here,” she said, shoving one of the bags into Scott’s arms, “I have to count all this money from the vending machines. The student council gets fifty percent of the profits for the end-of-the-year dance. Come and help me.”

Scott nodded. It was kind of nice being asked—or rather told—by Hailey to do something with her. Who knows what would happen next? Maybe he could see if she wanted to go to the movies and then . . . he gave his head another shake. *This is Hailey Rubenstein*, he reminded himself. *Nothing’s ever going to happen. Nothing*.

Hailey emptied the coins onto a large table in the cafeteria and the two got to work, sorting the quarters, dimes, and nickels into separate piles. Hailey’s hands flew around the table while Scott tried to keep up. He was starting to work up a sweat when he finally took his jacket off and hung it over a chair. He paused and watched Hailey’s green eyes search for quarters, her long red hair tucked behind her ears.

She glanced at Scott and grinned. “You look tired. Long day for you?”

"Yeah, well, no. I didn't sleep much last night or the night before on the plane ride home."

"Plane?"

"Yeah, I spent the winter holidays with my dad in Uganda."

"Uganda? What were you doing there?"

"I was exploring some caves with him. He's an archeologist, and sometimes we go places and check out a dig or a cave or whatever."

"That's so cool! You are so lucky! I would love to go to Africa. I've always thought about going there and working in an orphanage. You know, when I'm a doctor I'm going to join Doctors Without Borders and go over there. They can use all the help they can get. And hey, if I have the skills, why not?"

Scott watched Hailey's eyes grow intense. Beauty, brains, compassion. All of Scott's NO WAY stop signs were buried like a mammoth in a tar pit.

"Tell me all about it," Hailey said as she finished the pile of quarters.

With a newly discovered surge of energy, Scott sat down and gathered a handful of nickels. He told Hailey everything, from the way the people dressed in such intensely bright colors, to the different foods and how great everything tasted cooked in a clay oven, to how he could only drink soda and bottled water because the tap water wasn't safe to drink.

Hailey's eyes never left his face while he replayed his trip, but when he started to tell the story about the cave and the skeleton, and she reached across the table and grabbed his hand, his heart took complete control of his brain and sent any remaining inhibitions into the dark ages.

"No way! Weren't you scared?"

"No, I've seen plenty of skeletons before," he said, shrugging nonchalantly.

"That's just too cool," Hailey said.

Scott saw an opportunity he didn't want to miss. He told her about the frayed piece of leather sticking out of the skeleton's hands and how he'd painstakingly opened each of the fingers until the pouch was revealed. And how he gazed into the sack to see five polished green stones.

"So you think they're a talisman, a sort of good luck charm?" Hailey asked. "I sure would have loved to have seen that. I don't know if I'd be too thrilled about the skeleton. But the stones—that would have been cool to see."

"Really?" He reached into his jacket pocket.

"Hold that thought," Hailey said as she stood. "Do you mind waiting here? I have to go to the office and get some more coin rollers. I'll be back in a sec."

She walked out the cafeteria doors. He would show her the stones when she got back. It would be rather nice to see the look in those fine green eyes.

A muffled ringtone came from his pants pocket. “Hello . . . hello? Just a sec, Mom. The reception’s bad here. I’ll go into the hall.”

Scott walked out of the cafeteria and turned the corner into the hall facing the large outside windows.

“Yeah, I’ll be home right away. Just helping a friend.” A short pause followed. “Yeah, I can do that. Where is it?” He pulled a pen from his pocket and wrote on the palm of his hand. “The red ones and not the green. Got it.” Another pause. “No, I’m okay, just a little tired. Yeah, I’ll get to bed after supper. Love you too, Mom.”

Scott pocketed his phone and walked back toward the room. A high-pitched scream came from the direction of the cafeteria. He darted around the corner and ran into the room to see Hailey looking at the table where they had sorted the money.

The money was gone.

“Where were you?” Hailey demanded.

“I just went out into the hallway. My mom called and the reception was bad,” he said.

“You idiot!” she yelled. “I asked you to stay here while I went to get the rollers and you left the money here? Without someone watching it? How stupid can you be?"

Scott shrugged. "I was only gone for a couple of minutes."

"A couple of minutes? Well, that was plenty of time for whoever took the money!"

She stormed out of the room.

Scott turned to look at the chair where he had been sitting. It was bare too. Whoever had taken the money had decided to help themselves to his jacket as well.

"Shit!" he yelled, slamming his fist on the table.

He turned and walked out of the cafeteria, rubbing his arms. That it would be a cold walk home and he didn't have a hope in hell of getting Hailey to go to the movies with him were the least of his concerns. All he could think about was the small leather pouch and the five green stones that lay inside his jacket pocket, and the fact that he, more than likely, would never see them again.

Chapter 7

Sticks in a bundle are unbreakable.
~ Bondei proverb

Bruce trudged into his room and tossed his bag onto the bed. It landed with a thud.

"And you're not going anywhere until it's clean!" a voice yelled. "I'm sick of your room looking like a pigsty. I'm sick of you and your—"

Bruce slammed the door.

Loud footfalls came down the hallway. The door flew open. His stepmom stood in the frame, her arms crossed over her chest.

"Don't slam the door. I just put Ben to bed." She walked into the room and looked down into a crib sitting next to Bruce's bed. The boy was still sleeping. "Here," she said, tossing him a box of garbage bags. "Use these. And don't just leave them in your room. Put them in the Dumpster where the garbage belongs." She turned on her heel, then stopped and looked over her shoulder.

"Listen. I know I ain't your mom, and I know you don't like me telling you what to do. But get over it. Your dad certainly ain't around enough to tell you anything, so I'm the next best thing. And you better get that into your head."

Bruce glared. "Sh, baby's sleeping," he said, holding his finger to his lips, his mouth fixed in a smirk. He shut the door.

He glanced at his room. Empty chip bags, chocolate bar wrappers, and soda cans lay on the floor, on top of his dresser, and under his bed. Piles of dirty socks, underwear, T-shirts and jeans were shoved into the corners. A long string of electrical cords from the TV, video console, and speakers wound their way through the mess, overloading a power strip hidden under a pile of clothes. On his bed, a single sheet lay twisted and crunched into a ball beside a pillow sporting a well-worn Mickey Mouse pillowcase cover.

"So you want a clean room, huh? Well, you got it."

Bruce grabbed a pile of the clothes from the corner and carried it to the laundry room. After two more trips he had left a huge mound next to the washing machine. "That should keep the witch busy for a while," he muttered under his breath.

He returned to his room and pulled a garbage bag from the box. He opened the red tabs and walked around the room, tossing in a pile of chip and taco bags, candy wrappers, and soda cans. He picked up a dinner plate, thickly crusted with dried spaghetti sauce, stared at it for a second, then dropped it into the bag. A couple of forks followed and fell with a resounding clang on the plate. He added several glasses with chocolate milk scum dried at their bottoms, along with a mushy apple and a very fuzzy green orange.

Bruce crouched on his knees and swung his arm under his bed, bringing a pile of clothes and more garbage into the open.

He glared at the mound and blew his breath out of his nostrils in a noisy huff. He was not making another trip to the laundry room. That was for sure. With one hand he grabbed the clothes and garbage and shoved it into the bag. He tied the full bag, threw it into the corner near his door, and grabbed one more from the box. Another sweep of his arm under the bed brought a couple of beer cans into the light. Bruce picked one up and shook it. The half-full can of stale beer sloshed back and forth.

"Well, no sense in letting good beer go to waste." He walked into the laundry room and poured the contents over the mound of dirty clothes. "There. That'll make 'em smell better." He walked back to his room and turned his attention to the nightstand by his bed. With one sweep of his arm, everything, including several magazines, gum wrappers, and an alarm clock, landed in the green bag.

"No, I'm keeping you." He pulled out a magazine and stuck it under his pillow. "You're too fine, Miss September."

A piece of paper sticking out from behind the dresser caught Bruce's eye. He pulled out an old photo, folded, ripped, and forgotten from years past.

He unfolded the worn creases, then stopped and gazed at a picture of a younger Bruce with his arms wrapped tightly around his three-year-old brother. Behind them stood his mother, her arms wrapped around both boys, and farther back was his father, his arms enclosing everyone in a tight squeeze.

Bruce turned the photo over and read the words "Group hug," scrawled in his mother's handwriting. Gingerly, he ran his fingers over his mother's face, then his brother's, and finally his dad's. He stared at the younger version of himself.

He walked to the crib and stared at the baby wrapped in a blue blanket, sucking on its pacifier while it slept.

"Well, that ain't us anymore, is it?" Bruce said. He dropped the photo on the nightstand.

Bruce dragged the bag to his desk and pulled out each drawer, dumping their contents inside. The bag swelled as it filled with broken pencils, crumpled papers, bottle caps, and the debris of his troubled life.

"What the hell is this?" He reached into the bag and pulled out a small pointed stone. He held it in the palm of his hand while his thoughts raced back to a moment years ago, in first or second grade, or maybe even third, when a kid in his class brought an arrowhead for show-and-tell.

"Stupid kid," Bruce laughed. "All proud 'cause he found this with his dad and was gonna put it in the museum for everyone to see."

Bruce tossed it back into the bag, yanked the red pull tabs and tied it tight. He threw it into the corner near the door.

"She wanted a clean room. She's got a clean room."

He jumped on his bed, popped a video game in, then cracked open a can of soda. His fingers instantly found their place on the controller as he rushed his character up a beach to a bunker, keeping an eye open for any Nazis. Aiming his laser rifle at a brick wall, Bruce fired, sending a bolt of molten plasma at an unsuspecting Nazi soldier as he rounded the corner. He watched the guy disintegrate into a billion pieces. The corners of Bruce's lips lifted in a fleeting smile. “Survival of the fittest, man.”

A quiet knock came from the door. *Tap-tap, tap-tap-tap.*

“Come in, Theo,” he said, looking back at the game.

Bruce’s brother sat down beside him and moved in closer, wrapping his arms around him.

“What’s wrong, bud?”

“I wanna go see Mom.”

Bruce put down the controller. “How ’bout we go see her this weekend? We’ll take the bus early in the morning and stay with her all day.”

“I wanna go right now.”

“Well, we can’t. You’ll just have to wait.”

Theo laid his head on Bruce’s arm while Bruce wiped a tear from his small face.

“You stop that right now. I said we can go this weekend.”

Theo counted on his fingers. “That’s four more sleeps.”

“Yeah, four more sleeps. Think you can handle that?”

Theo gave a little nod.

“So what did you do in school today?”

“Nothin’.”

“That’s not true. You can’t do nothin’ in school. What did you do?”

Theo looked at the ceiling. He scratched his nose. “We played cats in the cupboard, and I caught Tommy and Ed and Cindy.”

“You caught a girl?”

“Yeah.”

“Aren’t you scared you got cooties now? Better check.”

“There’s no such thing as cooties. You’re just making that up.” Theo glared at Bruce and crossed his arms over his chest.

“Okay. Okay. You’re right, but don’t start going after the girls. Gotta let ’em come after you.”

“But it wasn’t Cindy’s turn to be it. It was my turn.”

“Never mind. You’ll get it someday.” Bruce picked up the controller and continued with his game. “So what else did you do?”

“Mrs. T. made us write about our Christmas. She’s so mean. She made me sit at the table all by myself ’cause she said I was talking too much.”

“Uh-huh.”

“She made me bring it home to finish. Wanna see?”

“Sure.”

Theo returned seconds later and threw a well-worn notebook onto Bruce’s lap. “Here,” he said as he pointed at his drawing with a chubby finger.

A very round Santa Claus sat in a sleigh pulled by eight stick-figure reindeer. A young boy, all head with a huge smile, held the reins. Two sentences were written below: "On Christmas day Santa ast me to hep driv his slay. It was fun."

Bruce gave Theo a shove. "So that's where you were all day? I thought you were hiding under your bed 'cause you didn't get the Xbox you asked Santa for."

"Nooooo."

Bruce gave his brother another shove.

Theo looked up and smiled. "And what did you do in school today?"

"Nothin'."

"That's not true. Nobody can do nothin' in school."

Bruce thought back to first period. "Well, I learned about a war going on far away from here, and people were carrying their kids on their backs and leaving their homes and—"

"That's sad. I wouldn't want to leave my home," Theo said, his face scrunching up. "But if we did, would you carry me?"

"You? You're too fat for me to carry!" Bruce said, pinching Theo's gut.

Theo frowned.

Bruce quickly smiled. "Just kidding, bud—of course I'd carry you. All the way. Now get to bed."

Theo grabbed his notebook and grinned. "G'night, bro."

"Night," Bruce said as he turned his attention back to his video game. When the door closed his thoughts returned to the last few minutes of his social studies class. "What a great morning," he said, smiling up at the TV screen, remembering the expression on Mr. Smeld's face as he tried to calm the class. He knew he really didn't feel that way about the war, but it was great to see the class, especially Hailey and Scott, getting so pissed off. He loved bringing out the best in everyone.

He put the remote down, grabbed his bag, and placed it on his lap. He opened it, pulled out two smaller white cotton bags, and emptied the contents onto his bed. A huge mound of coins formed.

Now what am I gonna do with all of this? he thought. *A little bit of beer money? Well, I'd have to exchange it for bills 'cause Blitz ain't gonna like a stack of coins when he buys a case for me.*

Bruce's mind filled with ideas on how he could exchange the coins. *A bank? No, that would be just looking for juvie time. Asking someone at a store?* No, he didn't think they would do that kind of thing. Bruce shrugged. He would have to face the fact that the money could only be used to buy stuff—not beer.

Waste of time, he thought. *Especially when I can find things for "free" most of the time.*

"Maybe it's not a total bust," Bruce said as he reached into his bag and pulled out a jacket. He remembered how easy it was to hide the bags of money under the coat while he made his way to his locker. "Good thing you were there."

He put his hand into one of the pockets and pulled out a package of bubblegum. "'Chew 4 U. A Tongue Sensation,'" he read.

Bruce popped a stick into his mouth. *Not bad,* he thought. *But maybe . . .*

He reached into the other pocket. "What the?"

Bruce pulled out a leather sack, took off the cord, and opened it.

As he looked at the polished green rocks inside the sack, only one thought came to his mind: *What kinda moron would carry a pouch of stones in his pocket?*

Instantly it came to him.

Scott Romo.

Bruce recognized the jacket from first period. Scott Romo and his archeological finds: the arrowhead, the trips he would go on and tell the class about during show-and-tell way back in primary school, and now these stones.

Such a pussy.

Bruce took one of the stones and rolled it around in his hand.

The world is full of too many assholes, he thought. *Scott Romo for all of his pussyness, his dad for leaving his mom for some new young sleaze, and his stepmom for trying to run his life.*

Bruce laid his head on his pillow. The last thought that came to his mind was that he didn't care if his stepmom yelled at him for wearing his shoes to bed.

"I've never felt so tired in my life," he said, already half asleep.

"Me neither," a young boy said as he looked at his small feet and the leaves and twine that bound them.

Chapter 8

When two elephants fight, it is the grass that gets trampled. ~ Swahili proverb

Bruce looked down at the boy. He was black—blacker than the midnight sky without any stars or streetlights shining.

The boy grinned, showing his white teeth. “Where are you footin’ it from?” he asked.

Bruce’s eyes widened as they darted from one place to another. He was walking on a dry, dusty dirt road, somewhere out in the country. Fields stood on either side of the road. But not fields of wheat or grass—more like fields full of tall, thick, leafy green plants. Almost like the plants he often saw in the large pots inside the principal’s office. The landscape was dotted, here and there, with huge bushy trees, their branches stretching as far as they could away from their trunks. And there were hundreds of people on the road, all walking in the same direction. Women carried babies in slings wrapped around their backs and balanced bundles tied in large sacks upon their heads. Men and young children herded goats and sheep and cows using sticks to direct their paths. One boy sat on the back of an old worn-out bike, his head drooping low, while a man peddled past a family who looked up wearily as he went by. And all walked silently, not saying a word.

Bruce stared at the boy again. *Where the hell am I?* he thought. *What kinda dream is this? Is this one of those dreams you dream when you think you're still awake*? He stared at the bright green trees and grass. "If it is, it's a very real one," he said to himself.

"I can tell you are not from here," the young boy said, taking in Bruce's white skin. "So where is your home?"

Bruce shook his head. If this was his dream, he should be able to wish this boy away. Hell, he could change everything: the place, the people, and this intense sun that was starting to make the back of his neck burn. He closed his eyes and tried to imagine more appealing dreams he could get into.

"You okay?" the boy asked.

Bruce opened his eyes. Nope. The boy was still there. Maybe if he imagined a little harder. Focus on something like . . . a nice car . . . a cold beer . . .

Miss September—anything but a dirt road and some little black kid.

The boy interrupted Bruce's thoughts. "You know, I have not seen too many of the white people before—but you are white white. You look like you stepped off the plane into Africa yesterday just."

Africa. So that explained everything. But why would he be dreaming about Africa? He hadn't been thinking about anything remotely African, except maybe in social studies class, but even then he spent more time thinking about Stacey Kobbs, the blonde girl he saw in his math class. *Why isn't she in this dream?* he wondered.

Bruce spit on the ground. He was going to hate this dream.

"My name are Oicho Charlie," the boy said, putting out his hand.

Bruce stepped back and sized him up. The boy's head barely came up to his chest. His eyes were dark brown, but the whites were tinted with red and pink. And the clothes he wore—if you could call them clothes—were just rags. Mud covered, ripped, you name it. Bruce's gaze traveled down to the boy's feet. They were covered with large leaves and tied up with thin pieces of tattered rope. Dark red spots, *Likely dried blood*, Bruce thought, stained through the dried coverings. *Must be some poor man's way of making shoes.*

"What are your name?" Charlie asked.

"It's Bruce. Just Bruce will do," he said abruptly. *This kid asks too many questions*, he thought. A faint rotting smell drifted up to Bruce, and his nose wrinkled. He looked briefly at Charlie's feet, and a wave of nausea hit him. He stopped in his tracks and looked away from Charlie, staring at the road ahead.

"Do you need a break? I mean, if you are tired we can stop for a rest. But I really think we should keep on going. I heard there is a town a little farther up the road. Some people met up with some traveler yesterday, and they said it was just a few mile ahead." The boy's voice lifted, and his eyes smiled as much as his lips did. "Are you going to the town to stay?"

"No," Bruce said. "I don't know where I'm going. I just got here, and I don't know what the hell is going on."

"Well, I do not think many of us do. Just stick with me, though, and we will get there together," Charlie said, reaching up to Bruce's wide shoulders to direct him on the way.

What the hell, Bruce thought. Besides, he didn't have much choice in the matter. What else was there for him to do? Sit on the side of the road under the scorching sun and wait until he woke up?

He kicked a stone on the road and watched it

land in the ditch. Taking a few steps forward, he stopped and waited for Charlie, who followed with quick short steps.

The pair walked on in silence, joining the hundreds that continued along their way. Here and there large trees grew next to the road. And each time they passed one, they found a group of people sitting under it, taking a short rest, finding some relief from the hot sun. Occasionally, Bruce could see small round huts with grass roofs in the distance, but no life was visible around any of them. All were quiet and empty and abandoned. The only sound came from the birds that broke the silence with their various calls and trills and tweets.

Finally, Bruce let out a big sigh and stared into the cloudless sky. He couldn't handle the quiet anymore. "So what happened to your feet?" he asked.

"I ran through some thorn bush," Charlie said, looking down as he carefully avoided stepping on the small rocks that covered the clay road.

"Why'd you do that?"

"To escape," Charlie said with a tone in his voice that questioned Bruce's ignorance. "It was my chance. And there was no way I was going to wait for another one. I had watched month and month for that moment, and no small, small ka-field of thorn was going to get in my way. Besides, when you run through a field of thorn, the cover is very good and not too many people want to follow."

Bruce tilted his head to the side and furrowed his brow. "Escape from what?"

Charlie stifled a laugh. "You really did get off the plane yesterday, yes? I mean, you are kidding me. Everyone around here know about Kony and the LRA. Why do you think we are all footin' this way? To get away from him and his army." Charlie's voice trailed off, and he became very quiet.

Bruce's eyes lit up. *Now this is finally getting interesting. A dream about an army? And war? Cool*, he thought.

He stepped in front of Charlie and stopped. "So this Kony guy and his army attacked your village, and you guys had to run away? How big is his army? I mean, does he use tanks and bazookas and machine guns?"

"No," Charlie said, "No. He use us kid." Charlie's head fell to his chest while his voice quieted with each word. He walked past Bruce.

Bruce followed. "What do you mean, he uses you kids?"

"He raid all the village. He take all us kid and force us to . . ." Charlie paused. He closed his eyes tightly, then opened them, only to stare at the ground. "He force us to do horrid thing, then he take us away and force us to raid more village. I looked for a chance to escape many, many time. But last week I had a chance to run away. We were raiding this village. Kony wanted us to take on many more soldier—children—and he wanted some grain because our supply were getting low. It was my troop job to force the east side of the village out. We ran ahead, but when I saw the field of thorn and the other troop heading into all the hut, I knew it was my only chance. I did not care if I got caught—I knew what they would do to me—but I got tired of the fighting and the killing. Many time I wished I was dead. It was escape or death. At that point, either was fine with me just."

Charlie paused and cleared his throat. "When I ran through the field, I was very glad for the height of the bush. I did not care that the branch whipped at my face or I was running on a bed of thorn—I just wanted the bush to surround me and cover me. And that is when everything changed. I heard more gunshot fired—but from the opposite direction. We were under attack. We were warned the government army might be there, but the LRA commander sent us in anyway. They always send all the young kid in first. That way the enemy waste bullet on us. Suddenly, it was quiet. Then I heard shout from the other side. Their commander was telling the men to check all the body and gather the gun. I knew everyone in my group was dead. Except me. But I still wondered if I was the lucky one. In many way I envied them. They no longer had anything to be afraid of.

"But I did. If the army caught me, they would kill me. I had no doubt about it. I saw it happen before. Many time. And then I realized something. My group was dead. No one knew who I was. I was safe. As far as anyone knew, I was just a young boy. I was no longer a soldier. I put my gun down, and I crept quietly away from the village."

Charlie lifted his chin and stared at the road ahead.

"But if you had your own gun, why didn't you use it on the guys who took you? I mean, it's easy, isn't it? You just aim and blast them away." Bruce cradled an imaginary rifle in his hands and pretended to shoot a round of bullets at an old man who was walking ahead of them. *"Ratatatatatatat!"*

Charlie shuddered. "No, it is not like that. You see, if I tried to do anything, they would . . . You do not understand just. I mean, you might think that at first when you get taken, but then you realize that if you try they will shoot you. There are so many of them. And you do not know. You never know who you can trust."

"But you must've had some pretty cool guns to use. I mean, did you have an M249 SAW, or an M4 carbine? Now those are guns. I saw an M4 once, but it was just a dud, you know, a fake. It didn't even fire real bullets."

Charlie shook his head. "I do not know what kind of gun it was. But what does it matter? A gun is a gun. It take away life. It kill."

Bruce stuck his hands in his pockets and shrugged. Charlie stared at the road. The two boys walked on in silence. A couple of small gopher-like creatures poked their heads out of their holes.

"Hello, little *ongere*," Charlie whispered. The pair stared at Charlie for a second before diving to safety.

"Listen," Charlie finally said, "I cannot foot as fast as you. I am holding you back. Go on ahead just. That way, if you get to the town before night, you can find yourself a good spot to sleep, maybe get some food for yourself."

Charlie stopped in his tracks and waited for Bruce to go on his way.

"Yeah, whatever," Bruce mumbled.

Bruce walked past several more trees and a well a few feet away from the road. Farther ahead he came upon a couple of thatched roofs sitting atop several posts. The logs leaned precariously under their load, the grass roofs slanted to one side. A huge tree stretched its branches out over a packed clay ground, a pile of blackboard slates leaning against its trunk.

He stopped. In the distance he could make out the bare outlines of a group of buildings. The town Charlie had told him about was coming into view. Bruce turned his gaze to the field that surrounded the large tree and grass-roofed shelters.

A large group of children and men and women walked toward him from the field. *More people,* he thought. *Where are they all coming from?*

The group moved at a fast pace. Bruce narrowed his eyes as he focused on the men who led the way. The man in front wore dark green pants and a matching green shirt. The men that followed wore khaki-colored outfits. Bruce peered more intently. Black straps hung over the men's shoulders. Black straps attached to large rifles.

"Cool. Those are AK-47s. Look at 'em. They're . . ."

A group of young boys and girls moved out from the troop. Each of them held a rifle in their hands, the straps over their shoulders, their fingers resting lightly on the triggers.

Bruce's mouth hung open in mid-sentence as an awful realization came to him: this was it, the army Charlie had been telling him about.

The hair on the back of his neck stood up on end. This was not good. He quickly turned around and glanced back. The group of people, including

Charlie, was well behind him—at least a hundred yards. And the dip in the road kept them hidden for now, but not much longer. Bruce glanced from the group of soldiers, to the weary travelers, and back again.

What do I do? he thought. He looked into the grass fields that lay on either side of the road. *They have nowhere to hide.*

"Okay, Bruce. Wake up. Wake up. It's a bad dream. Wake up!" he said to himself.

He blinked and shook his head. He stared ahead. The group was still there.

"Come on. Everyone knows you can wake yourself up when you're in the middle of a nightmare. Wake up, Bruce!"

He slapped his cheeks. They were coming closer. He turned around slowly and walked back toward the group. *No,* he thought, *I'll just be leading 'em into everyone. This is stupid. Think, Bruce. Think.* The two groups moved closer and closer to each other. Bruce stopped and turned away from the road, toward the field. He ran.

"Eeh! Look!" a voice yelled.

Bullets whistled high over Bruce's head. Blasts of sand hit him in the face as bullets hit the clay ground, sending clouds of dust into the air. "Oh shit!" he yelled. He ran faster.

He glanced from one side of the field to the

other and saw a large clay-like mound that resembled a miniature mountain. He dove into the tall grass and crawled toward it.

"You're history, Bruce, buddy," he whispered. "How can you be so stupid? They know where you are."

The grass parted and the red mound came into view. Bruce inched his way around and hid behind it. *Lie still, Bruce. Lie absolutely still*, he thought. Voices came from the road.

"What are you doing?" a man yelled.

"I saw a boy out there. A *muzungu*, near that termite hill," a boy replied. A slight tremor came from his voice.

"A *muzungu*? Out here? Walking alone? A child?" the first voice said. "You are wasting bullet. Go out there and find him. Now." The words were spoken with such intense hatred and anger that Bruce's whole body froze with fear.

"Stay still," a small voice whispered just a few feet away from him.

He turned his head, straining to find the source. There, hidden in the grass, he glimpsed a stained and ragged T-shirt. *How the hell did Charlie get here?*

"Come on out, little *muzungu* boy," the boy teased. "Come on out of your tiny hole, little *ongere*."

Bruce listened to the sound of the grass as it parted obediently in the soldier's path. He listened to the cold sound of the rifle as it moved the blades from side to side, knowing that each step the soldier took brought him closer and closer to where he lay hidden. Bruce's throat tightened. His breath amplified and echoed as he covered his nose and mouth with his hand.

"Do not move," Charlie said softly.

Charlie crouched on his knees. He began to stand.

"No!" Bruce whispered. He grabbed Charlie's leg and pulled him down before Charlie could raise his head above the grass.

Suddenly, barking and laughter came from the roadside.

"You stupid *laming*!" the voice from the road shouted. "Is this your *muzungu*? This white mutt is the reason for your bullet? Get back here before I split you open and feed you to the mutt!"

Charlie froze. Bruce gave a silent sigh of relief. Both listened as the footsteps moved away.

"Move on!" the commander shouted. "We have long, long way to go!"

The boys listened to gravel crunching under the hard soles of the men's boots until it faded into the distance. A bird sent a loud *deed-deed-deed-deed-er-ick* call into the air until it was joined by another and another. Seconds passed, then minutes. Gradually the rise and fall of Bruce's breaths slowed and steadied. He pushed himself onto his knees and lifted his head to peer above the grass.

"No!" Charlie whispered, grabbing Bruce's arm. He mouthed the words "We must wait," forming each and every word clearly. Bruce heard them loud and clear. He lay back on the ground. Charlie pulled a blade of grass and chewed on its end. Several more minutes passed until finally the boy lifted his head cautiously above the grass. He nodded. Slowly, Bruce rose.

"You were gonna let 'em take you, just to save me. Why would you do that?" said Bruce.

"You would have done the same thing for me," Charlie replied matter-of-factly, turning back to the road.

Bruce stopped and stared at Charlie's back. He wasn't quite sure if the kid was right about that.

"Hey, Charlie. What's a *muzungu*?"

"It is what we call all you white people when you come to Africa. You are like you are lost all the time. Like a wanderer."

"Yeah, you got that right," Bruce said.

Chapter 9

A friend is someone you share the path with.
~ African proverb

One by one the heads of the travelers peered above the grass. They glanced from one side of the road to the other, to the field, and back again. Bruce laughed. It reminded him of the gophers he would see out in the countryside, hiding in their holes, looking this way and that for the hawks that often swooped down and grabbed them for their dinner.

"Eeh, you know you saved us," Charlie said, turning toward the town.

"What?"

"When the shot went off, everyone ran into the field and hid in the grass. You warned everyone," Charlie said with a grin.

"But it wasn't something I did. I mean, I didn't plan it. I was trying to save my—I mean—I didn't mean for it to happen. It just did."

"Oh, I know. But either way, you saved us."

Bruce looked away from Charlie and hung his head down in embarrassment. He didn't deserve any hero worship. He was only being stupid. And it happened to work out for the best.

"But there's one thing I can't figure out. How'd you get so close to me out in the field?"

"Eeh, I took a shortcut," Charlie replied. "It is always easy to walk in the field than on the rocky road. You know, it is soft soft on the feet. When I saw you ahead of me, I thought I should cut across the field and save some footin' just. Then I saw the group and I said to myself, 'Charlie, it could be LRA or government army.' I was not sure, but I have learned you always have to be careful. That is when I went farther into the field, and that is when I heard the shot and saw you running. So I stayed low and quickly moved toward you. That is all just."

That's all? Bruce thought. *The kid dismisses it just like that. As if it happened to him every day.* He shrugged. *Maybe there was something to this kid. But why spend any time dwelling on it? That required thinking—no sense doing something stupid like that. Besides, you don't think in dreams.*

He stopped and stared at Charlie, the sun, the fields, and the road. *Something's not right here*, he thought. *You don't feel in dreams.* He turned and walked into the grass and waved his hand through the tall blades. He felt the sharp, dry edges, just as he did when he ran through the field to hide from the LRA. He walked back to the road and grabbed a handful of dirt from the ground and threw it up into the air. The dust tickled his nose, just as it did when the barrage of bullets hit the ground around him. *Dreams don't feel this real, do they?* he wondered. *Or do they?*

He ran to catch up with Charlie.

The outline of the town drew nearer and nearer as they descended a large hill. A main road, from which several smaller roads branched off in a haphazard sort of way, led into the town. Small buildings, none more than two stories high, lined the roads, some painted in bright blues, others in girlish hot pink. *They must've had a sale on blue and pink paint about thirty years ago*, Bruce thought, seeing the faded and chipped walls.

Closer to the town stood the one and only gas station. Next to the solitary pump, visible from even this distance, was a bright pink building with a faded Shell gasoline sign nailed to the side.

Suddenly, Bruce smelled a horrible stench. His hand went to his face, covering his nose and mouth.

A strong taste of bile worked its way up to his throat, forcing him to gag and spit.

A body of a young boy, maybe nine or ten years old, lay on the road. A pool of blood, dark red, soaked into the ground next to him. Bruce staggered back and shut his eyes tight. A huge stork stood over the body, using its sharp large beak to rip apart the flesh. The bird was easily over three feet tall. Its white belly was stained with the same blood that covered its beak as it nonchalantly tore apart the dead boy's stomach.

"Ah!" Charlie yelled. He flailed his arms in the air as he ran toward the bird. "Get out of here!" he screamed, seething with anger. "Git! Git!"

The bird took little notice of the intrusion and went back to its meal.

Charlie picked up a large rock and heaved it at the bird's head. "Arrgghh! I said git!" he shouted. His whole body shook as he glared at the bird.

The stork hopped away, stood back, and waited, flapping its wings and clacking its beak in defiance.

Charlie knelt over the body and lifted the boy's head onto his lap. Some people stopped to look; others paused and murmured prayers as they continued on. Mothers and fathers pulled their children close to them and covered their eyes.

Tears streamed from Charlie's eyes, clearing pathways down his dirt-stained cheeks. They fell onto the dead boy's still face. Charlie moaned and rocked back and forth. He gently placed the boy's head onto the ground and stood. He walked a few feet from the boy's body, took a flat rock, and dug into the red clay earth. He dug furiously, driving the stone into the ground with all of his strength, yanking the dirt away.

Bruce looked past Charlie into the field. He didn't know how to react to the boy's tears and sobs.

Many long minutes passed until Charlie had dug a small grave—small, but big enough to bury the young boy's body in. Slowly and carefully, he placed his hands under the body, lifted it, and placed it in the hole. He took his ragged shirt and placed it over the boy's face; then he gathered a small handful of dirt and sprinkled it over the cloth until the boy's face was covered. He lifted each chunk of dirt and placed it gently on top of the body until the hole was filled. And then he made a cross. He took two sticks from a nearby bush, fashioned them together with a piece of twine from his foot, and placed it at the head of the grave.

He began to sing, softly and gently, a song that began and ended with tears.

"Wan wabinoki ngom,

Ngom wan wadok,

Tipu dok bot Lubanga,

Yom cwiny madit."

Charlie stood and looked toward the horizon where the sun was beginning to set over the town.

"Let us go," he said quietly. "It is getting late late."

Bruce followed. They walked together in silence, the song's melody still playing in Bruce's head. Finally, he broke the silence. "That song . . . what did it say?"

Charlie stopped and closed his eyes. He repeated the song, the lilt of his accent adding harmony to the verse.

"From the earth we have come

To the earth we must go.

Let your soul leave for heaven

Where sorrow will be no more."

"But the boy you just buried . . . who was he?" Bruce asked.

"I do not know."

"You didn't know him?"

Charlie shook his head. "No. But he did not deserve to die because he was too weak to carry the gun or the tin. And he deserve a grave."

Bruce stared back at the makeshift cross. He was confused. He could understand why a person would cry when someone close to them died. *But why would anyone cry over the death of someone they didn't know?*

Chapter 10

One who causes others misfortune also teaches them wisdom. ~ African proverb

"What the hell's going on now?" Bruce stopped and stared down the road that led into the town.

The women and children who had been traveling with him and Charlie ambled back and forth, carrying pieces of tin, wood, and plastic to where the men were setting up a group of makeshift shelters. They joined tin to wood with pieces of twine and rope, and hung torn pieces of plastic over long sticks, creating small enclosures that would provide some protection from the cool evening breeze.

Two small children, a boy and a girl, dragged a large piece of wood across the road and stopped momentarily to catch their breath. They readjusted their grip on the awkward load and walked backward as their tiny hands refused to let go of their newfound treasure. Weary teenagers lifted broken boards and torn pieces of tin onto their heads and carried them across the road until they dropped them at the feet of the men. Women busied themselves starting fires and preparing the evening's meals while their children brought yellow containers filled with water to the pots set out by the burning coals.

Charlie pointed to the area where the children were coming from. "*Gway!* There is a dump back there! Come on! Maybe we can find some plastic—and who knows what else!"

Charlie took off as fast as his injured feet could carry him. Bruce followed cautiously behind.

"A dump," Bruce muttered. "The kid is nuts. He's excited about a dump." He stood back and watched as Charlie rummaged and sifted through the debris. Throwing pieces of bricks and concrete aside, Charlie looked like a kid on a mission.

"Here!" he yelled, waving a large piece of clear plastic in the air. "Look! I found some!"

Bruce eyed the plastic, ripped and riddled with holes. "What good is that thing?" he asked.

"We will use it tonight to wrap ourself. It will keep us warm."

"You go ahead and do that," Bruce said. "You're not gonna catch me rolled up in some stinking sheet of plastic, no matter how cold it gets."

Charlie shrugged and looked back at the rubbish pile. "*Gway*!" he yelled again. "Can you imagine someone throwing this out?" He picked up an old ripped Spider-Man backpack, the kind a kid would bring to kindergarten, brushed it off, and threw it over his back.

"This is good!" Charlie said, grinning from ear to ear. "We are all set now. We have got some cover and a backpack for anything we need to keep for along the way. Now if there was only some way to get something to eat. Let us go into the town and see what we can find."

Bruce followed Charlie as he jumped onto a crumbling sidewalk that ran alongside the stores and the broken paved road. He smelled peanuts and corn roasting. His stomach growled.

"I'm starving," Bruce said as he watched a young man turning the corn cobs over an open fire on the edge of the road.

"You do not look like you are starving." Charlie poked at Bruce's belly and laughed. "Come on. Maybe we can find some work to do so we can buy something."

Bruce stopped in his tracks and stared as Charlie walked ahead.

You don't physically feel hunger in a dream, he thought. *You don't actually feel your stomach growl 'cause you haven't eaten all day.*

His eyes opened wider.

You don't smell in a dream either.

His heart pounded, faster and faster.

He thought back to the moment when they met up with the army.

And you don't feel fear like that in a dream.

The guns, the army, Charlie . . . it's real. But— Bruce thought back to his bedroom—*I fell asleep.*

Charlie stopped and turned. "What are you doing? Let us go."

Bruce looked at the man selling the corn, then at a woman walking past with her child wrapped to her back, then back to Charlie. "Are you real, Charlie?"

The boy gave a slight laugh. "Real? Course I am real. As real as you. Now come on. Let us see how we can get something to eat. My little stomach has been eating nothing but my spit for the whole day."

Bruce took in a deep breath. "Weird," he mumbled, "but cool."

He followed Charlie as he walked into an alleyway leading into a large marketplace. They passed by a couple of men playing a game, their hands quickly picking and dropping coffee beans into small cups carved into a wooden board. They passed stalls filled with many, many different items for sale: blankets, shoes, clothing, spices, dried beans, rice, and grain. A couple of vendors stood near several crates filled with fruit and vegetables. Bruce watched a man fill a woman's bag with oranges while another woman placed a large football-shaped green fruit or vegetable—Bruce couldn't tell what it was—in a basket on a woman's head. As the woman walked away, he couldn't help but stare.

"What the hell is that thing?" he asked Charlie.

"That is a jackfruit. They are very good."

"It's huge!"

"Yes. Big enough to feed a village. Including goat and chicken too."

Bruce laughed.

Farther down the way, a man walked away from a vendor with two live chickens tied by their legs, swung over his shoulders. Next to the chicken salesman, the carcass of a cow hung from a stall, where a woman pointed out the best cuts of meat she wanted for the evening's meal. Farther still was a long shelf covered with fish, whole fish, their eyes glazed over, staring blankly at the darkened beams hanging from above.

Bruce looked across and started to drool. He felt as if he were a little boy in a donut shop. Except this was no Tim Hortons. Lined up in neat little rows in the stall beside him were packages of cookies and chips, bottles of soda, and anything imaginable you could find at the local corner store.

"Over here," Bruce said. He pushed Charlie toward the stall.

A girl, about fourteen years old, stood behind the front shelf, poised and ready for business. Her brightly colored dress was clean and pressed, her short-cropped curly hair neatly pulled back with a matching scarf.

"Is there something I can get for you?" She gave Charlie a warm smile.

Bruce pointed to the top row. "How much for a box of cookies?" he asked.

As she turned to point out their various prices, Bruce didn't miss a beat. Within seconds he had unzipped Charlie's backpack, thrown in several bags of chips, a soda, and some crackers, and zipped it back up. He stood there, nonchalantly smiling at the girl when she turned around a few seconds later.

"Thanks," Bruce said, quickly taking Charlie's arm, "but we need to get going." He pulled Charlie off his feet as he headed to the exit.

"*Gway!* I was going to ask her if we could sweep around her stall for some food," Charlie snapped. "Why the heck did you do that? We could have had some supper."

"Get going," Bruce repeated. "I got it covered."

A large hand gripped Bruce's shoulder and spun him around. He stared up into the face of the blackest man he had ever seen in his life. The man towered over him. Bruce gulped.

"Put it back," the man said.

Bruce didn't move one inch. Beads of sweat formed on his forehead. His mouth went dry. He was two seconds from pissing his pants.

He walked back to the counter, opened Charlie's backpack, and carefully put everything back in its place. His hands shook. The girl looked at Charlie, her brow drawn tight, a look of bewilderment in her eyes. Charlie stared back at her, the same look mirrored in his.

"There is no reason for you to do this, Mandaca," the girl said, placing her hand on the big man's arm. "They have paid for it all. The money is here in the basket."

"It does not become you to lie so blatantly, Suzanne," the man said in a firm and demeaning voice. “Your mother would not be happy to see how quickly you give away your earning to any *lacan*. I saw it all happen. Next time, do not turn your back on a *muzungu*, let alone a beggar boy.”

The man shoved Charlie and Bruce out of the marketplace and onto the street.

Suzanne’s gaze followed their steps, her eyes darting from Charlie, to Bruce, and then to Mandaca.

Mandaca grabbed the boys by their shoulders and spun them around. “I am tired of you worthless parasite stealing from us. That is not our way. Now leave my town.”

Bruce cringed, hearing the emphasis placed on the word “my.”

“Yes, sir,” Charlie replied. He glared at Bruce, then lowered his gaze and stared at the man’s black boots.

“What do we have here, Mandaca?” A young man dressed in a brown uniform walked toward Bruce and Charlie. The man’s lighter skin contrasted greatly with Mandaca’s blackness, as did his thin and lanky body. But it was the rifle slung over his shoulder that grabbed the boys’ attention first.

“Have you caught some more *takataka* behaving as thief in your market?” he asked.

Mandaca frowned. "Yes, but I have dealt with them, Nunida. They will not be bothering us again."

"Oh, but I am sure they will," the man said. "What did you do? Give them one of your mean stare?"

"They are only children. And perhaps they are hungry. Let them go just, and they will not bother again," Mandaca said, towering over Nunida.

Nunida put his hand upon his rifle. "No. They will be coming with me. A night in the *jela* will do them some good."

Nunida took the butt of his rifle and stuck it into Charlie's ribs. The boy didn't need any coaxing. He limped ahead, his whole body slumped in resignation. Bruce followed. He was still shaking.

The boys walked down the road until Nunida pushed them onto a smaller side street. A red brick building bearing a faded sign, LIRA UGANDAN POLICE DEPARTMENT, stood at the end of a well-worn pathway. Another sign posted beside the door read LET US WORK TO GETHER HAND BY HAND TO END CRIME.

Nunida shoved the end of his rifle into Bruce's back. "Inside."

The boys entered the crowded office. Filing cabinets, their drawers open, were overfilled with papers jammed in haphazardly. Two worn desks were covered with coffee cups, dinner plates of half-eaten meals, newspapers, magazines, and more files. The larger of the two desks, positioned against the far wall, was missing one of its legs. A pile of files placed under its corner gave it an awkward tilt.

"Downstair," the officer commanded.

Partway down the stairs Bruce clamped his hand over his nose. The stench of urine and other human smells was overpowering. He held his breath until they reached the bottom of the stairs. It was no use; he gagged.

As he stood beside Charlie and faced a row of rusted iron bars, Nunida pushed the cell door open.

A solitary pail stood in the far corner. There was no bench, no bed, no blanket—just one light hanging from the ceiling and a small barred window that let in just enough light to bring their night's accommodations into dismal focus.

Nunida growled. "Inside," he said. He stuck his foot out and shoved Charlie into the cell. Charlie tripped and fell. Quickly, he stood up and wiped his hands on his pant legs. Bruce brushed past Nunida and jumped inside. The cell door closed with a resounding clang. The man turned and walked away.

Charlie limped to one corner and sat down. He buried his face in his knees and let out a deep moan.

"Stupid jerk!" Bruce said under his breath.

"Stupid jerk?" Charlie glared at him. "Stupid jerk? Who is the stupid jerk? What made you do such a thing? We were doing fine until you stole the food. Why did you do that? We could be eating roasted corn and maybe some rice and drinking water, and we could be sleeping outside in our plastic, staying warm—not inside this *jela* that reeks of *cet*!"

Bruce glared back at Charlie. "What're you talking about?" he said. "I tried to help us. We're both hungry, and if it wasn't for that huge gorilla we would've been just fine!"

"That huge 'gorilla' is the *lodito* of this village. He is to be feared and respected by everyone, like any good leader should. He could have thrown us in jail, but he took pity on us because he knew we were hungry. If the officer had not come by, Mandaca would have slipped some money or some food into our hand and sent us on our way."

"How the hell do you know all that? You've never seen the man before in your life. What does he care about us?"

"It is the way of my people. I know he would do that. I could tell. I could tell just."

Bruce walked to the opposite end of the cell and rapped his head against the wall. He was not in the mood for arguing with this kid. He turned his head as the sound of heavy footfalls came from the stairs.

Nunida peered into the cell and smirked at the boys. Another man, sporting a number of stripes on the shoulder of his uniform, stood back. He placed his hands on his hips and stared down at the boys.

Charlie rose and stood across from the chief, his gaze fixed at the large man's steel-toed boots. Bruce stayed in his corner. *Hmm,* he thought as he stared at the man's belly hanging over his belt, *betcha don't see too many of those in Africa.*

"So we have found a couple of thief in our town." The chief spaced his words out for emphasis. "Tell me, boy," he said, looking at Charlie, "where do you come from?"

"From Padibe, sir," Charlie replied, continuing to stare at the floor.

"Padibe, eeh? That village was hit by the LRA about eighteen, maybe nineteen month ago. Were you there when that happened?"

"Yes, sir," Charlie stammered.

"And were you one of the children who were taken?" the chief asked. The harshness in his voice began to waver.

Charlie lifted his gaze and studied the man's face. "Yes, sir."

"And how is it you have come here to the town of Lira?"

"I escaped, sir."

"And where are you footin' to?"

"I do not know, sir."

"Are you looking for your parent?"

"No, sir. They are dead, sir. My brother and sister may still be alive. But I do not know."

"I see." The chief rubbed the end of his chin, deep in thought. "Well, I suppose the safest place for you right now is in this cell. Come morning we can let you go. But I do not want to see your thiefing hand around here again." His voice grew sterner. "Is that understood?"

"Yes, sir," Charlie said with a small sigh.

"And tell your *muzungu* friend that he need to go home where his parent can teach him a thing or two about what belong to him and what does not."

"Yes, sir."

The chief turned on his heel and walked up the stairs. Nunida stared at his back and spit on the ground.

"Do not think you are going to get off that easy, soldier boy," he snarled. "I have seen the horrid thing Kony and his soldier do when he raid all the village. And do not lie to me and say you were 'forced to kill.' I do not believe it. Not one bit. You are *takataka* and your words are *takataka*. The chief may be soft on you, kid, but I am not." Nunida glared at the boys. Charlie turned his head and looked away. Bruce returned the officer's glare, his eyes hateful and repelling. Without another word, Nunida walked away. Charlie slumped to the floor and covered his head with his arms. His body trembled.

"Hey, don't worry," Bruce said. "We'll be outta here tomorrow."

Charlie's eyes narrowed as he flashed a look of contempt. "You have no idea what your stupidity has cost us, do you?"

He curled up in the corner and turned his back to Bruce.

Chapter 11

Three things cause sorrow to flee; water, green trees, and a beautiful face. ~ Moroccan proverb

Charlie sat in the corner of the cell, his back against the wall. He opened his eyes, rubbed his hands over his face, and looked out the barred window. The last patches of light were leaving the sky. Nighttime had come to Lira.

Charlie rose. The scowl on his face softened. *"Wala kuzingatia kichuguu wakati nimepata mlima kwa hoja,"* he said.

Bruce stood and stretched his cramped legs. "What did you say?"

"I said, 'Do not focus on the anthill when you have got a mountain to move.'"

"What?"

“It is a Swahili saying my mother used to say to me. It mean, do not put your eyes on the little thing when you have to work on the big thing.”

“And why are you saying that?”

“Because there are some thing bigger than you, Bruce.”

“What?”

“Do not worry about it.” He turned his head toward the footfalls coming down the stairs.

Bruce and Charlie looked out to see a beautiful sight. Suzanne, carrying a basket on her head, approached their cell. Charlie smiled briefly, and then his smile disappeared. He looked away.

“Mandaca asked me to bring this to you,” Suzanne said as she lowered the basket to the ground. She pulled a couple of small loaves from the basket and passed them through the bars. “Here. Take them. You must be hungry.”

Charlie stared at the two loaves, then tore his gaze away.

“Come. I bring them for you. And I have water too.”

Bruce walked across the cell and reached through the bars to take the loaves. He swallowed as he breathed in the smell of freshly baked bread.

Charlie’s hand clamped down on Bruce’s arm. “No. We are fine. You can take your basket and leave.”

Bruce's eyes grew wide. "What the hell are you doing? I haven't eaten all day. Stop being so stupid and take the bread." He tore his arm from Charlie's grip and took the bread from Suzanne.

"No!" Charlie yelled. He ripped the loaves from Bruce's hands and flung them out of the cell. "Do you not get it, you stupid *muzungu*? You steal from this girl, and then you take her food again—without any shame! Have you no idea what is going on here? Are you really that dense?"

Suzanne picked the loaves from the floor and handed them to Bruce. He didn't move.

"Take the bread just." Suzanne's voice was calm and reassuring. "Sometimes people will do desperate thing when they are hungry. It happen. You are not thief. Only desperate people doing desperate thing because they feel they have no choice."

"We could have done some work for you," Charlie said.

"I know." Suzanne reached out and touched his hand. "Now take the bread. You are hungry, and tomorrow will be another day."

Bruce paused. "I'm sorry," he said. He avoided Suzanne's gaze and stared at the cement floor. Then, taking the loaves from her hands, he gave one to Charlie. Suzanne passed a couple of bottles of water through the cell. The boys gulped them down.

"Here are some blanket you can use. It will be cool in here tonight."

Charlie took the blankets, briefly holding onto Suzanne's hands. *"Apwoyo matek, apwoyo matek,"* he said, the words catching in his throat.

Bruce stared at Charlie. It was obvious the kid was saying "thank you" in whatever language he spoke. And he could tell by the tone in his voice that he really meant it, as if he hadn't been the recipient of so much kindness in a long time.

Suzanne nodded briefly and looked at Charlie's feet. The leaves, once fresh and strong, were now dried and stained with old blood. "Your feet. You have cut them. Are they sore?"

"Yes. They are hot, and it hurt to walk on them."

Suzanne wrinkled her nose as she smelled the rancid odor. "They are probably infected. I know of this medicine my mom use. I will bring it tomorrow, along with some clean water and some cloth to wipe your feet. Will you still be here tomorrow?"

"Yes, we are here for the night," Charlie said, swallowing the last part of the bread. "The chief said he will let us out tomorrow morning."

"And where are you going?"

Charlie shrugged. “I do not know. Somewhere safe. Somewhere I can look for the rest of my family. I do not know.” His voice shook.

Suzanne’s eyes moistened. “You are one of Kony kid, yes?”

Charlie was silent.

“I thought this. Your eyes and your voice told me.” Suzanne paused, wiping a tear that had fallen onto her cheek. “Listen,” she said finally. “There is a camp some relief organization has set up not too far from here. I heard Mandaca mention it. The people from Padar have been staying there for the past few month. They find it safer there just. Some of them come to the city hoping to find work. But there really is none, so most of them return to the camp to stay there and wait it out just.”

Charlie’s eyes widened.

“It is about three mile from here. Down the main road. I know because many truck come here and pick up supply sometime. I think they may be coming tomorrow, and you could catch a ride with them.”

Charlie looked at his feet. “Yes, that would be good.”

“I need to get going now,” Suzanne said as she picked up her empty basket. “My mom will be waiting for me. I will see you tomorrow morning.”

Suzanne hurried off. Bruce and Charlie watched her go and listened as the *slap, slap* sound of her bare feet hitting the cement floor faded into the distance.

Charlie turned to Bruce. His eyes took on a distant gaze while he smiled. “I think God still love me, Bruce.”

“What?”

“Suzanne. She is an angel sent to us from God himself.”

The sound of heavy boots hitting the floor with military precision interrupted Charlie’s thoughts and brought him out of his daze. With nonchalant arrogance, Nunida rapped the cell bars with his baton. He stared into the cell, his eyes fixed on Charlie, then on Bruce, his mouth set in a hardened scowl.

He placed the iron key into the cell door lock and twisted it slowly. There was a grating sound, followed by a click as the tumblers fell into place. Charlie froze. Nunida pushed the cell door open a thumb’s width and smiled.

“Have a good night, boy,” he said as he walked up the stairs. “Sleep well.”

Bruce glanced at the cell door and grinned. He pulled it open and stepped into the hall. “Come on,” he said. “What’re you waiting for?”

Charlie stood still. He planted his feet firmly on the floor. “No. I am not leaving this cell, and neither are you. If you know what is good for you—which I sometime wonder if you ever do—you will spend the night in this hellhole with me.”

Charlie walked to the end of the cell and stood as far away as he could from the door. “Close the door.”

“Close the door? Close the door, he says! Are you outta your mind? Why the hell would I stay in this place tonight?”

“Because the moment you step out of here, you will be a dead boy,” Charlie said.

“What? Why the hell do you say that?”

“Because that is what people like Nunida do to murderer here. An eye for an eye, a tooth for a tooth, a life for a life.”

“But I haven’t murdered anyone!” Bruce yelled.

“No. You have not,” Charlie said quietly, lowering his eyes, “but I have.”

“But,” Bruce said, “you were forced to be a soldier. Forced to kill. You told me that yourself. You had no choice.”

“But I did have a choice,” Charlie said, his voice breaking. “I always had a choice. I did not have to kill anyone. I just wanted to live.”

Charlie sank to the floor and covered his face. Uncontrollable sobs shook his body. Bruce looked away and stared at the floor. His mouth opened, but the words weren't there. He took in a deep breath and felt his body grow smaller as the breath escaped. He didn't know what to say. He didn't even know what to think.

Finally, he walked over and crouched beside Charlie. "But anyone else would've done the same. I mean, if it means losing your own life, you'd do anything to keep it, wouldn't you?"

"Even killing your parent?" Charlie said. "Only a real coward would do that."

Chapter 12

Love has to be shown by deeds not words.
~ Swahili proverb

Bruce took a step back from Charlie. He was overcome with horror and disbelief. His head shook. *No, no, no*, he thought. This couldn't be happening. He knew Charlie. The boy who was prepared to give his life for him out in the grass field was not a murderer. The boy who buried the body of the young child soldier was not a killer. The boy who valued decency and honesty despite his empty stomach was a good kid.

Charlie looked at the expression on Bruce's face. "See. You are sick of me too. You look at me, and you are sick of the very sight of me. And I do not blame you. I do not even want to be me."

Bruce turned away from Charlie and walked to the end of the cell. His thoughts weren't clear to him. This was beyond him—or was it? He had heard those words before: "I'm sick of you." From his stepmother, his dad. Many times.

Finally he spoke. "I'm not sick of you."

Charlie lifted his head, wiped the tears from his eyes, and took a deep breath. His voice shook as he wrapped his blanket around his small body. "It was my selfishness and stupidity that killed my father. If I had gone to the town that night, like me and all my friend had done for many, many week, Kony would not have come. It was safe there, because Kony did not dare come into the town to get us. There were too many people, and the government army was strong there. But one evening I was tired of walking, and I wanted to stay at home just. For one night. That is all I wanted. It was such a long walk. Three mile. Three mile there in the evening and three mile to go home, and then to school before the full sun showed itself the next day. I wanted to play. I wanted to rest. I wanted to be home.

"When my mother told me it was time for me to leave, I argued with her. I said, 'No, mother. It is all right for me to stay. Kony, he is not here.' I pointed to the field where my friend had started a game of football. 'Look,' I said, 'there is a game. I will play the game, and then I will go. It will be all fine.'"

Charlie closed his eyes and he smiled in remembrance. "And it was a good game. We had not been able to play for such a long time that we must have looked like a bunch of goat let off their rope. And I remember thinking, as everyone was cheering and laughing, that I wanted this game to go on forever."

The smile on Charlie's face quickly vanished as the memory of the events of the evening surfaced. "When the game was done, the sun had already set behind the bush. I began to feel fearful. It was all good while the sun gave us light, but when the sun set I began to worry. Perhaps I should have left sooner. My mother gave me my blanket and a bit of food wrapped in a piece of paper, then she kissed me on my cheek and sent me on my way.

"I had only taken a few step when a torch flew over my head and landed on the roof of our hut. It turned to flame instantly. Then more torch fell. The people screamed and ran. Some ran to catch their children into their arm while other ran into the bush. My father, he ran toward me. His arm were open, ready to lift me and carry me away.

"I remember the look in his eyes when all the bullet hit him in the back and he dropped to the ground. Have you ever seen someone die in front of you, Bruce?"

Bruce shook his head.

"I remember when my *min maa* died. She was old. She lived with us for many year after my grandfather died. I remember how my father would lift her and hold her while I would spoon food into her mouth. And I remember how one day her breath slowed until there was not any more. There was *kwee* all around her. Beautiful peace. When my father died there was no *kwee*. His eyes showed only fear. My father was a great and strong man. I had never seen fear in his eyes ever before. And now, that is all that is left for me of my father."

Charlie paused. He tried to gather his thoughts.

"When the LRA rounded us up, they forced us to kneel down on the ground as the commander brought our parent forward. As my mother rushed toward me, I knew something horrible was going to happen. That is when they tied us together. Her hand and my hand, with a rope that cut into our skin and made us bleed."

Charlie moved his fingers across the scars on his wrists. He stared past Bruce, beyond the cell window.

"Then we were forced to walk. I do not know how long it was. It was day and day and day. Any of the children who could not walk were beaten by the child soldier, and I remember wondering, why did these boy and girl do these thing to us? Were they not children too? Were they not from the Acholi tribe? Were they not our brother and sister?

"I remember when they cut the rope that bound my mother and me, I wanted to rub my wrist and clean the blood away from them just."

Charlie stopped short. His words were stuck hard and fast in his throat.

"I was so stupid. I did not know what was going to happen next. That is when they took my mother and tied her to a tree. I can still hear her scream as they pulled her and kicked her and tied the rope around her. I remember seeing old blood on the tree, and I wondered why it was there. And then they gave all of us, me, my friend, and my neighbor, stick and rock. And we were told to beat my mother. I refused. And that is when the soldier took one of the girl and put a gun to her head and shot her, right there in front of me. Then the man said, 'Kill your mother or you are next.'"

Charlie stopped talking. Finally, he took in a deep breath and allowed it to leave his body in a convulsion of tremors.

"You know, Bruce," he said, now seeing the four walls that surrounded them. "My mom never screamed when we beat her. She did not cry at all. She just looked at me and she said, 'I love you,

Charlie,' and then she closed her eyes.

Chapter 13

Two ants do not fail to pull one grasshopper.
~ Tanzanian proverb

The sun had hardly shown itself when Bruce was startled awake by a foreign voice blaring over a loudspeaker from outside.

"Allahu Akbar. . .

Ashhadu alla ilaha illallah

"What the . . .?" Bruce looked up and stared at the window.

Ashhadu anna muhammadar rasulullah

Hayya alas Salah . . ."

"What the hell is that?" He looked at Charlie, still sleeping on the floor.

"Hayya alal Falah . . .

Allahu Akbar. . .

La ilaha illallah."

As the voice faded into the distance, it was replaced by honking horns and bicycle bells.

Women in long skirts and men in dress pants walked by the cell window. Uganda was waking up.

Bruce groaned as he sat up and rubbed his legs and shoulders. The blanket he had slept on lay scrunched up in a ball on the cold cement floor. He stood and looked out the bars of the cell window.

"So I'm still here," he said with a huge sigh. His shoulders sagged from the weight of the realization.

A million confused and anxious thoughts ran through his mind. He had to admit that when he realized that this whole thing—Charlie, the road, the army—wasn't a dream, he thought it was—How did he put it?—cool.

But the stinking jail and Charlie telling him about being taken by the army and having to kill his own mother—that was something he couldn't wrap his head around. *And who could? Who'd want to?* he thought.

Bruce rested his head in his hands. *I just wanna go home,* he thought. Then he gave a little laugh. He remembered a movie he'd watched with his younger brother, about a young girl who said, "There's no place like home. There's no place like home." Maybe if he tapped his runners together he could get home just like she did with her ruby shoes.

He let out a long sigh. *No, that's not gonna do it,* he thought. *But I can't stay here forever, can I? I gotta get home sometime.*

Charlie groaned as he turned in his blanket.

And what about Charlie? Bruce thought. *He can't escape this hellhole. He doesn't even have a home to go to.*

A door slammed upstairs, and Bruce was jostled from his thoughts. He turned toward the footfalls hitting the cement stairs.

"So did our dear children sleep well?"

Bruce glared at the smug, smiling face of Nunida as he peered into the cell. Beside him stood another man—a very large man, wearing the same brown uniform.

Charlie lifted his head and rubbed his hand over his eyes.

"Get up, boy!" Nunida yelled, pushing the cell door open. The large man smiled in amusement.

Charlie jumped to his feet.

"It look like it is your lucky day, boy. Amri here has told me he is heading out this morning, and he would be happy to give you both a ride to wherever it is you want to go."

Charlie rubbed his legs, trying to get the blood flowing.

"Finally. I can't wait to get outta this piss hole." Bruce smiled at Charlie. "Come on. Let's get outta here," he said. He put his hand on the boy's shoulder. "We'll go get an Egg McMuffin. It's on me."

Charlie stepped back from Bruce, allowing Bruce's arm to slip off his shoulder. He stared at the smirk on Nunida's face. "Where is the chief?" he asked.

"He is upstair waiting for you."

Charlie's eyes focused on Nunida, then darted to Amri, then to the cell door and back to Bruce.

Amri walked into the cell and pushed Bruce toward the door. "Out."

Bruce obeyed instantly.

"You too," Nunida said, pointing his baton at Charlie.

Charlie followed Bruce. He hesitated at each step as he climbed the stairs. They entered the small office. No one was there.

"I thought you said . . ." Bruce stopped in mid-sentence as Nunida swung his baton down on Charlie's head. Charlie's knees buckled. He fell to the ground.

Bruce reacted instantly. He rushed at Nunida and threw his fist into his stomach. Nunida fell to the floor, grasping at his middle. With a sudden surge of energy, Bruce was on top of him. He punched his face, grabbed his head, and pounded it against the floor. Nunida lifted his legs and rammed his boots into Bruce's chest. Bruce flew across the room and smashed into the wall. His head hit the concrete surface as he fell to the floor. A million colors flashed in front of his eyes.

Nunida stood and wiped a small trickle of blood away from his lip and smirked. "That is enough from you, white boy. Get up."

Bruce pushed himself up against the wall and stood. His knees shook. Charlie rose. His eyes conveyed only one thing: this was the end.

Amri sauntered over to Bruce, tapping his baton against the palm of his hand. He pulled a pair of handcuffs from his pocket and slapped one around Bruce's wrist. The tight metal bit Bruce's skin.

"You are not so strong now, little *muzungu*. Are you?" Amri laughed as he glanced down to put his baton into his belt.

Bruce grabbed Amri's face with one free hand and rammed his head against the wall again and again and again. Amri slid down the wall and lay very still.

Nunida snatched his rifle from his desk and pointed it at Bruce. His finger eased onto the trigger.

"There is nothing stopping me from shooting you right here, right now, boy. I can easily tell Mandaca you became very violent and my life was in danger. But it would be more convenient for me and the vulture if I take you out of the town first."

Nunida stepped over Amri's body and grabbed the open end of the handcuff on Bruce's wrist.

Bruce smiled. "You have big ears," he said.

A confused look crossed Nunida's face.

Bruce kicked the rifle from Nunida's hand. It flew across the floor. He grabbed Nunida's ears with both his hands and brought his head down, smashing his forehead into the man's skull. Bruce stumbled backward; the whites of his eyes rolled back into his head. Nunida slumped to the ground.

"Don't touch me or my friend again. You hear me?" He kicked Nunida in the stomach. Nunida didn't even groan. Searching through Nunida's pockets he found the key to the handcuffs, took them off and tossed them to the floor.

Bruce ran to Charlie, lifted him over his shoulder, and rushed out the door.

Once they were out on the sidewalk, he let Charlie down, placed his arm around his shoulders, and helped him walk.

"We need to get away from here as fast as we can, Charlie. Are you up to some fast walking?"

Charlie nodded.

"But don't look at anyone. And don't make it look like you're hurrying. Just walk with me, okay?"

Charlie nodded again.

The boys walked in silence, past the marketplace, past the stalls, past the hotels and the shops and the gas station, until they were well on their way to the outskirts of the town. Finally, slowing their pace, they stopped and looked back.

"Where did you ever learn to do that?" Charlie said with more than a hint of admiration in his voice.

"Uh, just something I learned from watching some old *Terminator* movies. But you know what, Charlie?" Bruce said, rubbing his forehead and swaying slightly.

"What?"

"No one ever wins in a head butt."

Charlie laughed, and Bruce thought it was the best sound he had ever heard.

He looked up and saw a small corner store. He had an idea. "Wait here," he said, leaving Charlie standing on the sidewalk. "I need to get us something."

Bruce rushed across the street.

He walked up to a clerk standing behind the counter, removed his leather belt, and showed it to the young man. "I need to get some food and some medicine. Will you take this in trade?"

The clerk nodded.

"Good."

Bruce looked at the shelves behind the counter. "Can I have some of those buns there? And those tomatoes look good too. And I'll take that green thing there," Bruce said, pointing to a melon of some sort. "And two of those big bottles of soda. And that box of cookies."

The clerk reached for a small box of Oreos on the shelf.

"No. No. Not that one. The big box. We're celebrating."

Bruce looked down the small aisle in the center of the store. "Now where can I find some healing ointment of some sort?" he said as he scanned the shelves.

He spotted a package of baby wipes and grabbed a box. He almost did a little dance. Just a step down from the wipes he saw what he was looking for: some Polysporin cream. The kind his mother had always used whenever there were infected cuts that needed to be dealt with.

Bruce placed everything on the counter and handed his belt to the clerk.

The clerk shook his head. "No. I will trade the belt for the food. The medicine will be extra. What else do you have?"

Bruce sighed. "How 'bout the shirt? I got it at a Rolling Stones concert. It's worth at least fifty bucks back home."

"Yes, that will do," the clerk said, grinning.

Bruce took his shirt off and handed it to the young man. He couldn't help smiling. *It's worth it*, he thought as the clerk handed him the bags of his new purchases.

Holding his pants up with one hand and the bags with the other, Bruce ran back to Charlie. "Come on! Let's find a spot to sit. I got some food for us!"

"*Gway*!" Charlie said, limping along, trying to keep up with Bruce. "Did you steal this stuff or what?"

Bruce stopped and stared at Charlie. He frowned.

"Geez. Can you not take a joke?" Charlie laughed. "And pull up those pant. There is nothing worse than seeing a white ass in the street of Uganda."

Bruce shook his head and grinned.

The boys walked until they found an acacia tree near the side of the road. Its large branches reached out from its trunk, creating a shaded area the size of a small house. They sat under the tree, allowing the tall grass to hide them from the view of the road. Bruce took the food and set out a meal like no other. Within minutes they ate the buns, tomatoes, and melon, and drank most of the soda. While they leaned up against the tree, devouring their box of

Oreo cookies, Bruce looked at Charlie and smiled. He felt good.

Bruce reached into the bag and pulled out the wipes and the ointment. "Here," he said, "let's clean up those feet of yours."

Carefully, he removed the string and dried leaves from Charlie's feet. He turned his head and held his breath. The stench was overpowering. He cleared his throat and forced himself to look at the swollen feet. He took a few wipes from the package and gently removed the dirt and dried blood and pus that oozed from the open and infected wounds. *How the hell did he even walk on them?* he wondered as he wiped the last traces of blood away. Charlie rested his back against the tree and closed his eyes.

"This will really help," Bruce said as he covered Charlie's feet with the cream. "I'll just rub it in a bit to get it deep into the sores."

Charlie smiled, his eyes still closed, his face tilted toward the sun.

Bruce wiped the last traces of the Polysporin onto his pants.

Now all we have to do, Bruce thought, *is walk to the camp in the hot African sun, being careful to watch for the LRA and the police. Should be simple enough. Except . . .*

Bruce looked down at his Nikes.

"Okay," he said, letting out a sigh. He took his shoes off and gently placed Charlie's feet into his oversized runners.

"I don't know how well you're gonna be able to walk in 'em, but at least your feet'll be covered and you'll have a chance to heal," Bruce said.

Charlie stared at his shoes.

"You know, you are not that bad, considering you are *muzungu*." He laid his head back against the tree and closed his eyes again. "How about we rest here for a bit and enjoy the shade from this tree just?"

Bruce sat next to Charlie, feeling the coolness of the tree's trunk against his bare back. The hot sun broke through the branches creating patches of sunlight on his feet.

He listened to the crickets in the tall grass. The soft *coo, coo* of a pair of doves in the upper branches of the tree added harmony to the musical ensemble, as did the rustling of the leaves as a light breeze blew through the tree. Bruce's eyelids grew heavy. Soon his eyes closed and his chest rose and fell with a steady rhythm.

Slowly, Bruce opened his eyes and stared. The lush green leaves and the rich blue sky were gone. A white ceiling and an off-kilter light were in its place. The sound of the crickets and the birds was also missing, replaced by the distant sound of a washing machine going through its spin cycle. Bruce glanced from the ceiling, to the walls, then finally to his hand drawn in a tight fist. He opened his fingers and peered into the palm of his hand. He saw a small pile of dust and tiny pebbles. He looked at his socked feet, his pants, and his bare chest and grinned.

"Cool," he said.

Chapter 14

In the moment of crisis, the wise build bridges and the foolish build dams. ~ Nigerian proverb

Scott stood back and surveyed the hole in the wall. "Next time you take your frustrations out, Scotty, make sure there's no two-by-four behind it," he said, rubbing his swollen knuckles.

Scott took a Beatles poster from another wall, repositioned it over the hole, and pushed the tack in. He made a mental note to sneak some plaster and paint from the garage and fix it before anyone noticed.

He walked into the bathroom and stared in the mirror. The face that stared back at him looked like something from a zombie movie. Or worse. Black under the eyes, hair plastered against one side of his head, while on the other side it stuck out in all directions, resembling some Gothic hairdo gone bad.

"Maybe it's time I became addicted to caffeine," he said, climbing into the shower.

Half an hour later, Scott was standing at the corner near his house, holding a to-go cup of coffee, waiting for Rob.

"Hey, you look like what my cat puked up this morning," Rob said.

"Thanks. Whenever I need someone to make me feel better, I'll be sure to come to you."

"What gives with you? Still jet-lagged?"

"Yeah, I guess, but you'll love this."

Scott told Rob everything that happened after school: Hailey, the money, the jacket, and the stones.

"I can't prove it right now, but I know Bruce took everything," he said, tightening his hand into a fist.

"And what makes you think that?"

Scott stopped in mid-step.

"You've got to be kidding me. Because that's what Bruce does. Since grade school he's stolen things from us. Don't tell me you don't remember the time he stole that toy car of yours. You were all tears because it was your day for show-and-tell and you couldn't find it in your pack. And who did we see with it the next day? Bruce. And what about that time when I brought that arrowhead I'd found in Arizona when my dad and I searched that burial site? It was something important to me. It was my first find. You don't think I was upset when that went missing?"

"Yeah, but that was years ago. Get over it, Scott."

"But there have been other times. How about all of those bikes that went missing from the racks, and that speaker equipment after that dance? Nobody could prove it, but we all knew who did it, so I'm not going to get over it. Bruce is Bruce. He's still a pathetic, stupid jerk. And no one stands up to him because everyone's afraid of him."

Rob shrugged. "Yeah, I have to agree with you on that one. But look on the bright side—at least you have Hailey out of your life. I wouldn't want to get tangled up with that woman."

"Yeah, I guess."

"Anyways, I gotta go. Coach wants us at the gym early so he can go over the plays with us. Meet me at my locker at noon. Dear Aunt Betty gave me some cash for Christmas. I'll treat you to lunch."

"Yeah, see you then."

Rob jogged down the pathway through the park that led to their school.

Scott sat on a bench, sipped his coffee, and sighed. Maybe Rob was right. Maybe he should let it go. Maybe they were just some old stones. Rob proved it when he held the stone yesterday and looked at him as if he had two heads when he asked him if something had happened. *And let's face it*, he thought, *I was feeling a bit strange in the cave, maybe even a bit light-headed from the stale air and the claustrophobia thing. And when you're in a cave, acting like Indiana Jones, some weird "visions" are bound to happen. And when you're tired and jet-lagged and wound up, wouldn't you want to believe they're something more? No, they were just ordinary stones that some kid, who was born a long, long time ago, thought were special good luck charms or something like that.*

Scott took a big gulp of coffee. But even if the stones were just ordinary, they were *his* stones, they were part of his big find, and he had to admit, he wanted them back. All he had to do was prove Bruce had stolen the money and get him to give the stones back. That's all.

He breathed in the cold winter air and blew it out. His shoulders dropped. "Yeah, that's all."

Scott got up and continued walking down the path. He eyed a soda can lying on the ground and kicked it. *Nobody stands up to Bruce,* he thought. He took a couple of steps and gave the can another kick. *He just keeps on pushing and shoving his big fat ass around.* He gave the can one final swift kick and watched it fly through the air. "Yeah, if only that was Bruce's head."

Scott stopped and looked down the pathway. There was Bruce, crouched on his knees, wrapping a scarf around his little brother's neck.

"Now imagine that. A moment of tenderness from good ol' Brucey boy," he said.

Scott watched as Bruce reached into his pocket and gave something to his brother. Quickly, his brother jumped up and gave Bruce a high-five and ran down the pathway to join some friends. Bruce then turned away from the school and started walking toward Scott.

Scott stared at Bruce as he passed him, watching him put his earbuds in and turn his music on. He could hear the rock bass ebbing from Bruce's ears.

"Shithead," Scott said as he headed toward the school.

When Scott reached the spot where Bruce and his brother had stood, a piece of black paper lying on the white snow caught his eye. It looked vaguely familiar. Scott picked it up and unfolded the wrapper. The bright red letters read "Chew 4 U A Tongue Sensation."

He crunched the wrapper in his fist and glared at Bruce's back. His blood rose to his face and pounded into his fists. "Son of a . . ."

He walked toward Bruce, each step faster than the other, until he saw him duck into a cluster of trees that surrounded the public washroom.

Scott followed and waited outside the door. The tops of his knuckles turned white as he clenched them and pressed them to his sides.

A minute passed. Then two, then five. His jaw ached from gritting his teeth. "How long does it take someone to . . . ?"

Slowly, Scott opened the door and peered in. He crouched down and looked under each stall. Empty, empty, then at the third one, two huge feet seemed to stare back at him.

He set his coffee mug on a sink counter, walked into the next stall, and closed the door. He stepped up onto the toilet, making a quick note of a broken hinge on the seat, then carefully positioned his feet on either side of the bowl. He peered down into Bruce's stall. The *boom, boom* from Bruce's earbuds bounced off the stall walls while he sat on the edge of the seat, holding the pouch of stones in one hand and a stone in the other. Bruce wrapped his fingers around the stone and held it for a few moments. He opened his hand, looked at the stone, and sighed. He placed the stone into the pouch, tied the cord, and put the pouch into his pocket, then walked out of the stall.

Scott took in a deep breath. *It's now or never.*

He pivoted on the seat. Suddenly, his feet slid out from underneath him as the hinge broke and the seat bounced and clattered to the floor.

"Crap," he exclaimed as one foot plunged into the toilet. The toilet seat bounced and threw a perfect ringer around his other leg. Instinctively, Scott kicked forward, and the toilet seat flew out of the stall. He threw the door open and half stepped, half fell out of the cubicle.

"What the hell?" Bruce spun around and pulled his earbuds from his ears.

Scott tried to muster a shred of dignity as he stood in a puddle of toilet juice and attempted to fix Bruce with a steely gaze. It didn't work. If Scott had a tail, it would have been stuck between his legs.

"You took my stones," he blurted out, the words caught in his throat. His legs weren't all that steady either.

Bruce turned his back, ignoring Scott, and reached for the door again.

This was Scott's only chance. The adrenaline pulsed through his veins, and he hated the Scott who always backed down from Bruce.

"Give me back my stones," he said, taking a step closer.

Bruce turned around.

"They don't mean anything to you. They're just talismans. Something I found in a cave. Give them back."

Bruce took the pouch from his pocket, glanced at it, and shook his head. "Forget it, Scotty," he said as he dropped it back into his pocket.

Scott glared and drew in a long noisy breath through his nostrils. "You have to get it into your thick head that you can't keep on lifting things from people."

Scott couldn't believe the words that were coming out of his mouth.

Bruce laughed. "Listen, Scotty, I know they're your stones. You can have 'em when I'm done with 'em. But for now, back off."

Bruce shoved Scott into the wall. A loud crack resounded in Scott's ears as his head hit the cement. He shook his head and stared at Bruce. He grit his teeth while his hand tightened into a fist. He struck Bruce square in the face. Bruce's eyes bulged with rage. He grabbed Scott's fist in one hand and yanked it down. His other fist flew into Scott's stomach. Scott dropped to the ground. His breath came in short gasps.

"Like I said, I know they're your stones, and you'll get 'em back. Later."

As Bruce turned to leave, Scott glanced at the toilet seat on the floor. He grabbed it as he scrambled to his feet and smashed it down on Bruce's head. Bruce toppled to the floor.

Scott glowered. His breath was loud and hard.

Bruce's eyes glazed over. His eyelids closed, then opened very slowly.

"Look, Scott"—Bruce drew in a shaky breath—"I know they're your stones. But I can't give 'em back to you. I need 'em."

Scott tightened his grip on the toilet seat.

"I know if I was to tell you why, you wouldn't believe me. But trust me on this."

Scott laughed. "Trust you? You want me to trust you? Isn't that funny. Now give me the pouch, Bruce."

Bruce grabbed the wall and slowly pulled himself up. His legs shook. "I said you can have your stones later. Now back off!" He pushed Scott into the wall. "Understand?"

He drove his fist into Scott's stomach. Scott doubled over, holding his sides. Bruce turned and walked to the door.

Scott grabbed the seat from the floor and ran. He lifted it over his head and swung it down on Bruce's head again. A loud crack resounded. Bruce staggered backward. He blinked once, twice, then closed his eyes. He fell to the ground.

Scott stared at the still body.

"Great, Scott. You probably killed him. Now you can add something else to your list of offenses: first, withholding archeological finds, now, first-degree murder." Scott leaned over Bruce and felt a faint breath come from his mouth. "Okay, strike that. Alive but unconscious."

Scott reached into Bruce's pocket and pulled out the pouch of stones. He smirked as he picked up the toilet seat and dropped it over Bruce's head. "That toilet seat really suits you, shithead."

He put the stones in his pocket and walked out the door. As he rounded a bend in the pathway, he looked at the empty school grounds. Classes had already begun.

"No sense in getting another pink slip," he said as he turned toward home.

Several minutes later Scott walked up the empty driveway and climbed the stairs to his house. He pulled out his key, unlocked the door, and stepped inside, quickly locking the door behind him. As he touched the back of his head, he felt a huge lump. He smiled. As much as he was hurting, he felt good. He had stood up to Bruce. He had brought him down. And he had gotten his stones back.

Scott opened the sack and shook the stones onto the kitchen table.

There were only four stones.

"What the?"

He put the stones back into the pouch, stuffed them into his pocket, and opened the front door. He stopped and thought: the chance that Bruce was still unconscious was slim. The chance that he was on his way over was not so slim.

"Guess it'll have to wait," he said as he closed the door and locked it again. He slumped down at the kitchen table and started to think.

When Bruce comes to, the first thing on his mind will be revenge. The courage that had filled Scott slowly started to trickle away. He could not stay clear of Bruce for the rest of his life.

But he had another thought, which surprisingly seemed to bug him more than the first: Bruce said he needed the stones. And he really looked as if he meant it. *Could it be?* Scott grabbed the pouch and emptied the stones onto the table again. He picked a stone, held it in his hand, and waited.

Nothing.

Scott sighed and put the stones back into the pouch. There was no magic.

He tried to push the image of Bruce's desperate look out of his mind, but he couldn't. After twelve years he thought he had the guy figured out. *Why was Bruce so anxious to have this pouch of stones?*

It was all Scott could think of as he threw his soggy pants and socks into the laundry hamper.

Chapter 15

If you have filled with pride, then you will have no room for wisdom. ~ African proverb

Scott cracked the door open to see Rob standing on the front steps. His goofy grin was bigger than usual. “Never leave any evidence behind at a crime scene,” he said, handing him his to-go cup.

“What the? How’d you get this?”

“Long story short, I went to the coach’s meeting and realized I forgot my jersey. So I rushed home and on the way back saw a crowd of people around the door of the men’s public bathroom. When I looked in, there were a couple guys helping Bruce up, sorta laughing. Something about someone using a toilet seat as a concealed weapon. Then I saw your mug and I realized what happened. I grabbed it and put it in my bag and left. End of story."

"Uh, thanks."

"So you gonna tell me what happened, toilet seat warrior?"

Scott's eyes narrowed to a sudden death glare. He sat at the kitchen table and told Rob everything, from finding the bubblegum wrapper, to fighting Bruce and taking the stones, to returning home to discover only four stones left in the pouch.

"So what are you gonna do? Because you know next time Bruce sees you, he's gonna kill you."

"Yeah, I know. That's why I stayed home today. I think I'll tell my mom I'm not feeling well. She'll just think I caught something on the plane, and she'll let me stay home."

"And how long do you think you can pull that off for?"

"Until Friday, and then I have the weekend. Maybe by then I'll come up with a plan."

"Hope so. It would really suck for the school to lose its toilet seat warrior."

Scott glared.

"I'll come by Saturday. Do you want me to bring you any of your homework?"

Scott shook his head. "No. I think I'll just work on my will and decide what to give to my next of kin."

*   *   *   *

By the time Saturday afternoon rolled around, Scott was stir-crazy. He was glad to see Rob when he finally showed up.

"So how did it go? Your mom obviously bought the idea you were sick, huh?"

"Yeah, but she was worried for a bit I had malaria. Good thing I convinced her I always had a mosquito net on my bed and I always used fly repellent, so she let me off easy."

"Easy?"

"My dad had a scare when the doctors thought he got it after a trip to Ecuador. He lay in bed for days with tubes stuck in him, sucking juice in one end and using a bedpan at the other."

Rob shuddered. "I got some news for you. Hailey was all happy and bouncing around Friday morning. That money that went missing showed up at the office, the same day Bruce came back after his 'mysterious' illness."

"Really? What gives about that?"

"You think that toilet seat on the head did something?" Rob asked.

"Maybe. But if it did, I wish I'd thought of doing it sooner. Like in first grade."

Rob laughed. "Or at birth."

"Hey," Scott said, grinning at Rob, "do you think I have a chance with Hailey now?"

"Do you seriously want another chance?"

"No," Scott said.

"That's my man. You're learning. You can be taught."

*   *   *   *

The time on Scott's alarm clock read 9:27. Sunday morning. Last day of hiding out. Scott grabbed his bathrobe and walked into the kitchen to see his mom and dad putting together their ritual Sunday brunch. His father was busy pouring the pancake batter into perfect circles on the steaming griddle while his mother flipped the bacon, frying it to a fine crisp.

"You feeling any better today?" Scott's mom asked.

"Uh-huh, a bit," Scott replied, throwing a pile of bacon onto his plate.

He grabbed a stack of pancakes and poured the syrup, watching it drip down the sides. There was more to the Sunday brunch ritual at his home than just the pancakes. It was a time to sit and chat about the week past and the week to come. His parents joined him at the table.

"You know, the workers at the cave site in Uganda have decided to start digging at the base of the caves we were in last week, Scott," his dad said, shoving a huge piece of pancake into his mouth.

"Really?"

"Since you discovered that skeleton there, they've got this idea there may be some sort of ancient village in that area. It's hard to know what they'll find, if anything at all. But I sure wouldn't mind going back there to see what they dig up."

"Can I come?" Scott asked.

"Of course. But that won't be for months."

"I had a really strange email this morning from one of our volunteers in Uganda," Scott's mom said, interrupting his thoughts about his future trip. "A woman I've been keeping in touch with runs the displaced persons camp just outside a small town in northern Uganda. I guess she must have had some time to email me from an Internet café when she was in town picking up supplies, because I don't hear from her all that often."

"Well . . ." Scott said, encouraging her to go on. Sometimes she could take the shortest story and drag it on and on for hours.

"Well," she continued, "she said the weirdest thing happened when she was taking down the names of the new arrivals as they were filing into the camp that evening. Turns out there was this boy, about twelve years old. He said he had escaped from the LRA and had ripped up his feet when he ran through a field of thorns. When she stood up from her table to look at his feet, she saw the most expensive pair of running shoes she'd ever seen. She figured if they sold them they would have been able to feed three hundred of the children in the camp for one day. She said she asked the boy where he'd gotten the shoes, and he told her an angel had given them to him. So she asked the boy, 'Since when does our angel Gabriel bring shoes to young boys?' And you know what he said?" His mom chuckled to herself. "He said, 'No, the angel's name isn't Gabriel. His name is Bruce.' Now isn't that the strangest thing? Imagine a boy making up that story."

Scott stared at his mom and put his fork down on his plate. His mind was spinning. The vision in the cave: the smoke, the heat, and the gunfire. The artist's story. Then the fight: Bruce holding onto the stones in the bathroom cubicle and desperately telling Scott he needed them. Now his mom's story: expensive running shoes, an angel called, of all names, Bruce. Trepidation grew in Scott until his hands turned sweaty and his face became flushed.

Could Bruce know something about the stones I don't?

"I'm not feeling well, Mom. I think I'll go to my room," Scott said, suddenly getting up from the table.

Scott's mom looked up from her pancakes. "Your face is all red. You still feeling ill? Why don't you go lie down, and I'll check your temperature."

He nodded and walked to his bedroom, closing the door behind him. He grabbed his backpack from his desk and threw it on his bed. As he sat on the edge of the mattress, he pulled out the pouch and opened it. Slowly, he took out a stone and wrapped his fingers around it. He waited.

Nothing.

As Scott placed the stone back into the pouch, his shoulders dropped under the weight of disappointment.

No, there was nothing to these stones.

His analytical mind began to reason with him. *A so-called angel in Uganda called Bruce?* There must be plenty of guys named Bruce in Uganda. After all, Ugandans liked giving their kids North American names. And expensive shoes? There were plenty of explanations for that too: a shipping container filled with clothes and shoes sent over from the States or Canada or some other better-off country was just one of them. The vision, well, he had already found several reasons to explain that.

And the story the woman told him. It was a myth. Nothing more.

But Bruce wanting the stones? There had to be a reason for that. The stones would have been simple stones to Bruce. He didn't know anything about where they were from, just that Scott had found them in a cave. He didn't mention the cave was in Uganda or anything else.

Well, he reasoned, *who could ever figure Bruce out?* Bruce was a pathetic excuse for a human being, a liar, a reject. Not an angel. He was plenty of things, but an angel? Scott laughed.

"There's no way in hell that could ever happen," Scott said, throwing the pouch onto his bed.

"And yet . . ." He grabbed the pouch and opened it up again. He picked out a different stone, wrapped his fingers around it, and waited. Nothing. He grabbed another stone and then the last one. The results were the same: a huge nothing.

Scott returned the stones to his backpack once more. As much as he wanted to dismiss the idea the stones could have some "magical" power in them, it didn't all add up. Maybe there was something to these stones, and maybe Bruce knew something he didn't. And then a new thought came to his mind: *I had the vision in the cave when I had all five stones.*

Maybe the magic only works sometimes and only when all five stones are together.

He took in a deep breath. *That would mean getting the last stone from Bruce,* he thought, as his breath escaped from him, leaving him like a deflated balloon.

But they're my stones, and if there's something to them I want them back, Scott thought. *And besides, it was my discovery, and why should Bruce have anything to do with it?*

He sighed. He would have to go to school tomorrow and face Bruce. And he would have to get the stone back.

"Maybe I should bring a toilet seat with me," he said.

Chapter 16

Unity is strength, division is weakness.
~ Swahili proverb

A huge wave of fear tumbled over Scott when the alarm clock went off and woke him. He rolled out of bed, already dreading the day. Monday morning had arrived. He was going to have to confront Bruce and get the last stone back.

"Maybe Bruce got hit by a bus," he said aloud, forcing himself to laugh.

He grabbed a piece of toast from the kitchen counter and looked out the door. Rob was sitting on the front steps.

"What are you doing here?" he asked.

"Just thought you might need some protection. Did you bring any weapons from your bathroom cache?"

"Very funny."

When they walked into the schoolyard, Scott noticed a few unusually admiring stares coming his way. "You didn't tell anyone about what happened, did you?"

"What, me? No . . . well, maybe I hinted at it."

"Hinted at it? What do you mean by that?"

"I may have casually said it was quite a coincidence that both you and Bruce were away from school on the same day."

A group of kids, hanging out near the door, stared at Scott. They didn't even try to hide their smirks.

"And I suppose you mentioned my new title?"

"Well, maybe."

"Some friend you are."

"But it's all good, Scott. Everyone's cool with what you did. You're like some sorta celebrity now."

Scott stopped and looked around the yard. Almost every kid in the school was looking at him except Bruce, who was leaning against a tree, his eyes closed, oblivious to everything around him.

"I'm getting that stone back right now," Scott said, walking toward Bruce.

"Hey!" Rob grabbed him by the arm and swung him around. "Don't be stupid, okay? This is Bruce we're talking about. He could do some real serious damage to you. Think about it. It's only one stone. You've got the other four, right?"

"No, it's more than that. I think . . ." Scott paused. "I think it's time Bruce stopped taking things that don't belong to him. Besides, I'm sick of being pushed around by him. He's got something of mine, and I want it back."

Scott shoved Rob out of the way and continued toward Bruce. He was through with being scared. Fear had kept him from doing what he wanted to do. He wasn't going to let it stop him again. Besides, his confidence had reached an all-time high now that he had a hundred pairs of eyes watching him. Scott stood in front of Bruce, staring at his massive frame.

Finally, he spoke. "I want my stone back."

Bruce opened one eye.

"There were five stones in the pouch, and I only got four."

Bruce stared down at Scott, his body blocking the morning sun. "You're pathetic, Scott. You sound like a little boy in kindergarten." His voice took on a whiny, nasal tone. "'I want my stone back! Mommy, he took my stone!'"

"No, you're the pathetic one, still taking things that don't belong to you. Haven't you learned anything?"

"Yeah, I did learn something: you're a bigger asshole than I thought."

Bruce reached into his pocket and brought out a small handful of fine sand and tiny pebbles. "Here, you can have your stupid stone."

Scott stared at the dark pile in Bruce's hand.

"What the . . ." he said, taking a step closer. "What did you do?" He drew in a deep breath and held it while his hands tightened into fists.

"I held it in my hand and fell asleep, and when I woke up it was like this," Bruce said, putting out his hand and fingering the tiny pebbles.

"Is that what happened?" Scott took a few steps then stopped and spun around. He looked Bruce straight in the eyes. "You lie," he said. He walked away. His hopes were as crushed as the stone that lay in Bruce's hand.

Bruce ran up to Scott and stopped him in his tracks. "Where was the cave you found the stones?"

"Why do you want to know?"

"No reason. Just wondering."

"In Uganda, in Africa."

Bruce's eyes widened. "Uganda?"

"Yeah, my dad and I were checking out this cave, and I found a skeleton holding them. But what does it matter where I found them? The stones are mine, and this is what . . ." He glared. "You know Bruce, you just don't get it."

"For someone who's so smart, you're acting really stupid, Scott."

"Stupid? You're calling me stupid? You are such an a-hole." Scott slammed his fist on Bruce's hand, and the remains from the stone fell and scattered on the ground. He walked away.

Chapter 17

Cross the river in a crowd and the crocodile won't eat you. ~ African proverb

Bruce sat on his bed and carefully placed the last of the pebbles he'd collected from the school ground into the palm of his hand.

"Stupid ass," he said to himself. "He doesn't even know what he's got."

He rolled a small pebble between his thumb and his fingers while his mind drifted. He thought about Charlie.

He had to admit that the little guy had grown on him, and he was worried about him. He didn't feel right leaving Charlie alone under the tree. Not that he had any choice. One moment he was there, the next he wasn't.

But out in the school yard that morning, an idea had come to him. Maybe the pebbles could bring him back to Charlie. Maybe there was still a little bit of power left. And that's why it was crucial to find the tiny rocks that fell onto the ground. Maybe, just maybe, he could see Charlie again and make sure he was all right. It was worth a try.

Bruce wrapped his hand around the pebbles and closed his eyes. He didn't have to wait long. Instantly, images of Uganda surrounded him. Darkened images, lit only by the half-moon that hung in the sky. He stood still to allow his eyes to adjust to the darkness. Faint humming and chanting sounds came from a clearing ahead of him. Slowly, Bruce made out the outlines of two bare-chested men, circling a pile of rocks and sprinkling water over the pile.

"Oh, holy water . . . *ni wire* . . . *ni wire* . . . purify . . . purify . . ." they chanted over and over again.

Bruce inched closer. He wondered if he had come upon a sacred religious ritual of some sort. He watched the men continue to circle the pile, walking in a trance-like state.

Why the hell are they pouring water onto a pile of rocks? Bruce wondered. Then, to his surprise, one of the rocks moved, and then another. Finally, his eyes adjusted to the dim light and he realized it wasn't a pile of rocks he was looking at.

It was a group of children, huddled together.

A small boy clung to a girl, his arms wrapped tightly around her neck. Tears coursed down the girl's cheeks, her sobs barely heard above the chanting. Next to her sat a girl wearing a bright yellow dress. Her dress was ripped and her face was bloodied. She stared at Bruce, her eyes fixed and dazed, seeing nothing, hearing nothing. Closer to the inside of the circle, a boy lay on the ground. The stillness of his body made Bruce take a second look. *Is he dead?* he wondered. A girl bent over the boy and gently ran her fingers over his face. Slowly, Bruce focused on a long rope that ran from one child to the next, binding each of the children's hands. He followed the trail of the long cord until he saw a very familiar face. Crouched down on the ground, like a beaten dog, Charlie lay staring into the stars. His eyes were swollen and tears fell from his face in a steady stream. His lips moved in unceasing petitions.

Bruce caught his breath. Nothing could have prepared him for this. He looked around and discovered he wasn't the only spectator to this scene. Several kids, fully armed, stood on the periphery and guarded the huddle. Bruce ducked down, trying to hide behind the group. He had to figure out a way to help Charlie.

The chanting stopped and the jungle was quiet. The girl's sobs came to an exhausted end. The men walked away and entered a hut. *It's now or never*, Bruce thought. *Who knows when they'll return?* He crawled on his hands and knees, feeling the cold clay ground. His hand inched forward and his fingertips touched a small pile of sand. He looked down at his hands. Even in the dim moonlight, he could see them shaking. He lifted his hand and brushed the sand away. It fell and landed on a soft white surface. His eyes grew wide and a disturbing realization came to him: he was back home. He looked down on his bed to see a pile of fine black sand.

The magic from the stone was exhausted.

There was no time to lose. Bruce ran toward the bedroom door and stopped. He glanced at the garbage bag sitting in the corner and ripped it open, revealing the arrowhead that lay on top. It would be a pretty pathetic excuse for a peace offering, but it was all he had. He grabbed it and ran down the hallway then rushed outside and sprinted the four blocks to Scott's house. He banged on the door, then stood there, gulping in the early evening air.

The door opened and Scott's dad stepped out. "Uh, hello, Bruce," he said, his surprise obvious.

Bruce forgot any manners he may have picked up in kindergarten. "I need to talk to Scott right now," he blurted out. "It's important."

Scott's dad took a step back and looked at Bruce. Bruce could tell he was confused. He knew the boys weren't exactly friends. "Uh, just a sec. I'll go look for him. Wait here. I'll be right back."

Scott's dad closed the door and left Bruce standing on the steps. Seconds passed. A minute. Then two. And three. By the time Scott opened the door, Bruce was already considering busting it down.

Bruce put on his "nice" face. "I wanted to tell you I'm sorry I took your stones, and I'm sorry I hit you and rammed your head into the wall," he said. It was short and to the point. *Not bad*, he thought.

Scott stared at Bruce for a long time and then started to laugh. Bruce stepped back and did a double take. He had *apologized.* Wasn't this where the good guy was supposed to say, "That's okay. I know you didn't mean it. We're cool."?

"You think that covers it all? You've been a pain in the ass ever since you pushed me out of your way to have the slide in kindergarten, Bruce. It's going to take a lot more than just 'sorry.'" Scott stepped back and began to close the door.

"Wait!" Bruce grabbed the door and held it. He collected his thoughts and decided to start over.

"Here," he said, holding the arrowhead out in his hand. "I'm sorry for everything I've done to you. Every time I pushed you or hit you or stole anything from you. I can see you don't wanna accept my apology, and I don't blame you. Truth is, I didn't just come over here to say I was sorry. I came 'cause I need you to help me." Bruce paused for a second. *It's all or nothin',* he thought.

"The stones you have can take you places, Scott. I mean . . ." He stopped. "I mean, they take you to Uganda. That's what happened to me last week. After I stole your jacket and found the stones in the pocket, I picked one of them up, and while I was holding it I suddenly found myself in Uganda."

Scott glared. His hand tightened on the doorknob.

"And while I was there, I met up with a boy—his name's Charlie. And he'd just escaped from this army where they'd forced him to shoot and kill. They even forced him to kill his own mother." Bruce's voice trailed off as he remembered Charlie retelling his story while they sat in the jail cell.

"I was there for a day and a night, but in the morning after we ate and I'd cleaned Charlie's feet, we decided to rest under this tree. We were tired and it was already hot. And we still needed to make it to this camp. But I never got to see if he made it there okay. Suddenly, I was back home, and all that was left of the stone was this pile of pebbles and dust in my hand."

Scott laughed. "You're good, Bruce. Have you considered taking drama this year?"

Bruce glared. His hand clenched into a tight fist as he hid it behind his back. He drew in a long deep breath, and another and another. *Calm down. Calm down, ol' Brucey boy, or you're not gonna get anywhere,* he told himself. Slowly, he opened his hand and dropped it to his side. *Just think.* He felt his face relax. *You need to convince him. Would you believe Scott if it was the other way around?*

"But something bad has happened to Charlie," Bruce continued. "I know 'cause I was there in Uganda again. I used the pebbles left from the stone, and they brought me there but only for a short while this time. Just long enough to see Charlie and all of these kids that were tied together and these men sprinkling water on 'em. I think—no, I know—he's been captured by the army again. And I got no way of helping him unless I can have one of your stones to go back to Uganda." Bruce placed the arrowhead in Scott's hand. "Can you give me another stone so I can go and help Charlie?"

A confused look crossed Scott's face. He stepped back and stared at Bruce for a long time. Finally, he shook his head. "You're pathetic, Bruce." He dropped the arrowhead onto the steps, turned, and closed the door.

Bruce stared at the arrowhead. A lump came to his throat as he remembered the look on Charlie's face as he lay on the ground. He'd thought things were going to turn out for Charlie. He'd felt good when he sat under the tree and watched him dozing off with a smile on his face. What happened? How did the army find Charlie again? Did they take him right after Bruce disappeared?

He picked up the arrowhead and placed it on the mailbox next to the door. He stared at a crack on the walkway and followed it until it stopped at the sidewalk. Without looking up, he crossed the street and began to walk home. He had to think of something he could do. He was really worried about Charlie. A person could only handle so much sadness and horror in life, and Charlie had been given a lot more than anyone deserved.

Chapter 18

Hurry, hurry has no blessings.
~ Swahili proverb

Scott turned the TV off and sat in the living room, staring at the blank screen. He couldn't get the image of Bruce's face out of his mind as he pleaded, almost begged him, for a stone. It was so unlike the guy. And the story Bruce told him. It was too bizarre. How could it possibly be real? Besides, he had tried each of the stones over and over again to see if he would have another vision like he did in the cave. But it never happened. The stones didn't have any power, and Bruce was a liar. That was that. Or was it?

Scott looked out the living room window as his mom pulled into the driveway. It was late already. She must have had some extra work to do—there was always extra work to do.

She opened the door, put her laptop on the hall table, and walked into the living room. She slumped into a chair, lay her head back, and drew in a long, deep breath.

"Tough day at work, Mom?"

"Yeah."

Scott sat down beside her and put his arm around her shoulder.

"Our office found out one of the internally displaced persons camps—the IDP camp we set up in northern Uganda for those who had to leave their villages—was raided by the LRA last night. They've killed seven of our workers, burned lots of the tents and huts down, and taken some of the children. About thirty, they think. They don't know. They're hoping they'll find some of them hiding in the surrounding bush, but they're not too hopeful."

Her face was stone cold.

"I'm sick of this, Scott. I'm sick of wars being fought by children. I'm sick of children being used as pawns by an insane man."

She touched Scott's cheek, seeming to reassure herself of his presence.

"I'm sick of this thing going on and on, like it will never end. Wealthy countries jump up whenever some dictator needs to be removed—all in the apparent interest of saving the people. It's a crock. They only do it if their own interests are at stake. The Philippines, Kuwait. You know why the governments go into these countries?"

He shook his head. He hadn't really given it much thought.

"Oil. That's why they're there. They want to make sure their oil is safe and sound. And you know what the problem is?"

This time she didn't wait for him to reply. "There's no oil in Uganda."

Scott's mom lifted herself up from the chair and began to walk toward the kitchen. "I'm sorry, Scott. I shouldn't be telling you all this. You're just a kid. The biggest of your worries should be acne and homework," she said, trying to lighten the moment. She smiled and leaned against the wall. "Maybe I should run for prime minister. Then you and I could run the country and get some politicians off their butts. What do you think?"

Scott walked to his mother and wrapped his arms around her.

She sighed. "I just can't get this image out of my mind. They're probably doing this horrid, supposedly holy ritual on the kids right now, sort of an initiation thing. They sprinkle water on the child soldiers, telling them it'll keep them safe from the bullets. The kids don't know what to think. They're young."

Scott stared at his mom for a few moments, then finally blinked. “Water? Sprinkling water?”

“Yes, it’s some sort of cultish ritual they do. Kony has a group of men and women he’s trained to perform the ceremonies anytime they capture a new group.” She paused. “I think I’ll skip supper tonight. I don’t have the stomach to eat anything right now.” She climbed the stairs to her bedroom.

Scott’s mind raced. *Sprinkling water. Did Bruce see the kids who were captured from the camp?*

He rushed down the stairs and into his bedroom. He grabbed his backpack from on top of his desk and threw it onto the bed. He sat down, took out the pouch, and removed the stones. As he wrapped his hand around a stone, his first thought was that maybe he should wait and talk to Bruce first.

But it was too late. Big mistake.

A warm breeze touched Scott’s cheeks, bringing with it the memory of exotic Ugandan weather. He breathed in the fresh night air, enjoying the familiar way it left his lungs full and alive. He looked into the dark night sky. “It worked. But why now? Why not before?” Scott whispered. A half-moon lay nestled in the clouds directly above him. The silence of his bedroom had been replaced by the chirping of crickets and the long manic *ooohhhhh-whup* of a hyena in the distance. All of these things pressed the replay button of his trip with his father, but this time there was a new element.

Closer to him, Scott heard a less feral sound coming from near his feet. In the darkness he could make out the sound of quiet breathing, interrupted by labored sobs and tired whimpers.

He froze. He had a pretty good idea of where he was and what was happening.

When his eyes adjusted to the darkness, he realized he was standing on the outside of a clearing near a stand of trees. Directly in front of him was a group of children, huddled together in a mass of bodies and rope. Scott stared into the eyes of a young boy and then at the bloodied face of a girl who looked to be about the same age as he was. His breath halted in a quiet gasp.

Every part of his body was on high alert. His eyes widened until they ached. Every muscle in his body tensed in anticipation of the worst. He knew he wasn't safe here and he needed to move right away. There would be guards watching the kids. Scott stepped backward and heard a loud snap as a dry twig broke under his foot. He had made his second mistake of the evening.

A huge arm wrapped around Scott's neck and squeezed. A man stuck the end of a rifle into his side, and Scott gagged as a he breathed in his foul breath.

The man let out a repulsive laugh. "Eeh, Seth! Remember the *muzungu* you saw out on the road? Well, guess what I got here!"

Chapter 19

To run is not necessarily to arrive.
~ Swahili proverb

Fear filled every bone and covered every bristling hair on Scott's body. He couldn't breathe. His mind was numb. He could not think.

Another man walked into the clearing and stopped in front of him. Instantly, all of the children became still, staring at the ground before them.

"See. I told you I was not seeing thing. A little white boy stick out in Africa like a white worm in a pile of dog crap," the man said as he let out an ugly laugh.

As the man leaned forward, Scott smelled the same repulsive reek of his breath. "So what is a pretty small white boy like you doing out here?" he said, clutching Scott's face with his massive hand. The man shook Scott's head from side to side, and he felt like a rabbit in the jaws of a pit bull.

"He is probably some kid of a white *padi*. Got lost. Too stupid to foot his way home to his daddy church in the dark. Is that right, little boy, little, little ka-boy?" said Seth.

Scott tried to think quickly. Would this be the best cover for him? What other excuse could he use for being out here in the evening? Slowly, he nodded in agreement, hoping the men would believe him.

"What are we going to do with the small boy, J.P.? I mean, we cannot let him go and we cannot use him just. He would give us away with that ugly white mug."

The man called J.P. stared at Scott, taking in every detail. Then he started to laugh. He reached down to the red Ugandan dirt, took a handful, and smeared it on Scott's cheek. "You know if we cover the ka-boy, we could use him, Seth."

Seth grabbed the dirt from J.P.'s hand and rubbed the coarse soil over Scott's forehead. Scott flinched as the rough dirt tore across his skin.

"Yes. That works," said J.P.

Seth grabbed a larger handful and slapped it on Scott's cheeks, grinding the soil into his white skin. The dirt flew into his nose and eyes. He closed his eyes tightly, trapping the small pieces of sand under his eyelids until they rubbed and scratched like sandpaper on an open wound. Again and again, Seth took more of the coarse red clay and rubbed it over Scott's face and head, all the time laughing.

Seth stood back and admired his work. "You know, J.P., I did a good job here. Best thing I have seen done to a *muzungu* for a long time." Then to the soldiers guarding the children he called, "Tie him up to a tree, and if anyone move, shoot them. We are going to eat."

They shoved Scott against a tree and jerked his arms behind him. Within seconds they lashed his hands together, and a large rope cut tightly into his wrists, making any movement painful and impossible. He tried to open his eyes. His breath cut short as the pain of a thousand needles stabbed at his sockets. He clenched his eyes shut and swore under his breath, cursing the men, the dirt, and himself.

"I am so stupid," he muttered as he heard the men walking away. "So stupid."

His head fell to his chest. Tied to a tree and practically blind, he was useless. And he was terrified. He knew enough about the LRA to realize he might never see home or his family again. Remembering the looks on the children's faces, Scott wondered just how much these children knew. Did they know the hell that was in store for them? Charlie, the boy Bruce mentioned, the one who had just escaped and was recaptured . . . he knew.

Slowly, tears began to well up in Scott's eyes until they flowed freely down his cheeks. He wasn't ashamed to cry. A moment of self-pity was just fine then.

Little by little, teardrop by teardrop, the sand began to wash away from his eyes. Opening them to half slits, he looked over to the children sitting huddled on the ground. Scott guessed there were probably twenty-five, maybe thirty kids. Charlie had to be in there somewhere. Straining his neck, he leaned forward from the tree, hanging from his arms.

One of the soldiers, a young teenage boy, pointed his gun at him. Scott stood back against the tree. It was the third stupid thing he had done already.

Scott peered into the group, following the long rope that bound the children together. He studied each child in turn, taking in all he could. He saw several young boys and girls huddled together, their faces pressed into each other's necks, seeking what comfort they could find. One teenage girl sat to the side, staring into the bush. Her face was bruised and swollen and her nose bloodied. Her dress was ripped from her shoulders. She held her arms to her chest, trying to keep herself covered.

Scott looked away. His sadness turned to anger as he began to realize the cruelty and disgusting things this army was capable of. He remembered his mom telling him how rape was used as a weapon in war. It defiled the women and girls in a country, and it did plenty to destroy families and their homes. He wanted to spit in the face of the man who did it.

He returned his gaze to another girl holding a small boy on her lap. With her arms bound together, she tried to offer as much comfort to him as she could by rocking back and forth. Scott stared at his small body; he couldn't have been more than seven years old. Revulsion coursed through Scott. He was sick. What person would use a child to fight his wars?

He caught a movement from the corner of his eye. He quickly straightened up as the two men returned.

Seth swaggered up to the children and yelled, "Get up!"

The children scrambled to their feet.

"Get up, I said!" Seth yelled a second time and kicked a young boy in the ribs. The child gasped and jumped to attention.

Seth motioned with his gun for the soldiers to go closer to the children. He pointed to the rope that bound the group together and jerked his head, commanding the soldiers to remove the ropes. "There will be no escaping. We know all your thought." He patted his gun. "Follow me. There is much work to do."

The children formed a single line and filed past Scott, marching and staring at the ground.

One child, however, lagged behind the others. Scott watched as the boy took off his shoes and handed them to a soldier. The soldier grinned and pushed the boy into line. He put his bare feet into the shoes and marched over to Scott. As the soldier untied the rope that bound his hands, Scott looked down to see the soldier's new shoes. A pair of blue Nike Air Maxs. They were the kind of shoes only a rich kid in North America could afford. The kind that could be sold to feed three hundred children in one day. The kind someone would give to a child whose feet had been ripped up by thorns while escaping from the LRA. Scott smiled to himself as he looked at the back of the boy marching ahead with the other children.

He had found Charlie.

Chapter 20

The heart of the wise man lies quiet like limpid water. ~ Cameroonian proverb

A small shaft of light appeared over the horizon, sending its beams through the trees, awakening the day. A lone bird let out a raucous laugh and then flew across the camp, its wings drumming the air with its steady beat.

Scott followed the group into the clearing and glanced around the compound, trying to take in as many details as he could. He never imagined the extent of the LRA. He had pictured small poorly assembled groups of untrained soldiers forcing children to carry arms and fight. But instead, he saw hundreds of children working with clockwork precision, each at their required jobs. Some were busy carrying supplies into makeshift tents while others worked in the fields, tilling the soil and digging up plants. Several girls tended to fires and worked over pots, cooking the day's meal. And still there were more children, some sitting on the ground inserting bullets into steel magazines while others cleaned and polished rifles or sharpened machetes.

Scott looked to his side, and his mouth dropped open as the group walked by a stockpile of weapons. Huge machine-like guns that were held up by sturdy metal tripods pointed their barrels in his direction. Crates stood piled next to them, along with several dozen AK-47s. An intense fear filled Scott and crawled over his entire body. This was not an army that used sticks and stones to kill. It was well equipped and could easily wipe out a whole village in minutes.

He followed the group until it stopped in front of several crates filled with straw. Seth pointed to a pile of bags on the ground beside the crates and gave his next order. "I want ten mine placed in each sack. When they are done, send J.P. to call me. We will do the training later." Seth turned on his heel and marched into a large tent at the end of the path.

As Nike Shoes opened the wooden crates with a crowbar, the other soldier sorted the children into groups and readied them for their work. The soldier reached into one of the crates and took out a small disk-shaped black object and placed it onto the ground. Quickly, the children began to remove the mines from the crates and place them into the sacks. The horrors of the past evening had quickened their response to the soldiers' demands.

Scott gathered a few bags in his arms and walked over to Charlie and knelt beside him.

"Here," he said, passing a bag to the boy.

Charlie took the bag and immediately began placing the mines inside. He didn't look at Scott. His face conveyed no emotion.

Scott inched closer. "Charlie," he whispered.

Charlie placed the filled bag on the ground and began to fill the second one.

"Charlie," Scott whispered a second time, bringing his volume up a notch. "I'm Scott. I know Bruce. He told me all about you. I don't know how we'll do it, but we've got to figure a way to get out of here."

Charlie continued placing the mines into the bag. He didn't respond.

"Charlie." Scott's voice was almost pleading now. "We need to get out of here."

The boy picked up his bags, walked away, and placed them at the foot of Nike Shoes. He crouched beside a girl and began to fill another sack. Scott's gaze cautiously jumped from Charlie, to the mines, and finally to the young soldier.

Within minutes the children had completed their job and a huge pile of sacks was sitting on the ground. J.P. strolled toward the tent Seth had entered. He called out, "Ready sir!" and stood to the side of the door.

Seth emerged alongside another man. After a few words were exchanged, Seth nodded and sauntered toward the children. "March," he said and led the children to a field in which several young girls were working the soil. Scott heard the command as "Maatch," but he knew easily enough what the soldier meant.

Seth pointed to the girls in the group and gave the next command. "Dig up the cassava and bring it to the fire." He turned to one of the young soldiers in charge of the girls. "Have them fill thirty sack after they bring in enough for the next meal," he said.

The boys left the girls and followed Seth to a large tree standing in the camp. "Show them how to clean the gun. I want all of them ready for tomorrow," Seth said, barking out his next order to the man leaning against the tree.

A group of young boys sat in a circle on the ground. Their faces and hands were smeared with grease as they worked on the guns that lay in a pile in the middle. One child was carefully ramming a cloth wrapped around a stick up and down the barrel of a huge rifle while another worked on reassembling a gun he had taken apart and cleaned.

The soldier in charge assigned each one from the group to a boy cleaning a gun. He pointed his rifle at Scott, then at a boy hunched over an AK-47 near the base of the tree. Scott hastened to his side and squatted on his knees. The boy turned his face to him and held out a stick and a rag.

Scott looked in horror at the young face. The boy's nose was gone. Missing. Cut off. All that remained was a ghastly scar of mismatched flesh and disfigured holes where the nostrils should have been.

"Take dis and wipe the barrel like dis." The boy spoke in a quiet, distorted voice.

Scott took the stick and rag, trying to avoid looking at the boy. The boy's face was hideous and the fear that it meant to provoke was very effective. He worked in complete submission, never daring to look up at the soldiers, never daring to speak unless necessary. A shudder passed through Scott and he closed his eyes. *Who would do such a cruel thing?* he thought as he quickly wrapped the stick and inserted it into the barrel of the gun.

For the next several hours Scott focused on his job, making sure he was always busy while the soldiers watched every child's every move. He listened carefully to the young boy's instructions but could never bring himself to look him straight in the eyes. As the hours passed by, the size of the gun pile began to diminish. When all of the guns were finally cleaned, Nike Shoes ordered them to carry the guns to a storage place. It turned out to be a mud hut guarded by two men carrying large rifles, standing on either side of the doorway.

Carefully leaning each of the guns against the inside wall, the children quickly filled the hut with the rifles as they filed in and out of the enclosure.

When all the rifles were finally stored away, the soldier gave another order. "Get to those tree"—he indicated the edge of the camp—"and get some wood. Pile it up beside each fire. And you, you, and you," he said pointing his finger at three boys, "you are doing the cutting. Grab a machet and get to work." Seth and J.P. turned on their heels and walked away.

The young soldiers led the way to the trees and stood with their guns aimed at the children as the three boys chopped down the trees and the children dragged the heavy trunks to the fires. Scott carried a log over and peered into an open pot cooking on the fire. His stomach growled. The smell was familiar to him: cassava, Africa's answer to the potato, a staple of every African meal, sometimes bitter, sometimes sweet, but always very filling. His mouth watered. He dropped the log onto the pile and returned to the bush, trying to forget the smell that clung to his nostrils. They hadn't had anything to eat or drink all day. But he knew it was best not to look forward to something that might not happen.

Scott picked up a freshly fallen tree, and Charlie grabbed the other end, lifted it onto his shoulder, and led the way. They dropped the log onto the pile and returned to the bush. Scott paused and looked into the forest to see the sun spreading its last rays before the evening. Suddenly, he longed for home as he realized the sun that was leaving him now would soon be shining into his bedroom window.

He closed his eyes. Terrifying thoughts filled his mind. Home. Would he ever see his home again? Or his parents? Did they even know he was away? Were they even searching for him? There were so many questions he needed the answers to. He knew nothing of the power contained in the stones. But Bruce knew. He knew they brought you to Uganda, but what else did he know? If only he hadn't been so stupid and had waited and talked to Bruce.

A scream interrupted Scott's thoughts.

A few steps away from him, a girl stood frozen in fear. A large thin snake had wrapped its olive-black body around the girl's arm. Scott recognized the snake instantly: a black mamba. *Very* poisonous.

While everyone stood absolutely still, the two soldiers slowly approached the snake, their guns poised and ready. The massive snake nonchalantly slithered over the girl's shoulder and around her neck, then down to the ground. It draped itself over the girl's body, both tail and head touching the ground on either side of her feet. Scott couldn't imagine the intense fear that must have gripped her at that very moment.

Strangely enough, however, his thoughts turned to the need to survive.

"Come on, Charlie. Let's go," he whispered, jerking his head toward the bush. "We may never have another chance."

All of the soldiers' attention was focused on the snake. They only had a few seconds to steal into the bush and run.

"Come on!" Scott repeated. He ran into the bush.

Rifle blasts tore across the compound as the soldiers shot at the snake. Scott darted in and around the trees, ducking under the low branches, flying over any fallen logs. Within seconds he was well into the bush. He glanced over his shoulder to see Charlie. Charlie wasn't there.

"Stop, white boy!" Nike Shoes yelled. Two rifles were pointed at him. The soldiers aimed their guns at the ground and sent a blast of bullets into the sandy soil in front of Scott's feet.

He stopped. He lifted his arms into the air and walked back to the clearing.

It was the fourth stupid thing he had done so far. "Oh, well," he mumbled to himself. "Tomorrow's another day."

Without hesitation Nike Shoes hit Scott over the head with the butt of his rifle. Scott's knees buckled and he fell to the ground.

"Stupid white boy," he cursed, spitting on his face. He grabbed Scott by his hair and lifted him so his feet dangled in the air and then threw him against a tree. He pulled his arms behind him, tying a rope around his wrists, securing them brutally tight.

Nike Shoes grabbed a stick from the ground and dealt a well-aimed blow at Scott's knees. Scott screamed. The soldier tossed the stick to one of the children and lifted his chin in a gesture that indicated he was continuing Scott's torture.

He walked toward Scott. Scott squeezed his eyes shut and braced himself. The boy grasped the stick with both hands and swung it down on his shoulder. Scott screamed.

"What are you doing?" Seth sauntered toward the group. He stuck his finger into Nike Shoes's chest and repeated his question. "What are you doing?"

The soldier dropped his gaze to the ground.

"The white boy tried to escape," he said quietly.

"And?"

"And we shot at him to warn him."

"You wasted bullet to warn him? You did not shoot him?" Seth's voice sounded like a growl. "Give me your gun."

Nike Shoes's hands shook as he took the gun off his shoulder and handed it to Seth.

"You see, children, you must never waste bullet. Bullet are precious. They are like gold or diamond. They are what we need to stop our enemy. Each bullet must make its mark. Come. We prepare."

Seth pushed Nike Shoes toward Scott and ordered him to untie the ropes. Scott limped away from the tree and collapsed on the ground.

"Now I will show you how it is done," said Seth.

He took the rope from Nike Shoes and shoved him against the tree, tying his hands behind his back. Then, taking a few steps back, he drew a line in the dirt and stood behind it.

"You see, children, if I am, for example, aiming to shoot a man in the leg, I must be very careful with my aim. It is not good to waste bullet."

Seth lifted his rifle, aimed it at the soldier's leg, and shot. Nike Shoes's screams pierced Scott's ears. A bright red patch of blood formed on his pant leg.

"Now you try," he said, taking a boy by the shoulder and putting the rifle into his hands. "Place the butt of the rifle against your shoulder. Take aim. How about you try for the arm?" he suggested casually. "And pull the trigger just."

The young boy's hands trembled. Nike Shoes's screams subsided. His body shook as he gasped for air.

"Come here. You can do it. I will help you." Seth wrapped his arms around the boy and supported the gun. "On the count of three, we will pull the trigger. One . . . two . . . three."

A second blast found its mark. Nike Shoes screamed. A bright red patch formed on his upper arm. Scott winced. He shut his eyes tight.

"That was good, no?" Seth said, thumping the kid on his back. "Who come next?" It sounded as if he was inviting the children to take turns to go down a slide at the school playground.

"I will." Charlie walked toward Seth and took the rifle out of his hands.

"Good. Good," Seth replied. "Now let us see you aim somewhere else."

Charlie looked up at Nike Shoes. His eyes searched Charlie, begging for compassion. Charlie took careful aim and fired. The bullet exploded in the soldier's heart, killing him instantly.

Charlie passed the rifle to Seth and walked away, staring at the ground. Scott turned his gaze from Charlie, to Nike Shoes, and back to Charlie. He blinked back the tears that came to his eyes.

"Good. Good," Seth replied, smiling from ear to ear. "That is how you do it. You must not ever waste the bullet."

Chapter 21

Wisdom does not come overnight.
~ Somalian proverb

The scene that surrounded Scott was something that belonged in a deranged horror film. To one side of him lay a dead mamba snake. Near the snake, the young girl, who had felt the snake's dry scaly body course over her own, sat rocking as spasms of terror convulsed her tiny frame. And directly in front of him, the dead body of the young soldier, Nike Shoes, stood at attention for the last time. Scott looked at Bruce's shoes on the boy's feet; their dark blue color was now dyed crimson red.

The children filed past the dead soldier. They glanced at the blood that spread in a large puddle on the ground and quietly continued on their way. The soldier would stand guard alone tonight.

Scott winced as he forced himself to stand. A young soldier poked at the mamba with the barrel of his rifle. The snake lay limp and lifeless. He hoisted it over his shoulders and called out to another soldier. "We will enjoy the meat tonight, eeh?" he said with a grin.

Seth led the group toward the fires, his massive arm hanging limply over Charlie's shoulder, each step filled with arrogance and authority. Scott followed. Several girls, bending over the pots, ladled a thick mash onto broad palm-like leaves and handed them to the children. One girl handed out small cups of water dished out of a battered tin pail. At the head of the line, Seth ordered the girl to give an extra ladle of mash to Charlie.

The line moved forward until Scott stood in front of the girl and could see inside the now empty pot. Seth grabbed the spoon from the girl and rapped the inside. The hollow ringing echoed across the camp. He threw his head back and laughed. The spoon fell into the pot with a resounding clang as he walked away.

Scott bit his lip to hold back the tears. He felt a gentle touch on his shoulder and looked down into the eyes of the young girl as she held out a small cup of water.

"Thank you," he whispered and gulped the water down. He turned and walked away.

He sat and looked out into the horizon and watched the last light from the sun disappear. A chill settled over the camp and he drew his legs closer to him. All he wanted to do was sleep.

Seth walked into the middle of the group and spoke. “Get your rest now. We will be doing more training tomorrow. Tomorrow is a big day for us.” He tossed a rope toward one of the soldiers. “Tie them up.” He turned and headed toward a nearby tent.

The harsh cords were pulled tightly over the children’s wrists, already raw from being bound night after night. The children huddled together into a familiar, tight group as they always did, using each other’s presence and warmth to find some comfort through the evening. Brothers, sisters, and friends searched for each other, grasping for any sort of familiarity that would provide some consolation. Three soldiers took their positions surrounding the group. They would have an uneventful night. No one would entertain the thought of escaping after all that had just passed.

Scott found himself positioned on the outside of the group. At his right side were the young boy and girl he had seen earlier in the morning. The young boy had crawled under the girl’s bound hands and lay asleep with his head pressed against her chest. Scott watched the two for a moment. *They must be brother and sister*, he thought. He was overwhelmed with an intense feeling of pity for them. The same sadness filled him when he looked at each of the children who surrounded him: the girl wearing the torn dress, the girls who had worked under the hot African sun all day digging up the cassava, and the boys who had cleaned and polished the weapons they knew they would be forced to use. Each of them could fill a book with the horrors they endured during the past day. And what about the other children? The boy with the mangled face? The thousands of children who had been forced to be a part of this army for years upon years? What were their stories?

He turned his face and caught a glimpse of Charlie, sitting an arm's length behind him. Scott looked away.

Charlie confused him. Had he read him right? Each and every thing Charlie did that day—giving his shoes to the soldier, ignoring Scott's urgent whispers to escape with him—reeked of passive loyalty to the army. And when Charlie placed the bags filled with the mines at the soldier's feet, it reminded Scott of a peasant leaving an offering at the foot of an idol. Worst of all, he'd killed a boy. He took a gun and shot a soldier in the heart. Killing him instantly. So cold. Just like the rest of them.

Scott lay on his side, resting his head on his bound hands. The pain in his legs and his head was beginning to subside. The bruises on his knees would be huge. *How am I going to explain that?* he wondered. In spite of the pain, his exhaustion was worse and his eyes slowly closed.

"Are all white people as stupid as you?" a voice whispered.

Scott's eyelids flew open.

Charlie was staring at him. "I said, are all white people as stupid as you?"

Scott shook his head. What was this guy getting at?

"You know, either you are really dumb or you do not care about anyone but yourself. What made you think you could run into the bush and get away like that? Do you not think we would have all done the same thing if it was that simple?"

Scott shook his head. He was confused.

"I know you are thinking I am a hideous killer like the rest of them. I can see it in your face. But you are wrong. You are the one who is responsible for that boy death. He could have shot you when you took off into the bush. But he did not. He only wanted to warn you. He was not a killer."

Scott looked down at his legs, imagining the bruises that were swelling on his knees. "Well, he certainly enjoyed using my knees for batting practice," he said.

"And what would you rather have? A few bruise on your precious little white body or to be dead in that bush right now, with the hyna eating out your innard and the vulture waiting for the leftover?"

"But I wasn't the one who killed him, was I?" Scott sneered at Charlie.

"You really are stupid, yes? He was like you and me. He was doing what he had to do to survive. He knew if you escaped he would be strung to a tree and beaten until he was dead. Along with some of the other kid here. That is what the LRA does to it disloyal soldier. And do you not realize that Seth was using him as target practice? First one arm, then the other, first one leg, then the other. He would have forced us to shoot him until he was dead. I ended it so he did not have to suffer even more. Seth is like a cat playing with a mouse. And you are the one who started it all. If you were not so stupid, that boy would still be alive right now."

Scott looked away and stared into the bush.

"Do you not have anything to say?"

Scott remained silent.

"Anything?"

"I didn't know," Scott said finally.

"That is right. You did not know, so stop acting like you do." Charlie turned his face and looked away. He lay down with his back toward Scott.

Scott sent his mind back to the scene. He began to understand. The shoes Charlie had given to the soldier were not an offering but a bribe for better treatment. He reached deeper. Charlie ignored his pleas for escape because he understood the psychotic evil that commanded this army. Scott didn't. He faced his ignorance. Charlie shot the boy, much like a person would to end the suffering of a wounded animal. Scott was ashamed. He was responsible for the young soldier's death. A huge weight fell on him as he faced his guilt. He shook, feeling the coldness that came from his core spreading to every limb, making his mind numb, his remorse bitter. He had never felt so awful in his life.

He closed his eyes and prayed it would all end and he would wake up in his bed, dismissing it all as a bad dream.

Chapter 22

Nobody is born wise. ~ African proverb

Scott woke long before daylight. He had not slept well, even though his body was exhausted and sore and begged for rest. His mind would not allow it. Dreams that tried to enter his state of unconsciousness were interrupted by images of ropes and guns, mangled faces and torn dresses, and a soldier's body with three bloodied holes.

Scott pressed his knees to his chest and rubbed his legs. "I'm still here," he whispered to himself.

He peered at the group of children beside him. Despite the darkness he knew where each and every child had found their spot to spend the night and who lay nestled in whose arms.

He stared into the sky. A faint outline of a darkened cloud appeared at the horizon, covering the stars. It crept closer and closer until the whole camp was under its dull gray mass. Scott shivered.

A large raindrop landed on his face. It was soon followed by another and another. The clouds burst open and the rain fell on the land.

Scott pressed his legs to his body and tucked his head over his knees. The rest of the children did the same. It was futile. Within seconds everyone was drenched. He peered out from under his arm. A silvery sheet covered everything. When he stretched his arms out in front of him, he could barely see the faint outline of his hands.

A small puddle formed around them. It grew and grew, mixing with the red clay, rising above their feet, and touching their ankles.

Then, as quickly as it began, the rain stopped. The sun lifted itself and sent its rays onto the land and the children, slowly warming their chilled bodies.

A multitude of caws, trills, and melodic notes filled the air as the birds awakened to a new day. The smell of the earth, as the rain mingled with the morning air, created a fragrance that only a person blessed to live in or visit Africa would know and love.

Scott's shirt and pants clung to him as he slowly stretched his legs. He looked in Charlie's direction and found the young boy staring back at him. Charlie looked away and stared at his bare feet. The animosity Scott had seen on his hardened face in the evening was now gone. Scott turned away. He couldn't bring himself to look at Charlie either.

"Minyo . . . minyo . . . can me . . . can me . . ."

A girl began to sing. The notes rose and fell, creating a soft, gentle melody. Scott turned his head and looked at the teenage girl in the torn dress. Her eyes were closed as her face lifted toward the sun.

"Can me Uganda minyo . . ."

The young girl who held her brother in her arms joined in the song, singing the words in English. Her voice added perfect harmony.

"Uganda sun, shine on us . . ."

"Ineno cwer cwing?" the teenage girl continued.

"Do you see our sorrow?" the young girl responded.

"Gin ango mabitime ki latino wa . . ."

"What will become of the children . . ."

"Ka dilco pe . . ."

"If they have no tomorrow . . ."

"Can me Uganda minyo . . ."

"Uganda sun, shine on us . . ."

"Coo, monki lotion dore . . ."

"All man, woman, and child . . ."

"Wek yom cwiny wa omeny . . ."

"Let our love be . . ."

"Piny calo ceng . . ."

"Like the sun . . ."

"Wan ducu pi ngom wa . . ."

"Unite and bind our nation . . ."

Scott closed his eyes. The sun's rays warmed his body and sent tiny stars dancing under his eyelids. The girls continued to sing.

"Wanongo yomwiny . . ."

"Find our heart . . ."

"Bin inen wan . . ."

"Search our soul . . ."

"Nyut wan ni ayela pe . . ."

"Show us peace inside . . ."

"Wek dano ducu onge in ayela pe . . ."

"Let this peace extend to all . . ."

"Walego nipe inen bal ma watimo . . ."

"Forgiveness we must ask . . ."

"Wan pe wotamo bal ma otimu . . ."

"Forgiveness we must give . . ."

Scott opened his eyes and looked around him. The children's faces were lifted toward the sun. Their eyes closed. Their faces content.

"Man, okego calo latin . . ."

"This I ask, as a child . . ."

"Alego pi omera . . ."

"For my brothers and . . ."

"Get up!" Seth's voice sliced the air.

The children jumped to their feet and stood at attention. Their gaze instantly lowered to the ground. Their day had begun.

“Take the rope off!” Seth shouted.

The ropes were removed and the children marched, following Seth until he stopped in front of a tree pockmarked with bullet holes. He lifted his gun and pointed it at the children, using it to separate them into two groups. One group, made up of the girls and the younger boys, was led to the fields to resume their work from yesterday. Scott swept his gaze over the boys in his group; his eyes stopped at Charlie. He, like everyone else, was staring at the bullet-riddled tree. Its once-smooth bark was ripped and shredded, exposing the whiteness underneath. The branches lay bare and gray and lifeless. Not a word was spoken.

“Today,” Seth began, “you will learn how to be a soldier. You will learn to fight and kill. You will learn we are a strong tribe and you are invincible. We are God army, and we will win this fight against all that is evil in Uganda.”

“Watch,” Seth continued as he slung his gun from his shoulder. “Put the clip into the gun like this, pull back here on the action, and then let go. Now your gun is loaded and ready to kill. Aim like this, and pull the trigger.”

A blast ripped through the air and was followed by a stifling silence. A lone bird rose up into the sky, its indignant cries falling on them.

"See?" Seth said as he lowered the gun. "It is easy. Now you do it, *muzungu* boy," he said with a smirk, grabbing another gun and tossing it at Scott.

Scott caught the gun and stood in front of the tree. He felt its weight as he straightened the barrel and put the butt against his shoulder. He had never used a gun in his life. It felt incredibly cold. He pulled back on the action as Seth had demonstrated, aimed at the tree, pulled the trigger, and fired. Instantly the gun recoiled, lifting the barrel into the air, throwing the butt into Scott's shoulder. He winced.

"Ha, ha, ha!" Seth laughed. "Our *muzungu* boy is still only a ka-boy. Let us show him how a grown Acholi boy does it." He grabbed the gun out of Scott's hands and passed it to Charlie, who set the gun to his shoulder and fired. The bullet made its mark into the tree. Charlie stood poised, his legs firm in their stance. He passed the gun to Seth and backed away.

One by one each boy fired the gun, leaving their bullets embedded in the tree. And every time, Seth praised the boys. "Yes, yes. It is good we use these bullet to practice. You will become a fine soldier. Look at the strength you have."

Scott wanted to puke. He wondered how insane this man could be. If anyone deserved to be shot and spit on, it was him. Definitely. And then he wondered, *If Seth was this insanely cruel, what was Kony, the leader of the Lord's Resistance Army, like?*

Seth took the last of the bullets from the rifle and placed the gun against the tree. He picked up a bag and carefully pulled out a hand grenade and set it on the ground. "A good soldier make sure he cover his trail. Watch this."

He placed the grenade into a groove in a tree and wrapped a thin piece of vine around it to hold it in place. Then he took a wire from his pocket and carefully attached it to the pin of the grenade. He stepped backward until he came to another tree and wrapped the wire around its base.

"The trick is to pull the wire like so just," he said, testing the tautness of the wire. "Then, when it is tripped"—Seth made a noise sounding like a bomb going off—"you have at least one dead man who is not on your tail anymore."

Seth removed the grenade from the tree and returned it to the bag. He opened a large white bag, the kind used to hold flour or grain, turned it upside down, and spilled out a couple of dozen oranges. Scott stared at the fruit; the smell made his mouth water instantly.

Seth pulled out a knife, stabbed at an orange, and expertly carved off the peel with a quick twisting motion. Transfixed, the boys watched Seth bite into the orange. The juice dribbled down his chin as he made deliberate smacking noises. He dropped the peel onto the ground, stabbed at another orange, and tossed it to Charlie, then to each child until he gave the last orange to Scott. The reason for the order was obvious: who was favored, who was not.

The boys bit into the fruit, but no one stopped to savor it. No one smacked his lips and sucked in the fresh juice. No one paused to enjoy a rare meal. Food was only sustenance, nothing more.

Before they could gulp down their last mouthfuls, Seth ordered the boys to march. He led them to the same hut they had stored the guns in after cleaning them the day before. Five soldiers, older teenage boys, joined the group and followed Seth's orders to pass out the guns. Again, beginning with Charlie, the order in which the guns were handed out to the boys showed who the favorites were.

"No," Seth said, grabbing the gun intended for Scott. "You will need this instead." He tossed him a long wooden-handled hoe, the same kind the girls had used in the fields to dig up the cassava. "I have got a different job for you."

Each of the boys took their place in line and followed Seth. A soldier stuck the barrel of his gun into Scott's ribs. Scott quickly found his place and marched.

When the group stopped, he realized they had returned to the spot beside the bush where they had gathered the firewood the previous night. The corpse of Nike Shoes was still tied to the tree. A hoard of blackflies swarmed over the body.

Seth sliced the ropes and stepped back. The body fell to the ground.

He pointed at Scott. "Dig a hole and throw it in. And make it deep. The last thing we need is for some hyna to show up. The rest of you, follow me. It is time for you ka-boy to learn how to be real Acholi soldier."

The boys marched behind Seth and disappeared into the bush. Scott couldn't help but wonder what was worse: being trained to be a soldier and kill, or being left behind to bury the dead.

"Get to work!" A soldier pointed his gun at him.

Scott lifted the hoe over his shoulder and walked toward the body. He would dig the hole next to it. It would save him the gruesome task of having to drag the corpse any distance.

He stopped mid-step.

He smelled a horrendous stench. He covered his nose as he stumbled backward, trying to keep himself from doubling over.

The smell was like rank, rotting meat mixed with a sweetish, putrid perfume. Scott remembered a CSI episode in which a body was found decomposing in a forest. The TV scene was a child's fairy tale compared to this.

"Get to work!" the soldier repeated.

Scott forced himself to move closer to the body, fighting every gag reflex that threatened to empty his stomach. He threw the blade of the hoe into the ground and managed to tear up a small piece of earth. The ground was hard and packed. It was going to be a difficult job.

As he tore each small chunk of clay from the ground, Scott replayed everything that had happened to him since he arrived in Uganda. As each muscle strained and every drop of sweat fell from his face, he was challenged by the realization of his failures.

He hated himself. He hated himself for being such an idiot and getting caught when he first arrived in Uganda. And he hated himself—no, despised himself—for being responsible for ending a person's life. He knew he hadn't pulled the trigger. But it was his stupidity that had led to the boy's death. The image of Charlie shooting the soldier burned fresh and raw in his memory. The sound of the rifle blast as it sent the bullet into Nike Shoes's heart and the sight of the boy's body twitching seared themselves into his mind forever.

And he hated himself for thinking so little of Charlie. How dare he think he understood him. He had assumed Charlie was weak and had become like many of the others, abandoning all that was good in the need for survival. But he was wrong. Charlie was the bravest person he had ever known. *Would I have been able to end the boy's life, saving him from further torture?* The answer came with one word that pointed an accusing finger at him: no.

Scott stood and wiped the sweat from his face. He stretched his back and surveyed his work. His hands were covered with blisters and his mouth was parched, but the hole wasn't even close to being large enough. He looked at the body of the boy again. He would have to make the grave almost six feet long. And how old could he have been? His age? Older? Maybe, but not by much.

Scott turned his attention back to the hole. He couldn't look at the body anymore. He drove the blade of the hoe into the ground and ripped up the dirt. Over and over again he thrust downward, throwing his anger and hatred and misery into each blade mark that scarred the earth.

When the sun had finally lifted high into the sky, Scott surveyed the grave and decided it was large enough.

"Here. I will help you put him in," the young soldier said as he placed his gun against a tree.

While Scott lifted the legs, the soldier placed his hands under the shoulders, and together they carried the body to the grave. Scott laid the boy's legs down and glanced at Bruce's shoes. Before he could think of what he was doing, he pulled the shoes off the boy's feet and placed them on his own.

The soldier stared at the rubber boots on his own feet. "Does not matter to me. The higher rank all have the gum boot. They save the foot more. Take them if you want. They are no use to us."

"Thanks," Scott said.

The soldier lifted the body by the shoulders. "We can put him in gently if you hold both his leg while I walk to this end."

They placed the body into the grave and began to fill in the hole.

"Did you know him?" Scott asked the soldier boy.

"No."

"Not even his name?"

The boy shook his head.

"Do you know where he came from?"

"No."

Scott looked down at the boy's face, slowly allowing the dirt to fall through his fingers until it covered the face completely.

"It is best not to get to know anyone here," the soldier boy said. He threw a huge pile of dirt into the grave and walked back to his post.

The tears came slowly, and Scott allowed them to fall into the boy's grave. Somebody needed to cry at this boy's funeral. And in a very strange way, Scott was glad he could.

Chapter 23

Between true friends even water drunk together is sweet enough. ~ African proverb

There wasn't time for more tears at the boy's grave.

"Come," the young soldier said, "we must go to the camp."

Scott led the way down the path while the soldier followed, his gun pointed at Scott's back.

"Where are we going now?" Scott asked as they passed a group of soldiers.

"Shut up and get moving," the boy answered, shoving his rifle into his back.

Scott gave a quick nod. He knew where things stood between them now. Nothing had changed. The boy was a soldier, and he was a captured child—and a *muzungu* at that.

The pair walked past the many groups of children working at their different jobs until they came upon a mud hut with its door covered by a dusty and torn sheet.

The soldier boy knocked on the wooden post next to the door and called in. "I have the *muzungu* boy here."

A man drew the sheet to one side and glanced out the door. Scott recognized the soldier as J.P., one of the ones who had captured him the first night he had arrived in Uganda.

J.P. grabbed him by his shirt and pulled him into the hut. He shoved him down onto the floor. "On your knee."

Scott obeyed. His hands shook as he pressed them to his sides, trying to keep them still. His eyes slowly began to adjust to the darkness of the room.

"Here he is," J.P. said, directing his voice to a man sitting in a large chair. "He showed up one evening at the camp. Not too long after we returned from Lira."

"So you think he is some *padi* kid? Turned loose from the church, eeh?" A massive hand gently rubbed Scott's cheek. "Poor small child. You must be frightened. All the way from your *maa* and your *wora*." The man rose from his chair and circled Scott, pausing on occasion to rub his fingers over the stubble on his chin.

Suddenly, he grabbed Scott's hair and jerked his head backward. "But you are not with your mom and your dad now, are you?" The man laughed, spraying bits of spit on Scott's face.

Scott stared into two narrow dark eyes. He caught his breath. He recognized the face. He had seen it many times when he spent those hours researching child soldiers and the Lord's Resistance Army. He had seen it on the Forbes list of the ten most wanted men in the world. And he had seen it smiling, surrounded by children, young children, holding AK-47s and staring stone-faced into the camera. He was looking into the eyes of Joseph Kony, the leader of the LRA, the man responsible for the deaths of thousands and thousands of children. He was looking into the eyes of the devil himself. Scott trembled. He broke out in a cold sweat.

"He will be of great great use to us tomorrow," Kony said, shoving Scott's head to the ground. "It is good you did not kill him last night when he tried to escape. Keep someone watching him at all time. We talk tonight. I have a new plan."

J.P. lifted Scott by the back of his shirt and hoisted him into the air. He thrust him out of the door and called out to the boy soldier waiting outside. "Tie him up and keep him with you at all time. Then bring him back here tomorrow at noon."

Again the ropes sliced into Scott's raw wrists, and again he winced as the soldier tightened the ropes.

"Walk!" the voice behind him commanded.

He forced himself to move.

The pair walked through the camp, past a group of children filling magazines with bullets, a couple of girls emptying water jugs into a large metal pot, and a lone child crying as he held on to his mother's leg.

They came to the clearing. "Over there," the soldier said, pointing to a tree. "Sit."

Scott leaned his back against the tree as the soldier wrapped more ropes around his body and pulled tightly around his arms and chest. The soldier knelt down beside him and leaned toward him.

He whispered into Scott's ear. "Do not move. If you escape—which I doubt you will—but if you even let the thought to come into your mind they will kill me and many other. You do not know what Kony is like. Seth and J.P. are nothing compared to him." He spaced his last words out for emphasis: "Do not move." He stood and walked to the edge of the clearing and leaned against a tree.

Scott's head fell to his chest. He drew in a deep breath and then another and another. Despite the tightness of the ropes, his body was shaking. He closed his eyes.

"Oh God, what have I gotten myself into?" he whispered under his breath.

He stared into the bush where Charlie and the other children had marched. His gaze followed the empty path until it turned and was swallowed by the trees.

Suddenly, he thought of home. He pictured his mother and father. He saw them at the breakfast table, his mother pouring the coffee and his dad stuffing a pancake in his mouth. Their faces were smiling. An empty hollow in Scott's chest grew and grew.

I can't be stuck here forever, he thought. *Bruce came back, so there's got to be a way. But how?*

He tried to think of anything Bruce had said that would help him. *He said he was under a tree and then suddenly he was at home. What did he do to make himself go home? What? What?*

He created a list in his head: *Bruce took the stones on Monday night. I saw him the next morning with his brother. I stole the stones back, but there were only four. He had to have gone to Uganda that evening and then returned home before that next morning. But he said he was there for . . . what? A day and a night? That doesn't make sense. He was only gone for one night, not . . . it doesn't make any sense.*

But maybe . . . Scott's thoughts went off in a different direction. *Maybe the stones control how long you stay. Maybe I have no choice. Maybe . . .* Scott sighed. He was trying to make sense of something that didn't make any sense. And he knew he wouldn't get anywhere with that.

An image of Kony's narrow dark eyes flashed in front of him. He heard the leader's voice: low, gentle, then suddenly becoming strong and violent. He heard the words loud and clear as if he was still in the hut and Kony was staring down at him: "He will be of great great use to us tomorrow . . . It is good you did not kill him . . . Keep someone watching him . . . I have a new plan."

It was obvious something big was going to happen soon and they needed him. That's why it was imperative they kept him tied. But what did they want him for? What good was he? He was just a young *muzungu* boy. And then Scott understood: they thought he was the child of a white missionary, a pastor at one of the churches. They were going to use him as a hostage. They were going to use him so they could negotiate for something.

But what? What would Kony want? What could he expect to get from a missionary? Bibles? Hymn books? Scott laughed. No. But what did

Kony need the most? What was most valuable to him? It had to be something like . . . weapons! That's what he wanted. More weapons. And it would be just like Kony to demand that a pastor from a church provide him with money in exchange for his own son so he could purchase more weapons to kill more people and more children. A shiver ran through Scott's body, visibly shaking him. *How could anyone be so insanely evil?* he thought. He closed his eyes and took in a few deep breaths. He needed to think because he wasn't the son of a missionary, and there wasn't a father in Uganda who could buy his freedom.

The sun lowered itself onto the horizon, sending bright shafts of red light streaming through the trees. But still there was no sign of Charlie or the children.

It wasn't until well into the night that Scott heard the shuffle of bare feet and watched the dim outline of the group of children approach him. Silently, the children sat on the ground in front of him and placed their arms before them while the soldiers bound their hands for the evening. Even in the blackness of the night, Scott could make out the outlines of each child's body and face. And there, sitting before him, was Charlie, staring out into the trees, his eyes blank and lacking any emotion.

"Psst," Scott whispered. "Charlie, are you all right?"

The boy continued staring, his eyes fixed straight ahead, his mouth drawn tight.

"Charlie, listen. I'm worried. Kony is here. They brought me to him. I think he's going to hold me for ransom. He thinks I'm some pastor's kid, and I think he wants to exchange me for some money so he can buy more weapons. I don't know what he's doing, but he said he had a plan and they were going to talk about it tonight. Do you know what's going on?"

Charlie's head dropped. He drew in a long and unsteady breath. His voice came out in a cracked whisper. "I am so tired. I am so tired of the gun and the bullet and the death. Of seeing death every day. I want to die right now just. I do not know what is worse—wondering when the moment will come when I will be shot, or death itself. I think it is the waiting that is the worst part."

Charlie paused and looked at Scott. "The hyna will be feasting tonight," he continued. "Seth made us use the ka-boy and his older sister for target practice."

Scott caught his breath. He was numb.

"No." He shook his head and he gasped for air. "No. The little boy and his sister? Why? Why would he do that?"

"Why not?" Charlie replied. "Why do they kill any of us? They kill us when we are too slow carrying the supply to the next camp. They kill us if they suspect we are trying to escape. They kill us when we are following order, and they kill us when we are not."

Charlie looked up into the bright Ugandan stars. "I wish he had used me instead of them. I am so tired of death. I just want to die."

Scott followed Charlie's gaze and looked at the stars. They were brilliant. He had never seen such a beautiful night sky. He shook his head. It was strange he could look up into the stars and focus on their beauty when so much misery surrounded him.

"But you can't give up," Scott said, returning his gaze to him. "There must be a way for us to escape. Bruce told me you'd escaped before. How did you do it then?"

"I was lucky. During the last attack on a nearby village, I managed to escape when the army ran up against us. But I was only lucky. I still do not know how I managed to run without being seen."

"So if we attacked another village, there could be another chance?"

"Yes," Charlie replied, "but there have been many kid who have been shot in the back that way."

Scott saw the image all too clearly.

"They plan to attack the camp in Lira soon," Charlie said. "There are thousand of people living there who have escaped from their village because of Kony."

"How do you know they're going to attack?"

"Because they have been grouping. All of the smaller unit have been gathering here for the past few week. More weapon and ammunition have been carried here from up north in Sudan: gun, land mine, grenade. I was wondering when Kony was going to arrive. He must have been angry when they attacked the camp a few day ago and only came out with thirty kid. He is here to make sure they do it right this time."

Charlie took in a deep breath and then let the air fall out. "He will put our group in the front. We will be the one to lead the attack. The government army will not want to shoot the young children. Their hesitation will be good for us. But there will be less chance for us to escape because we will have the other on our tail."

Scott reached his foot out and gently tapped Charlie on his leg. "But you can't give up. We'll think of a way to escape."

"But I do not want to escape again," Charlie said flatly. "What do I have to escape to? My mother and father are dead. I have a younger brother and sister, and even though they do not understand what is going on they understand enough to hate me. If they are still alive. All my uncle, aunt, and cousin, and any of my friend left in my village, they hate me too. I was to blame for my parent death. And when we were forced to return to my village and attack, I was responsible for taking more children and burning the hut down and killing more people. I am tired of being a coward, killing other because I selfishly want to live." He paused. "No, I cannot forgive myself for what I have done. How could I expect anyone else to?"

Scott stared at the bloodstained shoes on his feet. If he had been forced to do the things Charlie was forced to, would he have? He didn't even want to go there. The horrors were real. Very real. But what he knew about Charlie he admired. And for that, he wanted him to hang on and not give up.

"Charlie," Scott began, "I buried a boy today who would be living if it wasn't for my stupidity. I didn't know his name, and I don't know where he's from. I don't know anything about him. But I was the only one who cried at his grave. And I'm thinking the only reason I cried was because I felt so ashamed. So horrible and so angry with myself. I need to know if you can forgive me for what I've done."

Charlie looked at Scott and sighed. "I forgave you a long time ago."

"Then why can't you think others won't do the same for you?"

"Would you?"

"I already have."

Scott pushed his toe down on the heel of his shoe and pulled it off. He did the same with the other. "Here," he said, sliding them over to Charlie, "these belong to you. Bruce would never have given his shoes to just anyone."

Charlie pulled the shoes closer to him. "You know, when I first was made into a soldier in this army, I learned of the way each man or boy showed his rank. Rank is very important here. It is what decide how much you eat or if you eat. If you sleep with a roof or the rain cloud over your head. Those who have top rank do not wear it on their sleeve. They wear it on their feet."

"What?"

"Anyone who has spent time in the bush know there are many danger on the ground, and a pair of boot give great protection. That is why you see some men wearing the gum boot. They are protected. They are top rank."

"That's just weird, Charlie."

"Yes, I know. But I am glad you are giving me running shoe and not rubber boot."

Scott laughed.

"I think I will get some sleep now. We will talk about escaping tomorrow."

Scott nodded and rested his head against the tree, looking up into the sky. He had to admit that the stars were so much nicer to look at in Uganda than at home—though less so when you were tied to a tree and being held hostage by an insane man. Nonetheless they were still beautiful.

A warm breeze lingered over Scott's face, his body, and his bound arms. He reached down to the ground and traced his fingers over the hard clay earth. His dad had told him the people in Uganda thought the earth was red because it was covered with the blood of many, many innocent lives lost. Now he understood. Sifting the dirt through his fingers, he watched the tiny grains fall to the ground until he closed his eyes and drifted off to sleep.

When he awoke the warm breeze was gone, and the Ugandan dirt lay thousands of miles away. A small pile of dust and pebbles remained in his hand.

The stone had worked its magic.

Chapter 24

If you want to go quickly, go alone. If you want to go far, go together. ~ African proverb

Scott jumped up from his bed and glanced at the four walls of his room. A surreal feeling washed over him like a giant wave until he shook his head and rubbed his hands over his eyes. He smiled, but only momentarily. The pouch of stones on his bed caught his attention.

He grabbed the stones and ran out of his bedroom and out the front door, catching a glimpse of his mother and father sitting at the table, sipping their morning coffee. Quickly, it registered: while he had spent two days and only one entire night in Uganda, only one evening had passed in real time. *Weird*, he thought, but that was all the time he spent pondering the power of the stones. He had more important things to deal with.

One block, two blocks, now three. Scott ran as fast as his legs could carry him until he reached Bruce's front door and rang the doorbell. Seconds, feeling like minutes, passed before Bruce's face appeared at the window. He took one look at the expression on Scott's face, soiled with red dirt, and stepped outside, closing the door.

"Let's go to your place," Bruce said, glancing at the rope burns on Scott's wrists. "We can talk there. It'll be more private."

Half walking and half running, they made their way to Scott's house just as his mom and dad were heading out the door.

Scott's mom looked at Bruce, then Scott, then back at Bruce again. It was hard to tell what puzzled her the most: the dirt on Scott's face, or Bruce being with him.

"I forgot my books!" Scott yelled over his shoulder as he ran past them into the house.

Bruce followed, giving Scott's parents an uncomfortable smile.

"And I'll be staying at Bruce's tonight. We've got a project to work on."

Bruce looked at Scott's mom again with another half-hearted smile, as if he wasn't too sure how receptive she would be to that idea.

"Okay," she replied, shrugging. "Strange . . ." She shook her head and closed the door.

Scott turned the kitchen sink tap on and stuck his face under the stream of water. He gulped at it greedily. It flowed down his chin and neck, wetting his shirt. He plunged his head under the tap, soaking his hair and face. All the while Bruce crossed his arms in front of his massive chest and stood staring at Scott, shifting his weight from one foot to the other. Finally, Scott stood, gasping for air.

"Well," Bruce said, "how's Charlie? Where is he? What's happened? He was taken by the army? Right?"

"Yeah, the army's got him. But he's okay. For now. But we need to get back to Uganda right away." He placed the remaining three stones on the table.

"Just wait a sec. First you need to tell me everything."

"Okay." Scott took in a deep breath. "When I got there it was dark and all I could see was this group of children. As soon as I saw them, I knew what had happened. My mom gave me this book about Kony and the LRA. Kony's this guy who formed this army—"

"Yeah, yeah, I know 'bout Kony and the LRA. Met some of 'em already. Anyways, go on."

Scott paused. "You met them?"

"Yeah, not up close and personal, but their bullets and I had a close call."

“Really?” Scott was puzzled and more than just a little surprised.

“Yeah, I’ll tell you about it sometime, but tell me about Charlie.”

Scott told Bruce everything about his time in the camp—from getting caught, to the army preparing for another raid and Charlie’s group being forced to lead everyone into the battle, to Kony believing Scott was the son of a pastor and wanting to ransom him. As he retold everything, the whole story seemed incredibly far-fetched. No wonder he’d had trouble believing Bruce when he tried to tell him about the stones; he had enough trouble believing what had just happened to him.

Bruce shook his head. His voice rose in intensity as he spoke. “They put Charlie in charge of a group and he has to lead them on the next raid? But he’s not a soldier. He’s just a boy. A boy. Why the hell would they do that? It’s a death sentence. He’ll get shot.”

“Yeah, I know. But that’s what the LRA does. It puts the kids up front so the government soldiers don’t want to shoot them. Then the kids are forced to shoot. If they don’t, the other soldiers from the LRA will shoot them from behind.”

“So the kids have no choice. They get shot in either the front or the back.”

“Yeah.”

"That's just"—Bruce paused, searching for the right words—"cruel and stupid." He wiped his hand over his eyes and stared at the floor.

"Yeah," Scott agreed.

"Okay," Bruce said, "tell me more. When does Charlie expect the raid to happen?"

"Soon. The groups have been gathering for the past few weeks, and he expects it to be a really intense one. They've gotten more supplies—guns, grenades, and mines—and Kony wants to do it right this time," Scott said, reaching for a stone.

His hand stopped in mid-reach as a knock came from the door.

"Scott! What the heck are you doing? We're gonna be late!" Rob walked into the kitchen and stopped, staring first at Bruce, then a soggy Scott, and finally the stones. "What are you doing? We're late. You didn't meet me at the corner."

Scott drew in a deep breath and let it out. "Rob, you remember the stones I found in Uganda?"

"Yeah?"

"Bruce and I have found something really, uh, interesting . . . umm, almost magical . . . about them." Scott paused, trying to find the right words. What could he say to convince Rob he was telling the truth? He decided the up-front approach was always the best. "The stones can take you to Uganda."

"What?" Rob shook his head in disbelief.

"It's true. First Bruce went, and then when he told me what had happened to him I didn't believe him—but then I did. My mom told me about this ritual, and that's exactly what Bruce had seen when he went back the second time—so I knew he was telling the truth. And so I held one of the stones, and before I knew what was happening, I was in Uganda. But we have to get back there right now or Charlie—this boy we met—is going to get killed."

"What? What are you talking about?" Rob asked.

Scott grabbed an apple off the table and took a huge bite out of it. "He's been abducted—again—by the LRA, the Lord's Resistance Army. They take children from their families and force them to be soldiers. They're horrible. And they're going to do another raid, and they're making Charlie's group lead it," he said as he continued to devour the apple.

"Charlie's group? What do you mean by a group?" Rob asked.

"A group of soldiers, kid soldiers, and they've all been trained to shoot and set grenades, and since they're the newest group they have to lead the raid. They've got the youngest children."

Scott threw his apple core into the garbage and reached for the stones.

"Wait." Bruce grabbed Scott's hand and held it still. "As much as we need to get there quickly, we need to make a plan first."

Scott nodded. A plan would be a good idea. It would save getting caught—again.

"Now tell me, when you left Uganda where were you?" Bruce's voice was calm and had that air of taking charge.

"Tied to a tree. Beside Charlie," Scott said, holding out his wrists.

Rob's eyes widened as he looked at Scott's wrists and saw the rope burns. "What the . . ? Are those . . . ? But how . . . ?"

"And I need to get back there right away because if they find me gone they'll start killing the other kids, including the boy who's supposed to be watching me," Scott added.

"What are you talking about? Killing kids?" Rob plunked himself down on a chair and covered his face with his hands. Slowly, he lifted his head and peered at Scott and then Bruce. "What kinda place did you go to?"

Bruce ignored Rob and continued thinking aloud. "So when we go back, you wanna arrive at the tree, tied up beside Charlie, right?"

"Well, that's not really what I *want*, but that's what's going to have to happen."

"Okay. So you're looked after. Now what about me? Where'll I land?" Bruce asked.

Scott shrugged. "Where did you land last time?"

"Beside Charlie."

"Well, that's probably where you'll land this time. He'll probably be sleeping. Everyone's tied up in a group and sleeping right now."

"Sleeping? Well, that helps me a lot. It'll be dark, right?"

Scott nodded.

"Then I have a pretty good chance of being able to sneak off and hide somewhere. Are there any bushes nearby, or is it a big open field?"

"It's near some bush. About ten or twenty yards away from where Charlie is."

"Okay. Then I'll have to create a diversion when I sneak away." Bruce grabbed a couple of apples and tucked them into his pockets. "These'll work."

Scott and Rob looked at Bruce. They were both confused.

"What? Haven't you ever watched it on TV? If you wanna get the bad guy to look the other way, you throw something near him to catch his attention. And then while he's looking, you sneak away," Bruce said as if it were obvious.

Scott shrugged. It was good enough for him. "Okay, so you land beside Charlie, you hide in the bush, and then what do you do next?"

"I head back to the camp and warn everyone."

"And how are you going to find the camp?" Scott asked. He was catching on.

"If Charlie's awake I'll ask him to point me the way. If not, I'll follow the trail the kids made through the bush. A group of kids walking through the bush is bound to make some marks."

"But it's been days since they traveled through the bush. The trail will be gone by now," Scott said, the voice of reason coming through.

"Got any other ideas?"

"No."

"Then this one'll have to do until we can think of something better."

"Yeah. But what about me? I mean, what do I do once I get there?"

"I don't know. Not much you can do tied to a tree. You won't be able to do anything until you're freed."

"But they're not going to free me," Scott said in exasperation. "When they bring me to the church and try to negotiate with the pastor there, he's not going to say, 'Yeah, that's my kid. Will you take this week's offering in exchange for him?' No. He's going to take one look at me and say he's never seen me before in his life. And then they'll kill me because I'm no use to them anymore."

Bruce nodded. The kitchen was filled with silence.

Finally, Rob spoke. "Okay, this is really creepy, guys. And you know what really creeps me out here?"

"What?" Scott asked.

"I believe you. I don't know why. Maybe it's the marks on your wrists. Maybe it's because I've always trusted you, Scott. But for some strange reason I believe you. Except this is scary. You're talking about guns and grenades and an army that likes to kill children. And you're children. *We're* children. And you're acting like you can just go back there and save this boy, Charlie, like in some sorta action movie." Rob paused, then looked at Scott with a mixture of fear and concern. "Think about it. What do you think you can really do?"

Scott stared back at Rob in silence. His mind was still whirling as he tried to think. Finally, he spoke up. "I don't know how we're going to do this. All I know is, we have no choice. Nobody else is doing anything. And we can't let them raid the camp again."

"But there's just the two of you," Rob said. "How are you going to go up against a whole army?"

"I'll go and get help from the people in the town nearby," Bruce said, "after I warn the people in the camp."

"And you think they'll believe you?" Rob asked.

"Yes," Bruce said firmly, staring Rob down. "And we can't waste any more time talking about it. Something needs to be done. There are three stones left. So you can come too. Three's always better than two," he said, challenging Rob.

"Come on," Scott said, grabbing the stones. "Maybe we don't have a good plan, but we'll just have to make it up as we go. We have to get back there now. If we don't, it'll be too late. Come on. Let's go to my room. We can leave from there."

Scott led the way down the stairs into his bedroom. "Rob, you stay with Bruce. And listen to him. He knows what he's doing."

Bruce glanced at Scott, and his eyebrows lifted a notch.

Scott opened the sack and dropped the stones onto his bed. "Now all you need to do is put the stone in the palm of your hand and hold it real tight. Let's do it all together, okay?"

"One, everyone pick up a stone," Scott began.

Bruce and Scott each grabbed a stone and held it in their hands. Rob reached down to the bed hesitantly and picked up the last one, cautiously cradling it in the palm of his hand. His hand shook as he held his breath.

"And two. Squeeze!"

Bruce and Scott closed their eyes and squeezed their stones.

"I can't do it!" Rob shouted. He dropped the stone into Scott's shirt pocket.

Bruce and Scott disappeared.

Chapter 25

Milk and honey have different colors, but they share the same house peacefully. ~ African proverb

Scott breathed a sigh of relief when he felt the ropes wrapped around his arms and chest once again. He was back, and the moonlit night sky reassured him he had arrived in plenty of time. Bruce crouched down and gazed at Charlie, lying sound asleep on the ground, oblivious to all that was happening around him. He smiled at the young boy, then glanced around.

"You think maybe Rob will change his mind and come later?" asked Bruce.

"I doubt it. He gave me the last stone before we vanished. It's here in my pocket."

"Why the hell did he do that?"

Scott shrugged.

"I gotta go," Bruce said, reaching into his pocket and pulling out the apples. He scanned the area. Two guards stood beside each other, leaning against the trees. Without hesitation, Bruce threw the apple so it landed directly behind them. Both soldiers spun around and looked into the bush.

"Stop!" one shouted.

Bruce scuttled across the clearing. He paused at the edge and then threw the second apple, this time farther past where the two soldiers stood staring into the darkness.

"Cover me!" the soldier yelled as he crashed through the bush, breaking branches and making a tremendous racket. It worked perfectly to cover the sound of Bruce's own footsteps and twig snapping as he ran in the opposite direction. Bruce jumped behind a huge log and lay down. It was too risky to go any farther. Not yet, anyway.

Seconds later, the soldier returned. "It was probably a hyna or something that smelled the blood from that body they buried over there," he said to the other soldier. "We better check all the kid."

The two came closer to the group and walked around, trying to count the kids in the dark.

"I think they are all here. But check the bush over there."

Scott froze as he watched the soldier walk toward the bush where Bruce had been moments ago. He crossed his legs to keep from peeing his pants. Instantly, he knew what to do.

"Hey!" he shouted. "I need to pee real bad. Can you let me up?"

"Go piss right there," the soldier yelled back at him.

"Aw, come on, guys. I can't pee sitting down here. I'll make a mess."

Both soldiers turned their backs to the bush and walked over to Scott. While one untied him and the other pointed a gun in his face, Scott spoke in an unusually loud voice. "You know, I've never seen such beautiful stars like the ones you have here in Uganda," he remarked, looking up into the sky.

Both soldiers followed his gaze.

"And your moon. You know, the moon doesn't look this bright or this huge where I come from."

"Yeah, yeah," the soldier holding the gun at his face said indifferently. "If you have seen one moon, you have seen them all. Now go pee."

Scott's arms were pulled in front of him as he was led away from the group. Fumbling to undo his zipper, he felt extremely awkward peeing in front of two strangers, especially one who pointed a gun in his face.

"Yeah, you know, that water can go right through you sometimes. And speaking of water, whereabouts do you guys get your water? Do you have a well near here?" asked Scott.

"What is it to you?" The soldier stared down his gun at him.

"Oh, I was just wondering if you had to send the kids very far to get the water for everyone. But maybe there's a creek near here you get it from. You know, that's something I haven't done for a long time. Swum in a creek. I mean, it would feel really nice right now, hey? Swimming under the moonlight, diving into the cool water. Do you guys know how to swim? I learned how when I was a young kid. I took swimming lessons at the local pool. But you probably never took lessons. My friend never took lessons, and he can swim just fine. He told me that when he was only four years old his mom threw him into the lake and told him to teach himself how to swim. He must have been really freaked out. I mean, he was only—"

"Shut up, white boy," the soldier with the gun said, shoving the barrel of the rifle into Scott's face. "You are annoying me."

Scott shut his mouth, walked back to the tree, and sat down while they wrapped the ropes around his body again. He didn't say another word. He had peed in front of two soldiers while one held a gun to his face, and he had talked his fool head off, risking his life while Bruce sneaked away into the bush. The soldiers returned to their posts and leaned against the trees.

"The *muzungu* is strange strange, yes?" one soldier said to the other.

"Yes, I do not see why we have the white boy. What use is he to us?"

"I do not know. He has the brain of an *ongere* in his head."

The soldiers laughed.

Scott suppressed a smile. *Way to go, Scotty boy. You did it*, he thought. *Now stop shaking.*

He leaned his head against the tree and tried to think of what he could do next. But he dismissed each idea quickly. There were too many risks, not only to him, but also to the rest of the kids. He had to admit Bruce was right. There was nothing else he could do. He had to sit and wait it out.

He closed his eyes, and fatigue drew him into a deep sleep.

"Scott. Scott, wake up."

He opened his eyes to see Charlie sitting across from him. The sun was beginning to show itself on the horizon while the glow from the moon in the west was fading into the brightness of the sky.

"I thought you were going to be gone when I got up," Charlie said.

"I was," Scott whispered. "But I came back and brought Bruce with me."

Charlie's eyes grew wide. "You brought my angel Bruce with you?"

"Yeah." Scott laughed to himself. "I brought you your angel. But he's hiding in the bush right now. He's going to the camp to warn them."

"How is he going to do that? Does he know which way to go?"

"No. But he'll figure it out. Don't worry."

Charlie looked out at the pathway to see several soldiers heading toward them. They wore nothing except their green pants. Their chests and feet were bare. "Get up, everyone," Charlie called out to the group.

The children stood at attention as the soldiers entered the clearing. They each carried two pails and set them down on the ground before removing the ropes from the children.

Scott strained his neck and peered into the buckets. A cup of water would do wonderfully right now. But instead of water, he saw a muddy greenish-brown mixture.

"What's in the pails?" he whispered to Charlie.

"It is camouflage mixed with water. They are going to do the purification ceremony now and get us ready for the raid. They always do it before we head out."

"Does this mean you'll be raiding the camp tonight?"

"Yes. That is what it mean."

The soldiers dipped their cups into the pails and poured the colored water over the children's heads. Each child stood absolutely still.

"*Ni wire, ni wire*, purify, purify.

Kan latin, kan latin. Shield the child, shield the child.

Gwok, gwok. Protect, protect.

Kan latin, kan latin."

The men chanted in unison, circling the children until they had emptied the buckets.

When this part of the ceremony was completed, a small pail of yellow-colored oil was set in front of Scott. Each soldier scooped out some of the foul and smoky-smelling grease and walked back toward the children.

"Kwany sati ki komi!" shouted one soldier.

Immediately, each child took his shirt off and laid it on the ground.

Again, each child stood absolutely still while the soldiers smeared the oil over their foreheads, chests, and backs. All the while they continued to chant:

"*Rubanga, in ma lacwec,*

in ma ingey o jami ducu, gwoka.

Mighty God, mighty God, in your greatness,

protect and shield, protect and shield."

The largest of the soldiers stood in the middle of the children and began to speak. "You have been trained in the way of a true Acholi warrior!" His voice bellowed above their heads. "You are now a soldier in the Lord Resistance Army! You are protected for our next battle. All bullet that come your way will turn around in midair and return to their origin and kill the cursed soldier who tried to shoot you. But if you think of fleeing, the bullet will find you and you will die. This is what has been told to our leader by the Great Spirit."

Scott could not believe what he was hearing. It scared him to think someone could actually tell children such lies. But looking at the faces of the kids as they listened to the soldier, he was more scared to think they actually believed him. How would they know? They were only children.

The soldier continued to speak while the other soldiers gave each of the children a small bottle of water, each containing a long narrow stick. "You must carry this bottle with you into battle. It is your protection. When the bullet start to fly, each of you must dip the stick into the water and empty the bottle like this onto the ground."

Scott peered through the children's legs and watched the soldier pour the contents of the bottle onto the parched clay ground. Immediately, a small stream formed and made its way toward their feet.

"In this way you will create a river, and all of the bullet that come your way will drown. You will be safe, unless you try to escape."

Scott could not contain himself. He struggled to stand, but the ropes were too tight. "Don't believe him!" he shouted. "The bullets will kill you! Run away! You need— "

The butt of a rifle came down on Scott's head. His warnings were silenced.

Chapter 26

A single bracelet does not jingle.
~ Congolese proverb

Scott cracked his eyes open and saw a blur of colors and shapes. The pain in his head intensified until it exploded in his brain. He felt as if he was going to puke. He turned his head and watched what little was in his stomach splatter on the ground beside him. The smell was nauseating, and he felt the bile in his stomach churn until it spewed out, leaving his stomach empty and hollow.

He leaned his head against the tree. He heard a faint hum. The sound became louder and louder until it grew into a dissonance of children's voices, chanting, the volume rising and falling, again and again and again. The children's eyes were closed and their heads bowed. They sat perfectly still. The only movement came from their mouths, synchronized, well trained, and obedient. The well-rehearsed prayer the soldiers had taught them flowed from their mouths effortlessly.

The scene reminded Scott of his childhood years in Sunday school. But the cultish and voodoo-like rituals the children had just experienced were far from any type of Christian prayer.

A voice came from above Scott's head. "Eeh! I did not kill you after all."

Scott could picture the sneer on the soldier's face. The ropes were pulled away from his chest, and a large hand grabbed his shirt and yanked him to his feet. "Go!" the voice behind him commanded.

Scott glanced at Charlie. Charlie's eyes opened, revealing an anxious look. A quick smile lifted his cheeks and then was gone before he closed his eyes and resumed chanting.

"Maatch!" the soldier yelled. He rammed his fist into Scott's back.

A million stars flashed in front of Scott's eyes while he had the strange sensation a vice was squeezing both sides of his brain. He willed his feet to take one step at a time. Stumbling, he caught his balance, using every bit of strength he had left to keep himself from falling. He staggered across the compound until they came to the mud hut with the dirty sheet covering the door.

Two young men in their early twenties guarded either side of the entrance. One stood over six feet tall. The other, although much shorter, made up for his lack of height with a fierce scowl that would send any hyena to its den. Both wore tall rubber boots. Gum boots.

"Watch him," the man commanded.

The soldier pulled the sheet aside and walked into the hut. Scott stood still and waited. The voices inside were muted and low, the words indistinguishable. The only thing Scott could gain from the voices was the tone. The soldier who had commanded him to march was now being given orders. The second voice inside was definitely Kony's, and the authority it demanded made Scott feel as if all the courage inside him was pouring out as fast as the water he had seen pour from the bottle during the ritual.

The soldier pulled the sheet aside and walked out as quickly as he had walked in. "You are with me now," he told the taller of the two soldiers. "Fill your canteen. We have a long walk ahead of us."

Scott followed the guard before the commanding soldier could stick his gun into his back again. They stopped in front of several yellow plastic jugs and poured the water into the canteens they wore on the side of their belts. Scott swallowed; his mouth was parched.

"Here," the commander said, putting a container into Scott's tied hands. "Drink. We do not want you to pass out and have to carry you."

Scott gulped the water down, trying to fill every square inch of his stomach. Slowly, the pain subsided and his head began to clear.

"Come!" The commander grabbed the canteen from Scott's hands and pushed him forward. "We have to get there before nightfall."

Scott looked into the sky and noted the position of the sun. It was probably a little after noon. Night came to Uganda around 7:00 p.m. That meant five or six hours of walking under the hot African sun. It was going to be a very difficult walk.

They followed the main pathway through the camp. It was a flurry of activity. Children were busy placing guns into piles and filling magazines with bullets. They filled small sacks with mines and grenades. They filled canteens and set them aside. The place reeked of fear and trepidation.

The three walked out of the camp and entered the surrounding bush. The commanding soldier in the front set the grueling pace while the tall soldier followed Scott. Without turning around, Scott knew the end of the guard's rifle was pointed at his back.

"Don't worry," he remarked casually to his new bodyguard, "I'm not going anywhere. I haven't made any other plans yet." He paused. "You know, since we'll be together for such a long time, maybe we can get to know each other on a first-name basis. I'm Scott, and you are . . . ?" He glanced over his shoulder; the soldier glared back at him. "Okay. Well, that about sums it all up, doesn't it?" Scott made a mental note; the tall soldier was now "Dumb Butt 1." He stared at the back of the commanding officer. "Correction," he whispered. "Commander is Dumb Butt 1, other guy is Dumb Butt 2."

Hours later, when the sun was in front of them, they stopped to take a short break. The soldiers sat under the shade of a tree and pulled out thin dried pieces of meat from their pants pockets and began to eat. The color drained from Scott's face as he put two and two together. Dried meat, hungry soldiers, a black mamba shot two days ago . . . he quickly dismissed any thoughts he had of eating. He would have to be a lot hungrier to eat anything that was poisonous and slithered.

The commander grabbed a piece of meat from the soldier and threw it at Scott.

"*Gway*! What did you do that for, Dirk?" the soldier yelled.

"The kid need to eat. He is no good to us dead. Now give him some water from your canteen."

Scott stared at the grotesque piece of snake meat that lay in front of him. Images of the black snake slithering over the young girl's body came to his mind, and thoughts of keeping whatever was still in his stomach were gone. Scott bent over and heaved. He threw up over the dark red meat.

"Now look what he has done!" the soldier shouted, looking at Scott in disgust. "You ruined a perfectly good piece of mamba meat! Stupid white boy!" he yelled. He kicked Scott in the stomach. Scott clutched his belly and fell forward, gasping for breath.

"That is enough," Dirk said calmly, holding the soldier back from Scott. "He is just a white boy. What do you expect? But he need to make it to Lira alive and in one piece. Back off, or Kony will be dealing with you personally."

Scott stood and glared at the soldier. He wished he had more left in his stomach so he could give Dumb Butt 2's nicely polished rubber boots a puke bath.

A movement in the bush caught Scott's eye. He looked over the soldier's shoulder into the bush. White skin, brown hair. He smiled for a second. *Leave it to Bruce to figure out how to get to the IDP camp,* he thought.

Scott wiped his mouth with the back of his hand and turned around. As he stepped in line behind Dirk, he realized things were beginning to look up. Bruce was following them, and he, Scott, was safe. Dirk had said it himself. They wanted him alive and in one piece. He was no use to them if he was dead.

The hours dragged on as they continued to walk. Many times during the march, Scott's legs buckled and he thought they were going to give out. His body had suffered more than its fair share of abuse during the last few days. And the lack of sleep, food, and water intensified the agony of each mile. But every once in a while, a fleeting image of Charlie's smile would cross Scott's mind, and a newfound determination set in.

When the sun began to sink down into the Ugandan jungle, Scott could see the distinct outline of a building set in a clearing directly ahead of them. A large white cross that had been driven into the ground confirmed they had arrived at their destination. Scott breathed in a huge sigh of relief until he remembered he was a ransomed boy without anyone to pay his ransom.

The group made their way to the church door.

"Knock," Dirk ordered.

Scott banged on the door, his bare knuckles rapping on the hard wood. Within seconds he heard footsteps shuffling along the cement floor. The door cracked open to reveal a small thin man with red stubble poking up from his balding head. The white collar and the gold cross he wore around his neck verified he was the pastor of the church.

Before Scott could say anything, the soldier threw the door open, pushing the pastor against the wall. The commander picked Scott up by the scruff of his neck and pitched him into the room, slamming the door shut behind them. The soldier lifted the pastor by his shirt collar and hung him on a solitary peg sticking out from the wall. The man's feet dangled in the air like those of a slaughtered cow in a Ugandan marketplace.

"*Muzungu* boy, you are happy to see your daddy now?" Dirk laughed, watching the terrified look on the pastor's pale face.

The pastor looked down at Scott, his eyes showing nothing but fear and confusion. The soldier lifted his rifle to the pastor's head and started to laugh. "I just love watching these little white *opego* squirm." He clicked the trigger of his rifle. The man's eyes grew wide and beads of sweat formed on his forehead. "Come now, *Padi*, do you oink like an *opego* too?"

Dirk joined in the laughter.

"Don't hurt him!" Scott yelled, struggling to break free.

"What do you want?" The pastor's meek voice was drowned out by Scott's yells and the men's laughter. "What do you want?" he shouted.

"Everything," Dirk said, tightening his hold on Scott. "Everything—if you want your son back."

The pastor glanced from Scott to Dirk. Without hesitation, he nodded. "Okay. Just let me down from here."

The soldier lifted him off the wall and dropped him on the floor. He scrambled to his feet and eyed his captors. "I'll give you everything I have. But you have to believe me I don't have that much to give."

"Yes, we know that, *Padi*, but we also know you take an offering every week, and we would be happy to take that off your hand too."

The pastor walked to his desk in the corner of his office, a firm resolve in his steps. He reached into a drawer and pulled out a well-worn leather wallet. Its thinness confirmed the pastor's lack of finances. Scott winced at the sight.

"Here," he said, placing a small stack of paper bills on the table. "Take it all."

He turned to his bookshelf and pulled out a short wooden box sitting between two Bibles. He shook the box upside down, and several handfuls of coins fell out, along with a larger stack of bills.

"You must have more," Dirk said.

"As you can see"—the pastor waved his arm around the room—"I live a very simple life here. What you see on the desk is all I have."

Scott stared at the money on the table and swallowed.

"You are wasting my time, *Padi*." Dirk shoved Scott toward the soldier. He grabbed Scott's arm and twisted it behind his back. Scott winced.

Dirk grabbed the pastor and pushed him into a chair beside the desk. He pulled a Bible from the shelf and held the book from its binding, fanning its pages open.

Nothing fell out. He threw the book onto the floor and continued his search, pulling out book after book, tossing each one to the floor as its empty pages once again verified the pastor's claim to poverty.

Dirk paused and eyed the desk. He yanked the middle drawer open and dumped its contents on the top. A stapler, some pencils, and a pad of notepaper fell out. There was nothing of value.

"Come now," Dirk said, staring down into the pastor's face. "You must have more hiding somewhere. You know this is not enough."

The pastor returned the commander's glare and shook his head. "I told you this is all I have. If I had more I would give it to you."

The lines on Dirk's forehead gathered. He took a closer look at the man and smirked. "Let us see what you have in the church."

The pastor walked to a door at the corner of the room and opened it into the church. A flea market's variety of wooden benches and chairs stood arranged in organized rows while a wide aisle led the way to a small wooden table covered by a white cloth. A small wooden cross stood in the middle of the altar. The only wall ornaments were long open windows that revealed a purple haze left from the evening's sunset.

"There's nothing here you would want," the pastor said as he reached the altar, his arms spread apart, revealing his bare palms.

Dirk shook his head in disgust. With one hand he rammed the pastor's head onto the table, sending the wooden cross clattering to the floor.

"It is not good enough. Either you come up with something else, or we will slice your dear *latin* up into many little piece and feed him to the *winyo*. I think the vulture would enjoy feasting on your son."

The soldier picked Scott up by the scruff of his neck and dragged him toward the altar. He slammed his head into the wooden table. Scott stared into the pastor's eyes and blinked back the tears. Suddenly, the man's eyes widened. A large blade flashed in front of Scott's face and tore across his cheek. Scott screamed in pain, but his attempts to move were useless.

"You know, little *muzungu* boy," Dirk said in a quiet, calm tone, "I have been doing some thinking here. To us, all white people look alike. But there are something I see in your face that I do not see in your father face. Take, for instance, your nose. It is thin and narrow, like the nose of an anteater. But your father nose is more like an *opego*. It is round and large. I am thinking your father should have a nose more like yours."

Dirk raised his arm again and brought the knife down onto the pastor's face. He stopped short and rested it on the bridge of the man's nose. The pastor's eyes grew wide. His body trembled.

"No!" Scott screamed. He reached for Dirk's hand with his bound arms and tried to grab the knife. "No!" he screamed again. "He's not my dad!"

The soldier yanked Scott from the table and threw him across the aisle. His head hit the bench with a loud whack.

"He is not your dad?" Dirk marched over to Scott, wrapped his massive hand around Scott's neck, and lifted him up. Scott grabbed at the commander's hands and tried to pry the man's fingers from his throat. "Then where is your dad?"

Scott gasped for any air that could find its way into his lungs. He felt as though the heel of a soldier's boot was being shoved into his chest and his brain was going to explode like a grenade.

"He's at the camp in Lira," he said, wheezing. "The . . . IDP camp. He's . . . an . . . aid worker."

Dirk released his grip and dropped Scott to the floor. "So you have lied. And how do I know you are not lying again?"

Scott struggled to catch his breath as he rubbed his fingers over the red marks on his neck. "He's not my dad. I was with my dad at the IDP camp in Lira when you raided it. I followed you when you took the kids. My father doesn't know where I am." His voice shook. He doubted if his words held any conviction.

Dirk stared at Scott, then looked at the pastor standing beside the table, visibly shaking. "So you have lied to me. A man of the cloth, and you have lied to me."

Dirk strode over to the pastor and shoved his face onto the altar again. He brought the blade of his knife down and sliced the lips from his quivering mouth.

"You must remember, *Padi*, the tongue is a very vile thing. And your lip should always be on guard not to let any lie or deceit come from it."

Dirk hauled Scott from the floor and pushed him toward the door. Scott looked back at the pastor, his eyes wide in shock. The man knelt on the floor near the altar. Bright red blood ran through his fingers as he kept his hands pressed to his mouth.

They turned and walked into the office. The soldier grabbed the money lying on the desk and shoved it into his pockets.

"Get going!" Dirk yelled, jerking the rope that bound Scott's arms. "We have wasted enough time here."

Chapter 27

Patience can cook a stone. ~ African proverb

Bruce crouched behind a thick set of bushes and peered into the clearing. He stared at the backs of Scott and the two soldiers as they left the church and walked across a field toward a pathway. They disappeared from his sight as they traveled farther and farther into the bush.

Bruce drew in a deep breath and counted. "One, two, three," he whispered. He stopped counting when he reached fifty. Then he looked to his right and to his left and ran to the church.

He flung the door open and glanced around, allowing his eyes to adjust to the darkened room. Evidence of the soldiers' siege lay before him: books tossed to the floor, drawers emptied, their contents spewed across the desktop and the floor below.

Bruce crossed the room and slowly opened the door into the chapel. He peered inside. A small figure crouched at the altar. Bruce breathed a small sigh of relief. It wasn't a body sprawled on the floor.

"Hey! Are you okay?" Bruce yelled. He tore down the aisle.

The pastor grabbed the altar cloth from the table and pressed it to his mouth. Bruce knelt down and looked into the man's eyes. They were wide with fear, and his body shook uncontrollably.

"What the hell did they do to you?"

The pastor's attempts to speak only created garbled words as fresh blood spewed from his mouth. Bruce lifted the man to his feet and guided him out the church door into the night air.

"I need to get you to a hospital," Bruce said. "Is there a hospital in Lira?"

The pastor nodded, then pointed to an old bike propped up against the building. Despite the desperation of the moment, Bruce had to smile. The bike conveniently had a cushioned rear seat, created especially for carrying a passenger or two. A large white cross, painted on the fender, confirmed it as the pastor's bike.

"Great. How far is it to Lira?"

The man held up two bloodied fingers.

Bruce flew down the road as the pastor straddled the backseat. One hand gripped the cushion while the other pressed the bloodied cloth to his mouth. The gravel road became a red blur.

When they entered the town, Bruce slowed for a second. “Where to now?” he asked.

The pastor pointed to a yellow building ahead of them. A blue-and-white sign announced they had arrived at the Lira Hospital.

Bruce turned onto a pathway leading to the building and hopped off the bike. He gripped the pastor’s arm and led him inside. A mother and her young daughter, cradled in the crook of her arm, were the only ones sitting in a small room.

“Hey! I need someone’s help right now! Is there a doctor here?” Bruce’s voice echoed down an empty hallway. He yelled louder. “Hey! I said I need help here! This man’s been hurt. He’s losing a lot of blood!”

Within seconds a man came out of a far room and rushed toward them. “Here. Help me get him into this room,” he said, staring at the bloodied cloth.

Bruce helped the doctor lift the pastor onto the cot. Slowly, the doctor took the altar cloth from the man’s mouth. He drew in a quick, deep breath. Where once there had been two red lips lay a gaping open wound, crudely cut by a knife. Bruce turned his head and leaned against the wall. The room spun around him a thousand times. He stumbled out of the room and out the hospital door, then leaned against the nearest tree, gasping for air.

Minutes passed while he clung to the tree and tried to steady himself. Finally, taking in a deep breath, he shook the nausea from his body and walked back in.

"Where did this happen?" the doctor asked, keeping his attention on cleaning away the blood.

"In his church. I found him there, just minutes after the soldiers left."

"So Kony's come back again, has he?" He tossed a bloodied cloth into a pail and dipped another into a basin of water. "What did he do to deserve this?"

"I think the soldiers wanted money in exchange for my friend. I guess he didn't have enough."

The pastor nodded and tried to speak.

"Don't talk," the doctor said, placing a cloth over the man's mouth. "I'll clean this up as best as I can, and then I'll have to do some serious stitching. It's good you brought him here so soon. I've had some victims come here days later, and there's not much I can do."

"You've had this happen before?"

"Oh, yes. It's Kony's signature. You're lucky the soldiers didn't have any locks with them. I've had to cut a few locks off of people's lips too."

Bruce shook his head in disbelief. The insanity of this army was incomprehensible.

"Yes, that Kony is one bad *jok*."

"*Jok*? What's that mean?"

"A bad spirit. A witch. Everyone in Uganda fears him because they believe he has spiritual powers." The doctor scoffed. "The children fear he can see into their minds and know if they're thinking of escaping. They're terrified of him. All of that ancient African witchcraft can be very intimidating when you're just a little kid. Even the adults are afraid if they say anything about Kony he'll come for them."

The doctor filled a syringe with a clear liquid. Suddenly, Bruce remembered the job he had set out to do. "Pastor, I'm gonna have to leave you right now. But can I take your bike? I promise I'll return it."

The pastor reached out and grasped Bruce's hand, then nodded.

"If Kony's men are around, you really shouldn't be going anywhere, especially during the night," the doctor said.

"But I have to go to the IDP camp and warn the people there. Kony's gonna attack it tonight."

"And how are you sure of this?"

"Because I . . ." Bruce stopped mid-sentence. It wouldn't do to tell the truth at this moment. "Because I'm a good *jok*."

He ran out the door and jumped on the bike. His feet had barely touched the pedals before he was whizzing down the main street, flying over every bump and hole that was in his way. He glanced to his side as he rode past the garbage dump where Charlie had found the backpack and the piece of plastic. He laughed to himself as he pictured Charlie carrying his finds and the grin that extended the whole width of his face.

He biked past the marketplace and the shops, then glanced at the jail where he and Charlie had spent the night. When he came to an intersection, he stopped to let a line of trucks pass through.

"Look at this. The *takataka* has returned." A large hand grabbed Bruce's shoulder. He turned and looked into the eyes of a familiar but less than welcoming face.

"I was wondering where you headed off to. Been looking for a few day now. But a snake always return to it hole, yes?" Nunida's grip tightened. "You know, I do not like being roughed around. Especially by some white boy."

Nunida grabbed the bike and yanked it toward him, shoving Bruce onto the pavement. He threw the bike aside and grasped Bruce's arm, twisting it behind his back. Bruce stiffened.

"Now let us go," Nunida said.

Bruce spun around and kicked Nunida's knees. The officer staggered backward. Instantly, he threw his fist into Nunida's face. He heard a loud snap. The man swayed as his hand flew to his nose.

"You little . . ." he said as he took a step toward Bruce.

Bruce ran and grabbed the bike and jumped on. He hopped the curb and began to pedal away. Nunida rushed at him and threw his arms around his neck. He pulled him down and sent the bike flying onto the street. With one arm wrapped around Bruce's neck, he used the other to remove his gun from its holster. He pushed the end of his gun against Bruce's temple. "No, you do not." He removed his arm from Bruce's neck. "Hand on your head," he ordered.

Bruce obeyed.

"Now walk."

"No." Bruce turned around. "No. I'm not walking, and I'm not going anywhere with you. The only place I'm going is to the camp down the road from here. I have to warn the people. Kony's gonna attack there again tonight."

Nunida laughed. “Ha ha ha! Such a noble gesture. But how is it a simple child like you should know this?”

“Because . . . because I’m a good *jok* who wants to help.”

Nunida laughed even louder. “Now that is one I have never heard before. A white boy impersonating a *jok*? A good *jok* at that? Well, boy, the bullet in this gun does not care if you are a good *jok* or a bad *jok*. Come with me.”

Nunida pressed the gun into his head. Bruce turned and walked down the sidewalk, into the police station, down the stairs, and into the cell.

The cell door slammed behind him.

“Shit!” he yelled. He threw a futile punch into the air, aiming it at Nunida as he walked up the stairs. The officer’s laughter traveled down the corridor. Bruce held up his middle finger. “Shithead,” he said through gritted teeth.

He stood in the center of the room. “Calm down, Bruce,” he said. “Calm down. You’re no good when you can’t think.”

He drew in a deep breath and another and another. He walked to one end of the cell and back again, then stopped and stared out the grate. A steady stream of feet walked by. Men in fancy black work shoes, women in high heels, and barefooted girls and boys.

"Hey," he said, smiling. He looked out the window and waited until he saw a solitary pair of small bare feet. "Psst! Hey, kid!"

The feet halted in front of the window, and a young boy looked into the cell. He sucked on the end of a sugarcane stick. "*Gway*, what did you do to get yourself in there, *muzungu* boy?"

"Hey, kid. How'd you like to earn some money?"

The boy got down on his knees. "Sure. What have you got?"

Bruce reached into his pocket and pulled out a five-dollar bill.

"That is not money."

"Sure it is. Where I come from you could buy a huge bag of candy with this."

"Well, that is not going to help me here. What else do you have?"

Bruce shrugged. This kid was smart. Real street-smart.

"How 'bout this?" Bruce said, reaching down to undo his leather belt. It wasn't the first time he had given up a belt in Uganda.

"Now, what am I going to use your belt for? That thing is big big. It could wrap around me three time." The boy laughed.

"You could trade it in for something real nice. I know a guy at the store at the end of the road who'd be happy to trade it for several boxes of Oreo cookies."

"Really?"

"Really."

"Okay. What do you want me to do?"

"I want you to go to the marketplace and find a girl named Suzanne and bring her here. She has a shop that sells soda and chips and cookies and stuff like that."

The boy reached his hand into the window. "Give me the belt and then I will go."

Bruce shook his head. "You come back here with the girl and I'll give it to you when you've earned it."

The boy nodded and took off.

Bruce sat down in the corner of the cell and waited. Minutes passed, and more minutes, until the cell grew colder and colder and the flow of the passing feet slowed down to the odd passerby rushing home for a late-night supper.

"Psst!"

Bruce looked up to see the young boy peering into the window.

"I got the girl here. Now give me my belt."

Bruce looked up and saw Suzanne's familiar smiling face. He took off his belt and handed it up to the kid.

"You promised your belt to him?" Suzanne asked.

"Yeah. He wouldn't take the money I had."

"Here. You keep it." She handed it back. Then placing some coins in the kid's hand, Suzanne said, "Take this instead. A guy need his belt."

She bent down onto her knees and placed her head close to the grate. "How did you get in here again?"

"It's a long story, and I'll tell you later, but I need to get outta here. I need to get to the camp just outside the town. Can you get Mandaca to order Nunida to let me go?"

She shook her head. "Mandaca went to the city just south of here. He will not be back for a week."

"Great. Just great." Bruce sighed.

"But I can get you out. Just wait there," Suzanne said, running off.

Bruce returned to the corner of his cell. He slumped down onto the floor, placed his head on his knees, and let out a huge moan. Even if she was to get him out, would there be enough time to get to the camp and warn everyone?

He started to sing. It was the only thing he could think of doing that would keep him from going crazy while he sat and waited. "Ninety-nine bottles of beer on the wall, ninety-nine bottles of beer. Take one down, pass it around, ninety-eight bottles of beer on the wall . . ."

The minutes passed on.

"Fifty-two bottles of beer on the wall, fifty-two bottles of beer . . ."

And still the minutes passed.

"Nineteen bottles of beer on the wall, nineteen . . ."

"You really have some strange song where you come from." Suzanne smirked as she fit the key into the cell door. "Now come on. I do not know how long he will be out for," she whispered, opening the door.

"How the?"

"Sh." Suzanne put her finger to her lips.

Bruce followed her up the stairs and looked into the office. Nunida was slumped over his desk with a mess of white cream dripping down his chin.

"I asked him if I could bring you a plate of Twinkie. Naturally he said no. Then the pig decided he wanted to have them for himself. Stupid man. Does he not know how easy it is to spike a Twinkie?"

Bruce laughed. He liked this girl.

Chapter 28

War has no eyes. ~ Swahili saying

Bruce hopped on the bike. "You coming?" he asked.

Suzanne looked at the cross painted on the fender. "What are you doing with the *Padi* bike?"

"Hop on and I'll tell you on the way."

Suzanne sat on the cushioned rear seat and let her legs dangle to the ground. Bruce turned the bike onto the street and rode away. He told her about Charlie being recaptured and about the soldiers at the church and what they did to the pastor, then about the LRA's plan to attack the camp that night. He left out all the details of Scott and the stones and any magical disappearances and reappearances. It was difficult enough for him to believe the story, and he was part of it. How could he expect anyone else to believe it?

"This make me sad," Suzanne said. "And it make me angry. I do not understand it. And the horror they do. Why?" She was silent for a moment. "And Charlie. What is to become of him? He is a young boy. He should be playing the football and running and enjoying the life as all boy do. This Kony—he is a mad mad man. Who would take the lip from a man? Who would take the lip from a *padi*?" Her voice quivered. "And now you tell me the LRA will attack the camp tonight. The people there, they have nothing. They lost all in the raid. What could Kony possibly want from them when they have nothing to give?"

"More kids."

"Yes. You are right."

Bruce glanced at Suzanne. He tried to offer her a reassuring smile. "Hey, they haven't taken over the camp yet. And while we're here we're gonna do everything we can to stop it, right?"

Suzanne's eyes narrowed and she gave a quick nod. "Yes, we are," she said.

"I thought so."

A few miles down the road, Bruce stopped at the top of a hill to catch his breath. He looked down into the valley and saw the glow of several small fires.

"It is the camp," Suzanne said, leaning forward to get a better view.

"Then we've made it in time." Bruce paused and turned in his seat. "Suzanne, what's a *takataka*?"

"Takataka?"

"Yeah. It's what that Nunida guy kept calling me and Charlie. *Takataka*."

"He called you that? If you ask me, he is the *takataka*, not you or Charlie."

"So what's it mean?"

"Garbage, trash. You know, the stuff you throw out that does not have any use."

"Oh," Bruce said, staring back at the valley.

"But you are definitely not *takataka*. That is for sure."

He laughed. "Let's move."

They flew down the hill, and the grass and brush became a green blur. As they approached the camp, Bruce slowly applied the brakes, bringing them to the perimeter where several trucks were parked. He jumped off the bike and rushed toward a group of tents. "Hey! Is there anyone here?" he yelled.

A man walked out of a tent and shone a flashlight onto the pair. "*Gway*! You come here!" he shouted.

Bruce grabbed Suzanne's hand and ran to the man. "You gotta get everyone outta here," he said, gasping. "Kony's on his way with his army, and he's gonna attack tonight."

The man eyed Bruce and then looked at Suzanne. His dirty face and soiled clothes revealed he had already endured an exhausting day. He didn't look the type who would easily give in to some teenage boy's ill-informed and misguided notions. "And what make you believe this?" he asked.

Bruce tried to organize his thoughts. "A friend of mine was kidnapped by the army, and he told me they were getting ready for another attack."

"And where is your friend now?"

"He's still being held hostage."

"And how is it he tell you all this, if he is still being held as the hostage?"

"We—" Bruce stopped himself. It wouldn't do to tell the man he'd met up with Scott at his house back in Toronto. "He snuck away and told me, and then he went back before they knew he was missing."

"And what make you think Kony will attack?"

"Because he's peeved they only got a few kids from the last raid."

The aid worker shook his head, disbelieving. "Listen. I do not know how much truth is in your story—but we have hundred hundred people here. We cannot scare them to run into the bush with fear that Kony is coming. If you have no proof, how can I believe you? You are a kid just." He waited for Bruce to reply.

Bruce stared at the ground and sighed. "No, I don't have any proof."

"Well, then," the man said. He turned to walk back to his tent.

Suzanne grabbed his arm. "I know you think he is only *muzungu*, but he know what he is talking about. You must listen to him!"

"I do not care if he is *muzungu* or president. I am not going to listen to a kid tell me a faking story about his friend held hostage and Kony coming back. I do not see the truth in it."

"But it is true, and if you do not listen to him, more kid will be taken. How can you ignore that?"

"I will take the chance." He turned his back to Suzanne and Bruce and disappeared into his tent.

"Come on," Bruce said. "We'll have to warn them ourselves."

Suzanne pointed to a faint flicker on the hillside. "You think that is the LRA?"

"Yeah, I think so. They're probably waiting for Kony to give the signal. Who knows how close they are already. Let's go. We've got no time to lose."

Bruce and Suzanne ran past the aid workers' tents and into the camp. They stopped in front of the makeshift shelters. The faint light of the moon revealed hundreds of tents, filling the valley and extending up into the hills.

"How are we going to warn everyone?" Suzanne asked.

"Got any ideas?"

"We could run into the camp just and yell that Kony is coming."

"But they wouldn't believe us. They'd think we were just two crazy kids."

"Yeah. It is too bad we do not have any gun to fire and scare them to think it is the real thing."

Bruce scanned the camp and looked at the aid workers' trucks. He smiled. "You've gotta be the smartest girl I've ever met. We're not gonna warn 'em. We're gonna make 'em think the army's already here. Come on. I'm gonna need your help."

They crept past the aid workers' tents and back to the trucks. Bruce peered into each vehicle, looking for one with its keys still in it. "Great," he grumbled, "I gotta wire 'em."

He reached under the front grill and popped the hood open. It rose with a noisy creak.

"Sh," Suzanne whispered. They looked toward the camp. All was still and quiet.

Bruce turned his attention back to the truck. He glanced at the motor, found the distributor cap, and gave it a slight twist. Then he carefully closed the hood and returned to the cab. With an expert touch, he yanked the wires out of the ignition and began tapping each wire to another until he saw the dashboard lights come on. “Good. That’s one,” he muttered to himself.

He ran to the next truck and repeated his actions: pop the hood, twist the cap, and hot-wire the truck. Now he had two trucks ready to make some big noise. He grinned.

“Suzanne, I need you to go back to the camp, and when you hear something that sounds like gunshots going off, run around and start screaming that Kony’s here. Just scream it at the top of your lungs. You got that?”

“Got it,” Suzanne nodded and took off toward the camp.

Bruce jumped into the driver’s seat and touched the two wires together until the ignition lights came on. Then, he touched each wire to the two until the truck started. Instantly, the truck backfired and a loud bang echoed across the camp. Soon another followed, and another. Bruce rushed to the next truck, and within seconds the air was filled with more blasts and bangs, creating a sound like machine guns ripping through the camp. Bruce chuckled. He had actually learned something worthwhile in auto class.

Within seconds he could hear Suzanne's screams. "Kony is back! Everyone run! Kony is back!"

Soon a chorus of screams rose from the camp, beginning at one end and quickly rippling into the interior until the whole camp was in a state of panic. Bruce sat in the truck and listened as the noise intensified. Hundreds and hundreds of people ran screaming out of the camp; men and women carried their children, running into the bush or the fields or up the hill toward the town.

Suddenly, the door of the truck was wrenched open, and the aid worker yanked Bruce out of the door. "What are you doing?" he yelled, throwing Bruce to the ground.

"I had to clear the camp! Kony's coming, whether you believe me or not!"

Immediately, the sound of real gunfire filled the air. The aid worker's eyes grew wide as he reached down and pulled Bruce up off the ground.

"Everyone run!" he shouted. "Kony is back! Put all your kid in the truck!"

Bruce ran to each truck, lifted their hoods, and twisted the distributor caps back in place.

Children piled into the backs of the trucks and squeezed their bodies tightly together until no one else could fit. Aid workers scrambled into the driver's seats, and still more children piled into the cabs. The trucks sped off, racing up the hill toward the town, blaring their horns, scattering the people along the way.

"Get out of the camp!" the aid worker yelled at Bruce.

Bruce ignored the worker's warning and searched for Suzanne as the herd of people rushed out of the camp.

"Suzanne's in there!" he yelled, running into the crowd.

Bruce pushed his way through the mob and yelled for her at the top of his lungs. It was impossible to make his voice heard. The screams and the blasts of the rifles were almost deafening.

"Suzanne! Suzanne!"

He craned his neck, trying to see above the crowd, until he saw an old withered tree standing a few yards away. He climbed the trunk, stood on the highest branch, and scanned the camp. And then he saw her, about a stone's throw away, grasping the hands of a boy and a girl and pulling them toward the road.

"Suzanne! Suzanne!" Bruce shouted, waving his arms.

He jumped from the tree and ran toward her, dodging the people rushing against him.

"Come on!" he yelled, grabbing the boy's hand.

Suddenly, a barrage of bullets hit the ground in front of them.

"This way!" Bruce pulled the boy's arm and led them in the opposite direction, away from the mob, searching for any sort of barricade that could shield them. A bright light flashed over their heads. A torch landed on a tent beside them. Instantly, the tent burst into flames. The flames sent their sparks onto the surrounding tents, and within seconds everything was burning. Bruce and Suzanne tightened their grips on the children's hands and stared at each other.

"Where can we go?" Suzanne cried.

A child's scream rose above the clamor.

"Come on!" she yelled.

Again they heard screams, this time louder and more terrified.

Suzanne put her hand to her face and gasped. A woman ran out of a hut. Her hair was in flames, her body blackened and charred. She stumbled into the clearing, her arms stretched out before her, her eyes wide in shock. A young girl screamed. Her arms reached toward the woman but her feet stayed fixed to the ground.

Suzanne grabbed the girl from behind and pulled her to her chest, attempting to cover the child's eyes. The girl screamed louder, then kicked and clawed at Suzanne, trying to escape. The woman's body fell to the ground, then lay as still as a log on a kitchen fire.

"Stop!" she commanded, pulling the girl tighter to her chest. "There is nothing we can do, *latin*. You must come with us, child."

She tucked the young girl's head into her neck and brushed her fingers in a soft caress over the girl's dirt- and tear-stained cheek. She stepped away from the woman's body and ran toward Bruce.

"Come on!" he yelled. "This way!"

Suzanne and the children followed Bruce, running through the charred remains of the tents, covering their nostrils to avoid inhaling the overpowering smoke. Bruce stopped.

Directly in front of them stood a young boy. His legs were spread in a firm stance while his hand kept his gun level with the ground. He aimed straight at Bruce. He glanced at the charred remains of a body still smoldering on the ground and then back to the group. "Stay there!" he yelled. His voice was high-pitched and wavering. The gun shook in his trembling hands.

Bruce and Suzanne stood absolutely still. The children grabbed Suzanne's legs and clung to them.

The boy took a few steps forward, fixing his aim on Bruce, then Suzanne, and finally on the children. "Do not move," he said.

Suzanne stared into the young soldier's eyes, searching the child's face. "My *omera*, my brother, how can you hold that gun and act like a soldier who kill his own people from his own tribe?"

The boy's grasp on the rifle stiffened. "How dare you speak to me. You are a latin! A young child! I am an Acholi soldier!"

"No. You are a young boy. You are not a killer."

"I have killed many time! Now step back, or I will kill you too!"

Suzanne stood firm in her spot. "Why do you not put the gun down, my *omera*? You can come with us. No one will know. We can take you to Lira and find a safe place for you."

Suzanne put the child down at her side and reached out, her palms facing upward.

"I said, get back! Move it!" the boy shouted, stepping forward and pushing the butt of his rifle into Suzanne's chest.

"Please. I promise I will keep you safe. Just come with us." She kneeled down and stretched her hands out to the boy.

"No!" he shouted, looking over his shoulder.

Emerging from the smoke, an older boy walked toward them, pointing his rifle at them. "Tie them!" he said, tossing a rope to the first soldier.

The boy slung his gun over his shoulder and tied Bruce's arms together at the wrists. The rope cut deep. Then he bound the young boy and girl and grabbed Suzanne's arms.

"No! You do not have to do this!" Suzanne pleaded. "You can both come with us! We will hide you! Kony will not know! I promise you, he will not know!"

The young boy wrapped the rope around her wrists and pulled it tight.

"I can see it in your eyes. You are afraid of Kony. And you desperately want to escape. Now is your chance. Please." The tears fell from Suzanne's face as she pleaded, her arms still outstretched, her knees still bent.

"This girl is *kicira*. Kill her, and all of the evil in her," the older soldier said, taking the rope.

The boy took his rifle off his shoulder and aimed it at Suzanne's head.

"No!" Bruce yelled.

The boy pulled the trigger. Instantly, the blood hit Bruce's face. Suzanne's eyes met his briefly before her body slumped to the ground.

Bruce stared at Suzanne's lifeless body and the river of blood that flowed from her head and slowly soaked into the ground. It was as if it carried all that made Suzanne with it: her compassion, her gentleness, her laughter, and her smiles. Tears welled up and coursed down Bruce's cheeks. His breath came to him in short gasps. He could not tear his eyes away.

"Walk!" the older soldier yelled at him, yanking on his rope.

Bruce startled. He stared at the soldier. His voice came out in a forced whisper. "Why? Why did you do that? She wasn't going to hurt you. She only wanted to—"

"Move it! Now!" The soldier boy cut the rope from Suzanne's limp arms and pushed his gun into Bruce's face.

Bruce willed his legs to move as he staggered forward. He looked behind at the young girl who was once safe in Suzanne's arms and now staring at her corpse. "Run!" he yelled to her. "Run!"

The boy yanked Bruce's arms forward. Bruce spun around and followed the child soldier, feeling the butt of the rifle in his ribs. They walked until they came to the edge of the camp. By now, all that was left of the refuge were the charred remains of the sticks that had once held the makeshift tents. The gunfire had ceased except for the occasional shot that interrupted the wails rising from the camp.

Bruce looked around him. His heart dropped. Group after group of children, with their arms tied before them, were being forced to walk out of the camp. Fifty. Sixty. No, there were many more than that, he realized, as he looked into the distance and saw more children being led away.

He scanned the field and searched for any sign of Charlie or Scott. Then, to his surprise, he saw a boy walking toward him. The rifle slung over his shoulder and the strut in his step could have belonged to any of the more experienced child soldiers, but Bruce knew in an instant it was Charlie.

"You have another *muzungu* boy," Charlie said, approaching the group.

"Yes," the soldier replied. "I found him in the camp. I shot the girl who was with him. She was trying to convince us to escape with her."

Charlie stared up into Bruce's tear-stained face. "Good. You did well. Now leave this group with me. I will look after them," he said, dismissing the two boys. "Maatch, *muzungu*." He pointed his rifle at Bruce and gave a sharp tug on the rope.

Chapter 29

Show me your friend and I will show you your character. ~ African proverb

Bruce stared at Charlie's back as the boy, clad in his oversized Nikes, marched ahead of him. He wanted to be happy because he had found Charlie again. But he couldn't. An image of Suzanne's dead body flashed in his mind. It was as real and vivid as when he had stood looking down at it, feeling the splattered blood on his face. One moment she was there, begging with the young boy to let them go and promising him her protection, and the next minute she was gone. Her still eyes stared back at him. He tried to shake the image from his mind. He couldn't.

He glanced around. All that surrounded him—horror, death, and despair—was the result of a deranged and evil mind. There was nothing good here.

Charlie led them toward a group of children, huddled tightly together. Even from the distance Bruce could hear their sobs and whimpers. He turned around and looked at the young boy and girl behind him. He wondered how they could even see to walk, their eyes swollen from the smoke and their tears.

"What are you waiting for?" Charlie yelled at the two soldiers standing guard. "Put the rope on them! The sun will be up soon!"

The boys sprang into action and tied the group together with a long rope. Bruce winced as he watched the ropes tighten around their wrists, the rough cords cutting into their young skin.

Charlie took the rope that bound Bruce and the two children together, and joined them to the two groups, placing Bruce at the front.

"Now git," he said pointing his rifle at the young soldier. "These kid are mine."

The two boys slung their rifles over their shoulders and walked away. Charlie watched the boys until they were well out of sight. As the first rays of light were starting to bring the surrounding bush into focus, more and more groups of children filed past them, each group led by several soldiers, with others taking up the rear.

Brucc watched the columns of smoke rise from the camp. Two people emerged from the desolation.

Charlie followed Bruce's gaze. A tall soldier and a white boy walked toward them.

"Well, look at this!" Dirk shouted. "We had one *muzungu* and now we have two!"

He tied Scott's rope to Bruce and stuck the end of his gun in Bruce's face. He laughed. "Your daddy doing his Christian duty here and helping the poor Ugandan people? Well, lucky for us he came. Now we have two white boy, which mean double the shilling."

Bruce glared.

Suddenly, Dirk turned to face Charlie. "What the hell happened out there?" he yelled. He slapped Charlie across the head, knocking him to the ground. The boy scrambled to his feet.

"Why did you start shooting before I gave the signal?" Dirk shouted. He tightened his hand into a fist and hit Charlie in the face.

Charlie fell to the ground and covered his face. He didn't move. The blood seeped through his fingers and dripped onto the ground.

"They started firing," he said, wiping the blood from his hands on his pants. "The army must have known we were coming."

"How would they know that?" Dirk yelled.

"I do not know. We were very quiet. We waited in the bush like you told us to. But suddenly we heard gunshot and all of the boy started firing. I yelled for them to stop, but—"

Dirk kicked him in the stomach. Charlie fell to the ground.

"You *awubi ma laming*! You stupid boy! Now we may never find this kid father and get our ransom! Do you know that?" He kicked Charlie again. "Get up!" he yelled. "We are heading back to camp."

Charlie pushed himself onto his knees and slowly stood. He picked up his gun, took his position in the front of the group, and pulled the rope. Scott stumbled and caught his balance, then followed, taking quick little steps behind him.

Charlie stopped and turned. He stared at Dirk.

"Maatch!" Dirk bellowed.

"No." Charlie placed the end of his rifle at Scott's head.

Scott froze.

"What the hell do you think you are doing, boy?" Dirk lifted his rifle to his shoulder and placed his finger on the trigger. "I said, maatch."

"No," Charlie repeated.

Dirk took a couple steps forward. "Put the gun down, boy, or I will be bringing you to Kony myself."

Charlie laughed. "Now that is funny. You are going to bring me to Kony. Now you listen, Dirk. If this little *muzungu* boy does not come back with you, we both know what Kony will do to you. And there are many kid who would rather enjoy watching you have your lip locked together before they tie you to the *goyo* tree and beat you to death."

Charlie tightened his grip on his gun and rammed it into Scott's head.

"The way I look at it is like this," the boy continued. "The bullet that pass through the *muzungu* brain is going to make it easy through the other *muzungu*. So I will be making good use of my bullet. If you point your gun at me, I will blow both head off, and you will not have any hope in staying on Kony good side."

Dirk lowered his rifle.

"Now take the mag out and drop it."

Dirk pulled the magazine out and dropped it at his feet.

"And I will have the one in your pocket too."

Dirk dropped a second magazine on the ground.

"Kick them over here."

Again Dirk obeyed.

"Untie the *muzungu* and go. You can have him. The rest of the kid are with me."

Dirk pulled the rope free from Bruce. "I will remember this, ka-boy. The next time I see you, it will be at the *goyo* tree and I will be sure to deny you all mercy." He yanked the rope. Scott followed and turned his head and stared at Charlie and Bruce. Charlie's face offered no emotion. Bruce felt only confusion.

Dirk and Scott walked farther and farther into the field until they became a tiny speck in the distance.

Charlie sliced the ropes from the children's wrists. "Go," he said. "Go back to your camp and then follow the road to Lira. Hopefully, you will find your parent there."

The ropes that bound Bruce's wrists fell to the ground. "So you're letting Dirk take Scott?" he said. "Why'd you do that? He's as good as dead now."

"Do not worry about Scott. We will follow, and when it is night again we can set him free. If I did not let him take Scott, Dirk would have no reason to leave, and I would have to shoot him. And there has been enough of that today. Scott is safe. Dirk would not dream of hurting him. Now let us find a shady place in the bush and hide there. Maybe I can find something for us to eat. I am starving."

Bruce followed Charlie into the trees until they had walked far enough for the enclosing forest to cover them. Bruce had never been surrounded by so much green. The early-morning sunlight began to touch the leaves and trunks of the trees, bringing them into focus. Thousands of dewdrops captured the sunlight, filling the jungle with tiny beads of light.

Charlie stopped in a small clearing and drew in a deep breath of air. "Ah!" He sighed, looking up into the trees. "I have found us some breakfast."

He scrambled up the trunk. "Look out!" he yelled.

A ripe red mango fell from the tree, followed by one after another. Soon the ground was littered with mangos and the air was filled with the fruit's sweet fragrance.

Charlie jumped down and grabbed one of the fruits. He sat under the tree and leaned his back against the trunk. "Come on," he said, patting the ground beside him. "Sit. It is breakfast." He ripped the peel off with his teeth. "Here, eat," he said, offering one to Bruce.

Bruce took it and sat down. "Suzanne's dead," he said.

"Yes, I know."

Bruce's voice shook. "The boy just shot her. For no reason. She wasn't doing anything to him. She just wanted to help him."

"I know."

"But he could've come with us. We would've helped him. We would've brought him back to the town and tried to find his family."

"But he did not know that. And if he did, do you think he would risk the escape? He think Kony can see into his mind. He would not take the chance."

Bruce dropped the mango onto the ground.

"Her blood is on my face," he whispered. He wiped his hand across his cheek and stared at the dried blood on the palm of his hand.

"I know." Charlie moved closer to Bruce and laid his hand on his shoulder. "But there is nothing you can do. When a life is gone, it is gone."

Bruce thought of how well Charlie knew this. "Are you numb, Charlie? I mean, you've seen so much death. Do you feel it anymore?"

"Yes, I do. But I must not look at it again and again. I must leave it and find the good. Like you. You came back for me, yes?"

Charlie's words brought a smile to Bruce's face. "Yeah, I came back."

"But why did you leave?"

"I didn't have any choice. The magic in the stone was gone, and it was time for me to go."

"Is that how you get here? A magic stone?"

"Yeah. There were five of them. Scott used two, I used two, and now there's only one left."

"Do you think the magic in the stone has been used up and you will be leaving again soon?"

Bruce smiled. He admired Charlie for being able to believe in something as unbelievable as magic stones. “Yeah.”

“Will you be coming back?” Bruce detected a slight quiver in the boy’s voice.

“I don’t think so.”

“Why not?”

“’Cause I think you’re gonna be okay.”

“But you know you can come and see me even when I am okay.”

“Of course.” Bruce laid his head against the tree, closed his eyes, and sighed.

“Goodbye, my angel Bruce. *Apwoyo matek*. I am going to miss you.”

Bruce laughed. It was the first time anyone had called him an angel.

Chapter 30

However long the night, the dawn will break.
~ African proverb

Scott dropped the bag of grain and slumped to the ground. Every part of his body whimpered. He could not go any farther.

"Get up!" Dirk yelled. He kicked Scott in the ribs.

Scott clutched his side and gasped for air. "Stupid ass," he whispered.

He lifted the bag over his shoulder and staggered down the path. He had already witnessed children being beaten and their legs sliced for moving too slowly under their heavy loads. It was strange how things like that could give a person incentive to keep going.

Scott watched the sun start its descent into the tree line. He figured they must have been marching for ten hours—at least. They had stopped once and been allowed to drink from a small stream, but that had been hours ago. The camp had to be close by now. And when they got there, maybe they would cook up some of the food they had stolen from the IDP camp and have something to fill their empty stomachs.

He did a lot of thinking as he walked through the fields and pushed his way through the bush. He thought a lot about Charlie. On the one hand, he was happy and relieved Charlie had been able to escape, and he was glad Bruce was with him. But on the other hand, he felt betrayed. So many times he'd replayed it in his mind how Charlie had the chance to shoot Dirk and could have let them all go free. *But*, he thought, *there must be a reason he didn't.* And he couldn't see Charlie leaving him to the LRA. He'd come and rescue him.

Then there were the stones. He wondered when the magic would wear off and he'd find himself back home. He knew the stones controlled everything—where he arrived and when he left—but was there more to it than that? He knew he wasn't the same person he was before he held that first stone. That was for sure.

He began to replay the events in his mind, piecing together what he could from Bruce's story and his own memories. And he came to another realization: Bruce wasn't the same person he was before either.

The beginnings of a well-worn path appeared ahead of him. They were close to the camp now. He followed the others and dropped the bag of grain onto the ground where the other bags of food supplies had been placed. His legs wobbled as he stood, feeling the relief from dropping the heavy load.

"Move!"

The rifle barrel was jammed into his back, and once again Scott found himself walking to the same clearing where he had first seen Charlie.

"Sit," Dirk commanded.

Scott sat with his back against the tree while a soldier pulled his arms behind him and tied them together. Huddled before him was another group of children, bound together, lying exhausted on the ground. This group was much larger than the one he had first seen when the stone brought him to Uganda. Dirk circled the group and smiled.

Scott took in a deep breath and let out a long sigh. His head dropped to his chest, and he fell asleep instantly.

It seemed like seconds later when Scott felt a small tug at his arm. He opened his eyes and looked into the biggest brown eyes he had ever seen. A boy Scott guessed to be about three years old stared into his face, examining his white skin and fair hair.

"Hey, fella," he said.

The little boy continued to stare at Scott, looking at everything about him—his jeans, his soiled shirt, and finally, his blue eyes.

Across from Scott a girl ladled large spoonfuls of rice into the children's outstretched hands. She dropped to her knees beside Scott and held a spoon to his mouth. He bit into the food and gulped it down. Again she brought the spoon to his mouth, and again he swallowed the rice. When he'd received his share, she held a small cup of water to his lips and he quickly emptied the cup.

"Thank you," Scott said. "You're very kind."

The girl offered a small smile in exchange for his warm words. She stood and took the pail in one hand and the little boy's hand in the other. As she walked away, a bundle wrapped around her side revealed a small child resting snugly against her back. The boy stopped to take another curious look at Scott and waved. Scott forced a smile to his face and nodded. He closed his eyes and fell back asleep.

Chapter 31

He who learns, teaches. ~ Ethiopian proverb

Scott woke late in the evening as a faint breeze touched his cheeks. He looked up to see the evening stars and let out a huge sigh. He was still in Uganda. When was he going to go home?

A hand tapped him on the shoulder, and a familiar voice whispered into his ear, “Sh. It is me.”

Scott glanced at the soldiers guarding the group. Both were leaning against a tree, their mouths wide open, fast asleep. He felt a tug on the ropes that were tied around his wrists and was afraid—not for his own life but for Charlie’s freedom. “No,” he whispered. “Get out of here. You’re free.”

Charlie continued to work at the knots.

"Charlie. Stop. Listen to me."

The tugging at his ropes ceased. He felt the warmth from Charlie's breath near his ear.

"I'm okay, Charlie. I know I'll be going soon. And I'll be fine. I don't want you to risk anything for me. Now go."

Charlie crept around the tree and faced Scott.

"Do you know about the stones and how Bruce and I got here?"

The boy nodded.

"There's more to the stones than bringing us to see you. The stones change people. They make you better. They make you a better person. Each time Bruce and I left you, we changed."

Charlie nodded again.

"Reach into my pocket and you'll find the last of the five stones."

Charlie pulled out the small polished green stone and stared at it while it lay flat on the palm of his hand.

"Take it to Kony. He's the one who needs to hold it and be taken somewhere. He's the one who needs to change. Otherwise, this war is going to go on and on and another generation of kids are going to lose their childhoods, if not their lives."

"But what about you? What if you never leave?"

"I have a feeling I'll be leaving anytime now."

"And you will be gone just like Bruce, and I will never see you again?"

"I wouldn't be too sure about that. I have a feeling Bruce and I didn't come here for nothing. I think there are great things in store for you."

Charlie stared at Scott. He was confused.

"Listen. You've endured more hatred and suffering and pain than anyone else I know and you're still a good person. A person like you could teach so many others to be the same."

Charlie looked down at his shoes and then at the stone.

"Now, go. I know you'll find a way to get the stone to Kony."

The boy laid his cheek against Scott's forehead; his tears fell onto Scott's face.

"I believe in you, Charlie."

Charlie put the stone into his pants pocket and backed away. He darted into the bush.

"Stop!" Two soldiers ran toward Scott, their eyes fixed on the trees where Charlie had escaped.

"Hey, you! Over here!" Scott yelled.

The two soldiers halted and stared at him. Scott vanished into thin air, leaving behind a pile of knotted rope. The stone had worked its magic.

Chapter 32

If you can't resolve your problems in peace, you can't solve war. ~ Somalian proverb

"Wa la la la la la!" the soldiers screamed, running away from the tree that once held Scott. *"Jok! Jok!"*

Within seconds several soldiers ran to the clearing and stared at the tree. The two men pointed at it, waving their arms madly about them, their voices a mixture of jumbled Acholi, Swahili, and English. Soon the clearing was filled with soldiers, all looking at the tree, lifting the ropes and shaking their heads. Charlie couldn't stop laughing.

He inched his way through the bush, carefully stepping among the trees and brush, keeping well hidden until he had traveled halfway around the camp and stood staring at a set of huts. Seeing the center hut was the only one that had a sheet covering its door, Charlie knew he had found Kony. Two guards stood on either side of the door, one wearing a camouflage uniform, the other wearing solid green army fatigues. Both wore large rubber boots.

"Looks like I am up against the big meat," Charlie whispered.

He crouched behind the lower bushes and stopped to think. The faint light of dawn was beginning to peer through the trees. The silence of the bush surrounded him. All was quiet from the clearing where Scott had disappeared. Charlie imagined the soldiers huddled together, trying to fathom what had just happened and how they were going to explain the whole thing to Kony. He knew the beating tree would be kept busy come early morning.

He stood and walked out of the bush. *Two big guys against little me. Well, I have survived using my brains and I have lasted this long*, he thought as he strode over to the two soldiers.

"I need one of you to come with me and search the bush." Charlie swallowed, hoping the men would not detect the quiver in his voice. "The *muzungu* kid has disappeared. Everyone else is combing the south side, but I have a feeling the boy came this way."

The two soldiers looked at each other and smirked.

"Yes, yes, ka-boy," the soldier in the camouflage outfit said. "Whatever you may say." Keeping a straight face, he turned to the other soldier. "You stay here, Dave, and I will head out with the boss child and search for the missing *muzungu*. This child must have the rank of general the way he boss us around. But I do not see any of his star or his boot, do you?"

Charlie drew up his chest and looked the soldier straight in the eyes. "Shall I be telling Dirk you refuse his order to come with me?"

"If Dirk is so wanting of me to search for the *muzungu*, then he must come here and personally deliver the message to my face. He know I have order never to leave here."

"If that is the way you want it, then it is, but when I find the *muzungu* I am not going to be sharing any of the glory with you or anyone."

The two soldiers glanced at each other, then at Charlie from the corners of their eyes.

"And what make you so sure you will be finding the white boy?" the soldier in the green fatigues asked, leering down at Charlie.

"Because I was part of his group, and I watched him and his eyes and how they roamed the camp, searching. And many time I saw him looking onto the path that led north out of the camp. But if you are not wanting to help me, then stay here." Charlie turned and walked away.

The soldier in the camouflage uniform stepped away from the hut. "Show the way, ka-boy."

Charlie gave a brief nod and continued on his way to the edge of the camp.

Half a mile down the path, the soldier stopped. "The *muzungu* would have to be stupid to follow a path into the bush. Would he not think to hide in the bush and make his way out in that way?"

"Yes, you would think this, but the *muzungu* do not think like us. They do not know the way of the bush. They are stupid stupid in that way," said Charlie.

"Yes, these white men and their white man way. So stupid. They could not survive one night out here."

"I will see if he is anywhere near." Charlie leaned his gun against a tree and scrambled up its smooth bark. When he reached the crown of the tree, he scanned the area around and below him. "Is there any sign of the boy going through the bush to the right of you?" he called down.

The soldier peered into the dense foliage. "No!"

"How about on the left? I think I see some broken branch over that way."

As the soldier turned his gaze to the opposite side of the path, Charlie yanked a huge spike-covered green fruit from the tree and held it directly above the soldier. He released his grip. The massive jackfruit landed with a heavy thud on the man's head. The soldier fell to the ground and lay very still.

"What a waste of a good jackfruit," he said, sliding down the tree.

Charlie grunted and groaned as he pushed the soldier to the tree and sat him up with his back leaning against the mottled bark. He grabbed a rope from the man's belt and wrapped it around and around until it held the man tightly. With a quick movement of his wrists, he placed two very well-crafted knots in the rope and pulled it tight. "Sorry, my brother. You will not be here for long. You will be safe—unless the hyna get you."

Charlie slung his gun back over his shoulder and rushed back to the camp. His pace quickened when the hut guarded by the one soldier came into sight.

"We caught him!" he said, panting and holding his sides as he stopped before the soldier. "But the *muzungu* is hurt, broken leg or something. He cannot walk." Charlie took in a couple deep breaths. "We are going to need your help."

The soldier studied Charlie's face.

Charlie held his gaze. "Should I go to the lower part of the camp and find someone else?"

The soldier looked past Charlie, then toward the path. "No. You stay guard here. I will go." He took off.

Charlie grinned.

He turned to face the door and paused, his heartbeat so strong it pounded in his chest and echoed in his brain. He drew in a deep breath, pulled the sheet aside, and stepped into the hut. Denied of the sun's first creeping rays, the blackness inside was almost suffocating. Charlie stopped and listened. Directly in front of him, he heard the low rumblings of someone in a deep sleep. Inching his way forward, he felt ahead with his hand, shuffling his feet, slowly moving toward the man who lay before him.

Charlie leaned closer. He saw the outline of a cot and a thin blanket covering a person whose chest rose and fell in a steady rhythm. Slowly, the image became clearer until he could make out Kony lying on his back, one hand lying comfortably on his chest while the other lay stretched out on his side, its palm facing outward.

Charlie pulled the stone out of his pocket and held it in his fingers. He stared at Kony and paused. This was the man who had ordered his soldiers to turn him into a killer. This was the man who had taken everything away from him: his father, his mother, his home, his childhood. He had to pay. Charlie tucked the stone back into his pocket and reached for his rifle. He took the safety off and aimed at Kony's chest.

No, a voice whispered inside his head.

He placed his finger on the trigger.

No. There has been enough killing already. You know this.

He inched closer.

No. If you do this, what will it make you?

Charlie closed his eyes while he drew in a deep breath. He put the safety back on and hung the rifle over his shoulder.

He pulled the stone out of his pocket, then reached out to place it in Kony's open palm.

"What are you doing?" Kony grabbed Charlie's wrist and pulled him toward him. Even in the blackness he could see the whites of Kony's eyes, staring directly into his.

With one arm Kony threw Charlie to the ground. Suddenly a bright light shone into Charlie's eyes.

"What are you doing?" Kony repeated, pointing the beam of a flashlight at him.

Charlie looked at the man, then at the stone in his hand. The light sent a brief shimmer of silver over the stone. Charlie's eyes widened.

"I said, what are you doing?" The faint click of a gun trigger caught Charlie's attention.

"I have a gift for you," Charlie stammered.

He stood and took a couple steps toward Kony. It took every ounce of courage to keep his legs from buckling beneath him.

"I was given this stone. I was told to give it to you."

Charlie placed the stone in Kony's outstretched hand. The man turned the stone over and over, then ran his fingers over its smooth surface.

"And is there something I should know about this stone?"

"It has power in it, sir. It has the power to change thing."

"To change thing. Well, dear ka-boy. Change can be for the bad or for the good."

"Oh no, sir. This change is only for the good. Only good thing come from this stone."

"Then I must thank this person who gave you the stone."

"He is not here anymore, sir. He has left."

"That is too bad. A good deed should always be rewarded." Kony held the stone up to the light and examined it. "It is quite beautiful. Yes. I will consult with the spirit to see of what use it will be." He smiled. "You have done well. You are a good Acholi soldier. What is your name, ka-boy?"

"Charlie"

"*Apwoyo matek*, Charlie. Thank you."

"It gives me great happiness to do this for you, Mr. Kony," Charlie said as he lowered his gaze and stepped backward. He turned and walked out of the hut.

The sun now showed itself above the lower bushes. A girl stood near a small fire, arched her back, then wrapped her child to her side. Charlie could no longer rely on the darkness to cover him. He needed to leave, and he needed to leave now.

He walked toward the outer bush, away from the path, trying not to draw any attention to himself.

Just when he was wishing he could make himself invisible, a huge raindrop landed on his forehead, followed by another and another and another. Within seconds the clouds burst open and a torrent of rain fell on the camp, on the bush, on the fields, and on Charlie.

The whole camp was obscured by a thick sheet of rain. Charlie couldn't even see his hands when he put them out in front of him. Without hesitating, he ran into the bush. He jumped over the fallen logs, dodging the trees. He ran for all he was worth. The rain fell, hitting his face, soaking his body and surrounding him. And still Charlie ran and ran and ran. It wasn't until he knew several miles were between him and the camp that Charlie began to slow his pace. He stopped and placed his gun on the ground.

And then a strange sensation began to fill him. His legs pushed against the earth, his arms reached toward the sky. Charlie threw himself up into the air and grabbed at the rain. Again and again he jumped into the air and began to twist and turn and shout.

And then Charlie danced.

Because he could.

AUTHOR'S NOTE:

Joseph Kony and his Lord's Resistance Army (LRA) began abducting children and forcing them to fight in a war against the Ugandan government in 1987. For twenty years his army abducted children, and it is estimated that sixty thousand children were taken from their homes, classrooms, and villages and forced to kill or be killed. Some were as young as seven or eight years of age.

When I traveled with a group of World Vision volunteers to Uganda in 2008, Kony had left the country and the people were intent on returning to their villages and rebuilding their lives. I met hundreds of people who showed a determination and perseverance beyond anything I had ever witnessed.

And then I met Charlie, a former child soldier who was focused on rebuilding his own life. We talked about his past, but more importantly, we talked about his need to put the past behind him and move forward.

"Charlie," a woman in our group asked, "if you were to see Kony again, what would you like to say to him?"

He answered, "I would ask Mr. Kony to come out of the bush, out of hiding, and come and live with us."

I was stunned.

"Why would you do that, Charlie?" I asked.

"Because I forgive him," he said.

I dedicate this book to Charlie.

If you enjoyed this book, please leave a review online at Amazon.com, Amazon.ca and Goodreads. Even if you didn't enjoy it, your feedback is appreciated!

To receive notice of the next release in the Stones Trilogy go to: www.donnawhitebooks.com. To join in the conversation: www.facebook.com/donnawhitebooks

Glossary

While writing this novel I made great efforts to include common words and phrases of the Acholi tribe in their native Luo language. Sometimes, however, I used a type of street slang known as Uglish, a cross between Luganda and English. In other cases I used Kiswahili, because it was more suitable for that word or phrase at that moment. Sometimes it was difficult to find a suitable word because the word in Luo did not exist, and if it did, the meaning was lost in the translation. While the dialects of the people of Uganda vary widely from region to region and class to class, the dialect that is portrayed in this novel is an assembling of different styles of speech from various regions and various classes of the people of Uganda. If I have made any mistakes, I apologize. I am, after all, a muzungu, just.

Glossary of Acholi (Luo) words

apwoyo matek: thank you very much

bodaboda: motorcycle or bike taxi. Bicycle bodaboda's have a long cushioned seat for the passenger located behind the driver's seat. Women and girls often sit side saddle. The word is derived from the phrase "Border-border" which taxi drivers used to enquire if their customers wanted transport to the Kenyan border.

awubi ma laming: stupid boy

cet: shit

goyo: beat

gway: hey

gwok: protect

hyna: hyena, Ugandans don't pronounce the middle e

jago: village chief

jela: jail

jok: evil spirit

ka: little. For example: ka-boy: little boy, ka-field: little field

kabedo me kuc: place for peace

kicira: evil

kwee: calm, peaceful

lacan: a poor person

Lagoro Rock: A hill or rock in Lamwo, Uganda. Traditionally used as a place for cleansings, festivals, and other rituals. Still used to this day.

lajok: witch doctor - believed to possess great and evil power

laming: a foolish person

lamone: enemy

latin: child

lodito: Leader or elder. May be a government leader, clan leader, or mayor.

maa: mother

machet: machete, Ugandans don't pronounce the final e

min maa: grandmother

muzungu: literally translated it means "someone who roams around" or wanderer. Word used to describe first Europeans who came to Africa and appeared to be wandering or lost. Plural: bazungu

ni wire: purify

omera: brother

ongere: unstriped ground squirrel, lives in burrows, similar to the North American gopher.

opego: pig

padi: pastor, priest

takataka: Swahili word for garbage

tong: spear

tumu or **tyero**: sacrifice

winyo: vulture

wora: father

Author's Thanks

Thank you to my beta readers/editors for their skills, encouragement and insight in making this book what it is today. Brother Dave, sister Sandra, Jeannie Pendziwol, Heather Leighton Dickson, Erica Orloff, David Henry Sterry, and Caroline Kaiser: if it wasn't for you this book would have been deleted long ago and I would be back to my less than exciting life as a supply teacher and lion tamer.

Thank you also to World Vision Canada who sent me on this journey and without whom I would never have met Charlie. The dream became a reality because of you. Thank you.

And of course, there are many others. Thank you to Okwe David, Lakor Angela and Arach Janet for the Luo translations. Don't you just love how God puts people together? And thank you to Oroma Christine for the verification of the story. You made me know I was on track and for that I am very grateful.

And my family. Thank you Gary, Kira and Karl for your patience. Your ability to endure countless days of Kdinner, killer dust bunnies, bathtub rings and an ever absent wife and mother is commendable.

And God. Thank you for putting me on this journey to meet Charlie and giving me the words to share his story. Every day that you put a person in my path, or showed me something new, I was reminded again and again of your divine intervention. Thank you.

And lastly, to the grade eight girl who told me she hated me for showing her a world so cruel and horrid. You proved that my book is fulfilling its purpose: see the world, don't live in a bubble, and when you see injustices in it, don't sit on your butt. Do something about it.

ABOUT THE AUTHOR

Donna C. White is a teacher and author of the *Stones* trilogy. She resides in Canada with her husband and children. Visit the author's website at **www.donnawhitebooks.com** to find photo galleries, teaching resources, and much more.

A percentage of the proceeds from this novel will be given to World Vision Canada's programs to help former child soldiers receive medical support, counseling, education and, when possible, reunite them with their loved ones.

If you wish to make a donation to help these children, go to:

https://catalogue.worldvision.ca/products/2501

For more information about child soldiers go to www.donnawhitebooks.com

Now you know. Do something about it.

Made in the USA
Columbia, SC
01 September 2017